Praise for Carter Wilson

The Father She Went to Find

"Buckle up. Watch out. And don't try to predict *anything*! The supremely talented Carter Wilson has crafted a uniquely unpredictable and absolutely immersive story starring one of the most fascinating characters you'll ever meet. *A Beautiful Mind* takes a life-and-death road trip in this battle of wits, maze of psychological suspense, and heartbreaking family drama. I was riveted to every page."

—Hank Phillippi Ryan, *USA Today* bestselling author of *One Wrong Word*

"Carter Wilson has done it again. *The Father She Went to Find* is off like a shot from page one, and it doesn't let up. A road trip story with dizzying twists and turns, featuring a unique protagonist you won't soon forget, this book will keep you up until you reach the last page!"

—Andrew DeYoung, author of *The Temps* and *The Day He Never Came Home*

"In his latest page-turning and deeply psychological novel, Carter Wilson has deftly crafted one of the most compelling and unique characters you'll read this year. I was glued to every word!"

—Wendy Walker, bestselling author of *What Remains*

T0036364

The New Neighbor

"*The New Neighbor* is a dizzying descent into a Byzantine maze of psychological suspense. Carter Wilson proves once again why he is one of the best, most inventive thriller writers working today."

—S. A. Cosby, *New York Times* bestselling author
of *Razorblade Tears* and *Blacktop Wasteland*

"Damn you, Wilson. I was up all night with this book. The mysteries of Bury are perfectly placed, the tension is thick enough to drown in, and the pages fly by. Brilliant escapism. I can't recommend it highly enough."

—Stuart Turton, international bestselling author of *The 7½
Deaths of Evelyn Hardcastle* and *The Devil and the Dark Water*

"A truly suspenseful and gripping read. I was filled with anxiety and on the edge of my seat throughout. Bravo!"

—Alice Hunter, author of *The Serial Killer's Wife*

"I can never resist a book with a well-written unreliable narrator, and Carter Wilson nails just that in his tautly written thriller *The New Neighbor*. I couldn't bear to put this page-turner down until I figured out every single detail in Wilson's suspenseful and twist-ridden story of loss, mourning, and new starts that asks if money can ever buy happiness, and even if it does—at what cost?"

—Emily Bleeker, *Wall Street Journal* and
Amazon Charts bestselling author

The Dead Husband

woman running from her past and the detective determined to uncover her secrets."

—Julie Clark, *New York Times* bestselling author
of *The Last Flight* and *The Lies I Tell*

"Carter Wilson's *The Dead Husband* is a perfectly paced and expertly written thriller. The prose is as smooth as glass, and the pages fly by as fast as the reader can turn them. And then the ending provides a shocking jolt. This is a smashing story about families and secrets and all the things you don't want to know about the people closest to you. Read it!"

—David Bell, *New York Times* bestselling author of *She's Gone*

"[About] a rich family with shocking secrets in an affluent small town, Carter Wilson's *The Dead Husband* is *Succession* meets *Big Little Lies*, and I loved every bit of it. This marvelously crafted thriller is the perfect escape, so find a quiet spot and sink in—you'll be glad you did."

—Jennifer Hillier, award-winning author
of *Jar of Hearts* and *Little Secrets*

"Wilson unveils each revelation of some new betrayal with surgical precision en route to a bittersweet finale. A harrowing reminder that you really can't go home again."

—*Kirkus Reviews*

"[A] chilling standalone... Psychological thriller fans will be rewarded."

—*Publishers Weekly*

The Dead Girl in 2A

"Will grip you from the first chapter and never let go. A lightning-paced thriller reminiscent of Dean Koontz. I couldn't turn the pages fast enough!"

—Liv Constantine, internationally bestselling author of *The Last Mrs. Parrish*

"One of those books you devour in a single sitting. *The Dead Girl in 2A* promises a lot from the start and delivers in spades."

—Alex Marwood, author of *The Wicked Girls*

"With a story as riveting as it is mysterious, Wilson's *The Dead Girl in 2A* is a terrifying plunge into the depths of a childhood trauma rising back into the light. Wilson's characters are as deep as the mystery that surrounds them, and the fast-paced plot doesn't disappoint. This is not to be missed."

—R. H. Herron, international bestselling author of *Stolen Things*

"Carter Wilson's novels slip under your skin with the elegance and devastation of a surgeon's scalpel. In his latest book, Wilson weaves a gripping tale in which the present can die in a single careless moment, and the past is as unknowable as the future. *The Dead Girl in 2A* is a high-wire act, exquisitely balanced between shattering suspense and the sudden opening of our hearts. I couldn't put this book down. Bravo!"

—Barbara Nickless, author of the award-winning Sydney Parnell series

"Readers will be intrigued by this exploration of how scientific experimentation...goes awry, leaving a trail of bodies and few survivors behind."

—*Booklist*

"Wilson provides plenty of creepy and downright disturbing moments on the way to the unexpectedly heartfelt conclusion. Psychological thriller fans will be well satisfied."

—*Publishers Weekly*

"Dean Koontz fans in particular will find a lot to enjoy. A disturbing, propulsive, and satisfying thriller. Wilson is an author to watch."

—*Kirkus Reviews*

"Bestselling author Wilson delivers a solid stand-alone psychological thriller with a clever premise that brings to light the devastation of memory-altering drugs in psychological warfare research."

—*Library Journal*

"A deftly scripted psychological thriller of a novel, *The Dead Girl in 2A* showcases author Carter Wilson's distinctive narrative storytelling style and expertise. An original and intensely riveting read from cover to cover..."

—*Midwest Book Review*

Mister Tender's Girl

"Dark, unsettling, and full of surprises, *Mister Tender's Girl* takes the reader on a dangerous journey alongside a woman who must face the past she's been hiding from. A fast-paced, spine-tingling read—and a reminder that imagined dangers are just as worthy of being feared."

—Megan Miranda, *New York Times* bestselling
author of *The Perfect Stranger*

"This elegantly written, masterful thriller, by turns meditative and shocking, lyrical and violent, will keep you glued to the pages from start to finish."

—A. J. Banner, *USA Today* bestselling author of
The Good Neighbor and *The Twilight Wife*

"The writing is both gorgeous and gritty, and the story so enticing that I gobbled it up in one sitting. I can only humbly request that Carter Wilson hurry up and write some more."

—Sandra Block, author of *The Girl without
a Name* and *The Secret Room*

"Carter Wilson hits it out of the park with *Mister Tender's Girl*—one of the most suspenseful novels I've read in a long time. This book is a true page-turner, riveting on every level."

—Allen Eskens, bestselling author of *The Life
We Bury* and *The Heavens May Fall*

"Not since *Gone Girl's* 'Amazing Amy' has a character from a make-believe children's book been so richly imagined and realized, and led to such a twisting, seductive tale. *Mister Tender's Girl* forces Alice Hill out of her lonely, isolated world to confront the inner demons that arose after she became the victim of a violent attack. As Alice delves into the events surrounding the crime, she finds that the fictional Mister Tender may have been a very different man from what the world believed. Carter Wilson's latest novel will have readers checking outside their windows for monsters—and, like Alice, also looking for those that lurk inside themselves."

—Jenny Milchman, *USA Today* bestselling author
of *Cover of Snow*, *Ruin Falls*, and *As Night Falls*

"Chapter by chapter, Carter Wilson's *Mister Tender's Girl* compels the reader forward: another question, another mystery, another fear to be dispelled or realized. Start reading this thriller, and you won't stop until the end. That's how compelling, whether endearing or nefarious, the main characters are. And that's how talented a writer Carter Wilson is."

—Randall Silvis, author of *Two Days Gone*

"In spare prose, Wilson ratchets up the horror spawned by obsession to a bloody end. For those who tolerate intense, sometimes graphic fiction, this is mesmerizing."

—*Booklist*, Starred Review

"Wilson turns the creep factor up to eleven, balancing his prose on a knife's edge. A highly satisfying high-tension thriller."

—*Kirkus Reviews*

"A can't-put-down thriller that will reverberate with readers. The characters are well drawn, the plot hums, the creepiness level is high, and you won't see the ending coming. Fans of psychological suspense shouldn't miss this great thrill ride."

—*Library Journal*

"[A] taut, complex thriller..."

—*Publishers Weekly*

Also by Carter Wilson

THE
FATHER
SHE WENT TO
FIND

A NOVEL

CARTER WILSON

Poisoned Pen
PRESS

Published by Poisoned Pen Press, an imprint of Sourcebooks
P.O. Box 4410, Naperville, Illinois 60567-4410
(630) 961-3900
sourcebooks.com

Library of Congress Cataloging-in-Publication Data

Names: Wilson, Carter (Novelist), author.
Title: The father she went to find : a novel / Carter Wilson.
Description: Naperville, Illinois : Poisoned Pen Press, 2024.
Identifiers: LCCN 2023028384 (print) | LCCN 2023028385
(ebook) | (trade paperback) | (ebook)
Subjects: LCSH: Self-realization in women--Fiction. | Fathers and
    daughters--Fiction. | LCGFT: Psychological fiction. | Novels.
Classification: LCC PS3623.I57787 F38 2024 (print) | LCC PS3623.I57787
    (ebook) | DDC 813/.6--dc23/eng/20230710
LC record available at https://lccn.loc.gov/2023028384
LC ebook record available at https://lccn.loc.gov/2023028385

Printed and bound in Canada.
MBP 10 9 8 7 6 5 4 3 2 1

to Ili
the smartest girl I know

ONE

July 13, 1987
Eau Claire, Wisconsin
Monday

I REMEMBER EVERYTHING.

This isn't an exaggeration. As the few who know me would confirm, I'm not prone to hyperbole. And when I say I remember everything, I'm not talking about the events of this morning. Or yesterday. Or the whole of last week.

I remember everything since October 2, 1973.

Since the day I woke from my coma when I was seven years old.

Every meal. Every conversation. The lyrics of every song that entered my ears. Every word of every page of every book that passed beneath my gaze.

Every word of abuse.

And all the words of praise.

One of those outnumbers the other, but I'm not in the mood to report the score.

I have supreme eidetic memory combined with hyperthymesia—the ability to recall life events in great detail. It's exceedingly rare that a person has both these things.

Lucky me.

Thing is, my abilities sometimes haunt me, but not as much as one of my profound inabilities.

I remember almost nothing of my life *before* October 2, 1973.

I've seen photos. I've heard stories. I've been told *surely you remember* more times than I can count—okay, that's a lie; I've been told that 217 times in the past fourteen years.

But I *don't* remember. And when I try to, it's like trying to watch a movie through a crashing ocean wave.

And yet.

Every now and then, once every two years or so, I recall something of that lost period of my life. Usually, it's a small detail, like eating vanilla soft serve under a towering oak tree in the park near my house. These sudden memories will surface in good—but not vivid—detail. And, god, how I want these rare finds to be meaningful, to be revelatory of some greater truth, but my guess is they're just the result of an improbable synchronicity of firing synapses.

But today.

Today I had my most powerful recollection ever.

I suddenly remembered bits and pieces of a road trip I took with my father.

I was six.

We drove from Wisconsin to Los Angeles. I assume we drove back, too, but I don't remember that.

This recollection was the first time I ever saw my father within the confines of my own mind. No photos. No old Super 8 reels. It was the father I experienced as a little girl.

This memory.

This happened today.

Right before I turn twenty-one.

Right as I expect to hear from him, his annual birthday card.

Goddamn. This could be meaningful. It's going to be a good day.

TWO

HOURS LATER IT ALL turns to shit.

Worse than shit.

Shit can be cleaned off.

"I don't understand," I say into the phone. I'm just buying time to absorb his words along with the feeling of a razor to my belly. I clench my core with all my might, as if otherwise my guts would spill onto the linoleum floor of the institute.

A pause. Dr. Brock clears his throat on the other end of the line.

"Yes, you do, Penny," he says. "That's the thing. You understand everything. You always have."

His voice sounds different over the phone. Ten years, and I've never spoken to him anywhere but in person.

I grip the weighty receiver and resist the desire to smash it against the wall. "You never told me you were going to leave."

"I know. But this is a promotion. It's important to me. To my family. I'll still come back to visit from time to time."

I'm sitting on the floor of my private room in the institute, folding my legs beneath me.

"You've been my therapist since I was eleven. I can't start over with someone new."

"You won't be starting over. You're continuing all the work we've done over the past decade, just with a different psychologist. I know it won't be easy, but you can do it."

"But I don't want to."

"I know that, too," he says. "But it's important you do. And you already know Dr. Cheong. You'll be in fine hands with her."

I close my eyes, thinking how being in anyone's hands is not something I desire.

"This is completely fucked."

"Penny."

"And you didn't even stay to tell me. You just left. I don't know where you are."

"I'm in Washington, DC."

"What's in DC?"

"The National Institutes of Health. I'm leading a team that's going to produce the definitive text on savant syndrome. I suspect you'll feature largely in the book."

That razor in my belly? It just began shredding organs.

"I don't want to be in the book. I'm not a lab rat. I just want things to stay how they were."

"Everything changes eventually," he says, and what a frustrating group of words that is. "We've changed together over the years. This is just a new phase of our relationship."

I open my eyes, finding nothing of comfort in the light. "I can't believe you would do this. I trusted you."

I know this man. He's never one to say anything until he's chosen his words carefully, which can sometimes result in long gaps of silence. This is one of those times.

"I know how you feel about abandonment, and my intention is not to hurt you. As your friend and therapist, I know you're ready for this transition." Then he adds, "I'm not your father, Penny."

Wow.

"No," I tell him. "You sure as hell aren't."

"Our relationship might be changing, but your work with the institute isn't. It's important you continue your studies there, with Dr. Cheong. Probably two or three more years at most. And you want to spend those years setting yourself up for the best possible success. When the time comes, you'll have opportunities most people would kill for."

Kill. That's an interesting word choice.

"Maybe I'm ready to leave here now," I say. "Maybe I couldn't care less about opportunities."

Of course, I've been free to leave the Willow Brook Institute for the Brain at any time. My years here have all been voluntary; in exchange for getting an education far beyond what the Eau Claire public school system could provide, I've allowed Dr. Brock and the rest of the doctors and researchers to study my brain. This place? It's a boarding school for the brilliant, but rather than outrageous tuition, I pay in research. There's no question, I *am* a lab rat, though I'm treated as the most valuable rodent in the world.

"You're angry. I get it. I would be, too."

Fuck off, I want to say. But it doesn't take a genius to know those words won't change anything.

"Is there anything else?" I ask. The sensation in my belly is hardening already, like scar tissue tightening over a sutured wound.

"Yes. I have a new phone number, obviously." He tells it to me, and the numbers, like everything else, etch themselves permanently into my brain. "You can call me anytime, day or night. I mean that."

"I believe you."

"I just want the best for you, Penny."

I look out the window, thinking about irony. Specifically, the irony of how I know so much about the world yet have seen almost nothing of it.

I reply, "Okay."

There's nothing else to say.

I hang up, twisting the phone cord until it resembles a noose.

THREE

DR. BROCK SAYS I have abandonment issues.

He's partially right.

What I really have is an acute fear of desperation. And for me, desperation is any situation where you can't even hope for a good outcome. Where you have no control. No ability. All you can do is process the information and hold all the pain inside.

This is what I'm feeling now, sitting on the floor in my room with the knowledge that Dr. Brock is going away. That he's already gone away.

I feel fucking desperate, and I hate the world for it.

While there's no hope, I can do the thing that comforts me most— or, at least, distracts me.

I close my eyes and concentrate. Then I speak within the walls of my mind. *Hi, Dad.*

I wait for my father's voice, a creation of mine so vivid that, over the years, I've come to almost believe it's real. He left nearly fourteen years ago, but I've learned to summon him at will.

And then, just like that, he's here.

Hey there, Pen Pen. What's shaking?

This is bad.

What's happening?

I tell him about Dr. Brock and how it's making me feel. I don't even let him respond, knowing there's nothing he can do. So I ask him a self-indulgent question: *Am I going to die alone?*

Oh, sweetie, why would you say that? What a horrible thought. Of course not.

I know, like, ten people in the world. And the one I'm closest to just up and left.

That's rough, Pen. I'm sorry to hear that. But no, you're not going to die alone. You have an amazing life ahead of you.

None of this is helping. It's just me talking to myself, after all, and how the hell am I going to rationalize through these emotions?

So I change the subject.

I remembered something, I tell him. *From the before years.*

You did? What was it?

A road trip. I was six. Just you and me. Eau Claire to Los Angeles.

He chuckles inside my brain. *We had a good time, didn't we?*

Why did we take that trip? And where was Mom?

He doesn't answer. I'm always met with silence when I ask a question my subconscious can't answer, and no part of me recalls why we took the trip. Maybe he had some kind of meeting, a conference, and I wanted to go with him. He agreed, and we decided to drive instead of fly so we could see the country. I don't know. Whatever the reason, I recall many of the details of the journey itself. The places we stopped, things we saw. And notes. I remember writing notes.

You remember the treasure map? he says.

I do. A smile creeps over my face, and it's the first time I haven't felt horrible since the call with Dr. Brock.

He continues. *Everywhere we stopped, we found a place and left written messages for each other. Of course, you couldn't much write, so I have no idea what's on the paper you used. But I wrote you notes. Long ones. And we put our messages in empty pop bottles before leaving them in places only we could find. I kept a list of all the locations, figuring someday we'd recreate the trip and find all those bottles, like a time capsule or some such.*

What did you write in your messages? I ask.

A pause. *Well, I suppose, you're gonna have to find those bottles to see.*

An intriguing thought.

But I'm getting too wrapped in the past. Being too loving of a father who did the very thing Dr. Brock is doing now.

So I ask one last question, the one I ask every time I speak to him. The question that reminds me about how deceiving memories can truly be.

Why did you leave?

Like every time I've conjured him since the age of seven, his answer remains the same:

Dead silence.

FOUR

I'VE HAD HEADACHES BEFORE. Bad ones. Ever since I came home from the hospital all those years ago, I've been prone to them.

I feel one coming on now. Sometimes they go away before materializing into something with teeth. Sometimes the teeth come and feast inside my skull. I'm hoping now, as always, for the former.

The conversation with my father reminds me to check the mail. It's that time of year after all.

I leave my room and walk down the antiseptic corridor of the institute's east wing, just as I've been doing for ten years. My gaze remains fixed on the floor six feet ahead of me, my happy place. I'm in no mood to talk to anyone. Especially Dr. Cheong.

How am I supposed to open up to *her*? Hell, I didn't even tell Dr. Brock anything very private in our first eighteen months of talks. I don't want to share anything at all with someone new.

I reach the small office behind the lobby. There are a few dozen hanging folders where mail is distributed. I find the folder bearing my name, always the one in front.

PENNY BLY

And.

It's here.

A day early, even.

I reach in and remove the card, my breathing quickening.

As always, the envelope bears no return address. I check the postmark.

Westlake Village, California.

Last year was San Antonio. Kansas City the year before.

I forgo tradition and open this card today, a day before my birthday. These cards are the only communication I get from him all year, transmissions from a ghost. It's been a bad day; I can use this bit of cheer, hollow as it may be.

My dad never writes more than two sentences, but his few words are like a drug to me.

I sneak a nail beneath the flap of the envelope, which opens easily. There's nothing different about the outside of the card itself—they're always cartoonish and usually feature animals, as if I'm still a child. Sure enough, the card shows a koala in a birthday hat, clinging to a eucalyptus tree. Above the figure, the text says, *Hang on!*

I suck in a breath, hold it, open the card.

You're 21! shouts the blocky Hallmark text.

My brain involuntarily flashes as it always does, associating a color with the number. *Twenty-one. A deep brownish red, the color of pooled blood sitting for hours.*

I have a couple of other special things about me aside from the memory stuff. One is that I see numbers as colors, have ever since I fell down the stairs of my house when I was seven. That singular event changed the course of my life.

Numbers as colors.

Six is green, a freshly cut lawn, brilliant and commanding. Four is pee yellow, a bit passive. Nine? Deep-space black, rigid in its certainty. Three: white, blinding.

My gaze flicks to the left interior of the card. The familiar handwriting in blue ink, print, not cursive. Never cursive.

A split second later, I notice another difference in this year's card.

Not two sentences from him but four.

My heart leaps, but just a little because it's out of shape.

I read.

Pen—

Happy birthday to my little girl, who's not so little anymore. You're grown up now and smarter than I'll ever understand, so it's time to stop this pretending and admit we were never meant to be in each other's lives. These will be the last words you'll ever get from me. I think we both know it's best that way.

Love,

Dad

FIVE

I CAN'T BREATHE.

I can't breathe.

The card falls from my hand, landing koala up on the linoleum floor.

He's leaving me.

He's fucking leaving me.

AGAIN.

I try to steady myself, but gravity suddenly feels optional. So I sit, right here in this tiny office, and the tearing in my core, which began during my call with Dr. Brock, gets exponentially worse.

No. No. No. No. No.

I can't handle this, so I need to refocus. I'm smart. I can refocus.

It takes everything to push the thought of my father's words from my brain, and I accomplish this by picturing myself dying.

I do this from time to time.

It's a weird kind of meditation with me. I picture the end of my life, and for some reason, it calms me. I have a stock of go-to scenarios: being in a car crash, getting cancer, burning in a forest fire, drowning in an ocean.

I close my eyes and ask my brain for death, and it gives me an all-new scenario this time.

I'm in an airplane, plummeting from the sky, falling as fast as Galileo's stone from the Tower of Pisa, at terminal velocity.

I've never flown on a plane in my life, but I can sense it, *feel* it even, my stomach flipping over as hundreds of imaginary passengers' horrified screams fill the hot cramped cabin. I can smell their stinking, sweaty fear.

Will there be pain as the plane spears the ocean? Or maybe it'll break apart before impact, scattering passengers into the vast freezing sky, all those piercing shrieks swallowed by space.

I can see it clearly, and it's horrifying. Another reminder that we don't control our minds but rather our minds control us.

The plane doesn't break up.

It just missiles nose first, faster and faster, spinning, straining, shrieking—a comet making a murder-suicide pact with the ocean below. Any second now the plane will strike the water, and everything will mercifully be over. I'll go from genius to vapor in a forgotten moment.

Almost.

Almost.

Now.

The vision vanishes as quickly as it appeared, leaving me a little woozy.

I open my eyes.

I'm a bit steadier now. Death has helped. Again. Funny, that.

I spy the card on the floor, thinking about how strange it is that such a little thing is capable of producing such mighty consequences. I mean, this thing is just a flimsy piece of folded card stock with a koala bear and a few handwritten sentences. People throw away such things all the time.

But getting this card in the mail today?

I have a feeling it's like when I fell down the stairs.

An inflection point.

Everything as I know it is about to change.

Oddly, the oncoming headache has diminished, and I thank the universe for small favors.

SIX

THE CARD MARKS THE second time my dad has left me.

The first was when I was seven and comatose in the hospital.

My father, Jack Bly, is little more than a collection of vague memories, a tapestry of opaque images and sounds that never quite formed into an impression. So I created him in my mind, talking to him almost daily. Asking for advice. Sharing secrets. Yelling at him. Asking for his love. And this phantom father never confesses why he chose to leave me, but my corporeal father is at least consistent in his real communication. The yearly birthday card.

This card.

If Dr. Brock's phone call was a knife to my belly, the card is a ten-pound hammer smashing into my skull.

As I stare at my father's heartless message over and over, I can't help but think, *Why now?*

Why would he choose to stop contact now? He says I've finally grown up, but I turned eighteen three years ago. I've been an adult that whole time.

So why now?

Maybe he's sick. Dying, even. Or maybe he never cared at all and finally got tired of this singular annual obligation.

God damn it. *Why?*

I'm tempted to summon him, but I know I'll just be talking into an empty void. There are no answers inside my brain.

I look at that stupid koala and realize this is the sum of my fears.

I'm alone.

Totally fucking alone.

Unless… my brain says.

I flick my gaze up, scanning the walls of the small office, the white paint in need of touching up, the framed motivational posters in need of dusting.

Unless I go find him.

My chest tightens at the thought.

My life has been a sheltered one, my days mostly spent shuttling between my home and the institute. Rarely anywhere else. I've never been on my own, unless I count all the times my mother barely registers my presence.

I've never even traveled outside of Wisconsin except for this road trip I just remembered.

Can I take care of myself? Out there?

A smile tugs at my lips.

Only one way to find out.

For ten years I've heard nothing but how special I am, how I'm one of only seventy-five in the *world* with my level of abilities. *Of course*, I can survive out there, away from home. Survive and maybe even thrive.

Maybe even find the happiness I often think about, whose attainability I just as often question.

But yeah.

I'm doing this.

My skin crackles with electric anticipation.

Yes, I know. I need a plan. A direction. It's not like I'll just take a bus and hope to run into my father at some random stop. I know the odds of finding him are almost nothing, but the more I think about leaving here, the more I can't dismiss the idea.

Maybe the point of leaving isn't to find him but myself.

Maybe this is why I remembered our road trip today. To give me motivation to take one of my own.

I'm giddy.

Seriously, I'm fucking giddy. I don't remember the last time I felt this way.

Tomorrow I turn twenty-one, and that'll be the day I leave everything I know and head out into the world.

Twenty-one.

Yeah, I know.

The color of pooled blood.

SEVEN

July 14, 1987
Tuesday

HAPPY BIRTHDAY TO ME.

Standing in the spartan lobby of the Willow Brook Institute for the Brain, with the ever-present faint scent of cleaning chemicals dulling my head, it hits me that this'll be the last time I'll ever be here.

Dr. Cheong crosses the lobby, beelining toward me. She's relatively new to the facility, having arrived three months ago. I've spoken with her all of four times, the conversations never lasting more than a minute. I don't even know what she does, but it doesn't matter. Nothing about this place matters anymore.

"Penny, I was looking for you."

"Okay."

The doctor stands a full three inches shorter than me, but something about her expression makes her loom large. There's a severity to it. Perhaps impatience. She glances down at the bag in my right hand.

"Are you spending the night at home?"

"Yes," I say. It's not an absolute lie, just a likely one.

The doctor looks at her watch. "It's only two thirty. I was hoping to get some time with you this afternoon. I understand Dr. Brock updated you on some of the changes we'll be going through here?"

Some of the changes, like they're just adding pizza to the cafeteria menu. "Yes," I say. "That he's leaving and you're supposed to be my new therapist."

She nods, her face tense. "Yes, that's right. I know this kind of transition can be difficult, so I wanted to schedule a session right away. Can you postpone heading home for an hour so we can talk?"

"No, I need to leave." I can tell by her face that my tone is harsher than I intended. This happens sometimes; I'm not the best judge of social norms. "It's…it's my birthday today," I add.

This earns a smile. "Oh, I should have known that. Well, then happy birthday. Do you have special plans at home?"

"Something like that."

"Okay. Tomorrow, then. Let's say nine a.m."

"Sure," I say, just wanting the conversation to be over.

Dr. Cheong reaches out and puts a hand on my shoulder, and I think of Dr. Brock telling me I'll be in fine hands with this woman. "Good. It's important we start building a connection."

I stare at that hand, wishing I had the telekinetic ability to make it burst into flames. She gets the hint and removes it.

"Sorry," she says. "Dr. Brock told me you don't like to be touched. I guess… I realize it'll take some time to build that connection. As long as we're both committed to doing that, I think everything will work out just fine."

I don't bother to tell the doctor there'll never be any connection between us, and we face each other for a moment in awkward silence.

It seems fitting to do one last thing before leaving this place forever. I walk over to the reception desk in the middle of the lobby and ask Carla, the receptionist, for a piece of paper and a pen. Carla does as I ask, though not before insisting I give the pen back when I'm done with it; people are apparently always making off with Carla's pens.

I place the paper on the reception counter and let the pen do the work.

It takes about ten minutes.

I sense Carla leaning forward. "Can I see, honey?"

Not a big fan of the term *honey*. I push the paper toward her.

"Wow," Carla says, staring at my drawing. "I'll never understand your ability to do that."

"I don't really understand it either," I say.

I hand the pen back and return to the doctor, handing her the drawing. It's my parting gift, something to say *have a nice life*.

The doc's expression remains unchanged, but I see the wonder in her eyes, if only briefly. It always happens when people see themselves in one of my drawings. Dr. Cheong's portrait is a near-photographic likeness, down to the small mole in the lower-left corner of her lip.

"I knew drawing was one of your abilities, but I've never seen your work. I mean..." She exhales, then soaks in the image a bit longer, seeming to hold on to something within it.

When I draw someone, I believe I'm able to unearth more of that person's inner essence—their *frequency*—than what they project to the world. And when I drew Dr. Cheong, I saw a woman desperate to prove herself, perhaps at the cost of anything else.

"Though I have to say I look angry in this," she says.

"It's how you look. At least to me."

"Really? You see me as angry?"

I shrug. "I really need to go."

Dr. Cheong nods and offers a weak smile. Maybe she's unsettled by her portrait. It wouldn't be the first time. "Okay, Penny. Thank you for this. And see you tomorrow."

I say nothing, not even nodding in agreement. I just turn and complete my journey to the double doors at the entrance to the institute, which whoosh open at my presence for the very last time.

EIGHT

WHAT THE FUCK, DAD?

It takes twenty seconds for him to respond. *Hiya, Pen Pen.*

Here I am, lost behind my eyelids, where the dark is deep and cavernous. *Seriously, what the fuck?*

So I guess you got my card.

I hate you, I say, meaning it in the moment.

I don't blame you.

Why did you write that?

As usual, there's no answer. Never an answer when he's asked to explain himself.

I'm leaving today, I tell him. *Coming to find you.*

Is that so?

And when I find you, you're going to tell me everything. The why of everything.

More silence.

I think you want me to find you, I add.

More silence.

Do you even want to see me?

For a moment I think he's gone, vaporized from my imagination.

But just before I open my eyes, I hear this: *I can't think of anything I want more than to see you.*

Okay, then.

More silence.

But how in the world are you going to find me? he asks.

Good question. I've asked myself the same one a thousand times.

Well, there's the postmark. Westlake Village, California. Seems like a logical place to start.

Hmmmm, he answers, and I don't like that. But then he adds, *You just had the memory about the road trip. And the messages we wrote to each other. The treasure map. Maybe that's something.*

I also considered this. But it all seems so impossible. Like what, scribbled notes from sixteen years ago will help me find him? If those notes can even be found.

Where's the treasure map? I ask.

Silence. Of course, silence.

Then he says this: *The outside world, Pen, well, I call it the wild. Sometimes it's wondrous; sometimes it's a little scary. When ancient explorers made their maps, they'd mark any unchartered territory with three simple words:* there be dragons.

Yes, I know. I know a lot of things.

I guess what I'm saying, Penny, is to keep your eyes open out there.

I keep my eyes squeezed shut as the conversation swirls in my consciousness. *Are you saying there are dragons out there?*

His answer does not give me comfort. *Well, hell, sweetie. In the wild, they're just about everywhere.*

I open my eyes, disconnecting this preternatural phone call.

"I love you," I say, meaning it in the moment.

NINE

MY ABILITIES CAME FROM my mother. Don't get me wrong: I didn't inherit them. No, they came about when my mom pushed me down our fucking staircase when I was seven years old.

The only thing I remember from that night is my parents fighting, and while my mother never admitted to shoving me, sometimes I think I can still feel her hand square between my shoulder blades. Accident or not, Linda Bly is to blame for nearly killing me and making me special all at once.

My first memory of the after was waking in the hospital bed days later. A doctor explained I'd been in a coma, *a deep sleep*. But it hadn't felt like sleep. It hadn't felt like any time passed at all. I remember wanting to go back into the coma to find peace because out of the coma, there was only pain, a persistent whole-body throb, a dozen broken bones, and my mother's lies.

The girl always had two left feet. Must've tripped herself up. I found her at the bottom of the stairs, stone-cold out. I thought she was dead, to be honest.

But I said nothing of the truth. By then, I was more afraid of my mother than any old coma.

My first words after waking up: *Where's Dad?*

Mom said nothing to this.

My second set of words: *How long have I been here?*

Eight days, the doctor replied.

And that's when I saw it for the first time, and it was so real, I thought I was hallucinating. The red of the number eight—a swirling, roiling, violent fire fog—right there, plain as day. It faded in seconds, but it was *there*, right in front of the doctor's face.

I said nothing to the doctor or my mom about this.

It was a new special thing, just for me.

Numbers as colors.

And that was just the beginning.

TEN

HOME.

I step through the doorway of my house, my left foot landing on the singular creaking floorboard, greeting my weight as it always does, with resignation. The house looks even older today, even more worn than usual, the floorboards themselves a testament to neglect: faded stains and yawning gaps.

I've lived my whole life in this house. I sure as hell don't want to die here.

Cigarette smoke hazes the hallway leading into the kitchen.

I find my mother at the dining table, its surface a hard plastic peppered with the marks of tobacco embers, ashes that miss the ashtray when Mom's aim is either drunkenly off or she simply can't be bothered.

She's holding a cigarette and staring at the refrigerator. No, that's not quite right. It's more like she's staring *through* it.

I wonder what she's thinking.

Nothing pleasant, I suspect.

"Hey," I say.

"Hey."

She doesn't bother looking over at me. Even if she did, she probably wouldn't ask why I have my duffel bag with me, why I'm home today and not at the institute.

"Have you eaten today?" I ask.

A shrug. "I think so." A purple cotton bathrobe clings for its life to her bony frame.

"Want me to fix you dinner?"

"No," Mom replies. "Not really."

Next to my mother's leathery knuckles is a glass half-filled with clear liquid. Could be water. Most likely isn't.

"You take your meds today?"

"Pretty sure," she says.

"Okay."

I walk to the refrigerator, open it, and find nothing worth having. "I might go out later and get something to eat. Can I take some money from your wallet?"

No answer, which doesn't mean no.

I find her purse on a small table next to the front door. The faded-green leather wallet yields eighty-seven dollars, less than expected given Mom's unemployment check arrived just two days ago.

I take all of it.

Do I feel guilty? A little.

But I'm going to need the cash.

Upstairs, in my room, I pull out my canvas backpack from beneath my bed. It's a little smaller than the duffel bag but will be easier to manage. It takes me twenty-seven minutes to pack for a trip that might last a couple of weeks, might last forever.

Twenty-seven. Elephant gray.

As I leave my bedroom, I take one last turn and stare back inside because that's what people on TV do. In all the shows, characters always turn and give one last look, as if searching for some deeper meaning.

"Good riddance."

I'm halfway back downstairs when it hits me, the hard and cold realization that I might never walk these stairs again. Now I stop and stare, not looking for some deeper meaning but confronting my past one more time.

There, that's what shattered me.

I deposit my backpack by the front door and go back to see Mom, who by this point has made her way to the couch and is lying down, her eyelids drooping.

I kneel next to her. "Did you keep anything Dad left?"

Her eyes widen, just a touch. "What?"

"I had a memory," I tell her. "That he and I went on a road trip. I think I was six. Do you remember that?"

She moves her gaze away, back to the ceiling. "I've tried very hard to forget everything about that man."

She hates him for leaving us. I get it. I can't even imagine her fury if I told her about the card he sent.

"But you don't even remember me and him talking a road trip together?"

She shakes her head, but I'm not buying it.

"I think...I think we went on this trip." I recall my memory and study it, but it's tattered and frayed. "And that we left little notes for each other in different places, and he wrote those places on a piece a paper. Like a treasure map."

"Jesus, Penny," she says. "A treasure map? When are you gonna stop being a goddamn little girl?"

Whatever weight the insult carries bounces harmlessly off my well-hardened armor. I change tactics. "For my birthday I want to burn all traces of him," I say. "All the cards he's sent me, any photos, any evidence he ever existed. I want a clean start."

Her gaze is back, and she looks scared, like I've just woken her from a nightmare. "Are you serious?"

"I am," I say. "I can't shake this memory, and I'm sure it's real and that he wrote all these things on a piece of paper. I want to burn that, too. If it's here, somewhere in this house, I want to destroy it."

What she does next surprises me. She actually pulls herself from the couch and heads upstairs. I wait, wondering if she's merely put herself to bed, but a few moments later, I hear her feet on the stairs.

She comes back, collapses again on the couch, and hands me the piece of paper in her right hand.

"You two leaving on that fucking road trip was one of the worst times of my life," she says. "I don't know why I kept that paper. Burn it. Burn it all."

"So it *was* real," I say, mostly to myself.

Mom says nothing, but I can feel her thoughts swirling around us, and they all have poisonous barbed tips.

I look at the paper.

My god.

It's the treasure map.

ELEVEN

IT'S NOT REALLY A map, not in the traditional sense.

There are no boundaries drawn, no compass, no X to mark the spot, no areas of geography labeled *there be dragons.*

Just a sheet of lined yellow notepaper, the kind you'd stuff into a Trapper Keeper.

A piece of paper with writing.

The handwriting is my father's, but a younger version of it, a more careful and elegant version of what appears in my birthday cards.

There's a title at the top of the page:

Pen Pen and Daddy's Big Adventure, September 1972.

September 1972. I had just turned six.

The next line reads *Time Capsule.* And beneath that is a message from my dad.

Can you find our notes, Pen Pen? Maybe someday you will. Maybe we'll take this trip again and find them together. ♥ *Daddy*

I focus on those last three words of his message. *Find them together.* Someone who's intending to leave his family doesn't write such things. Of course, it could be he wasn't planning to at that time.

My gaze moves down the sheet, where there are five locations written out and numbered. Each is an address, the first one a Kmart in Minneapolis (*SW corner of parking lot, base of oak tree, buried about six inches*).

Note number two is in Rapid City. Number three is in Denver. Four is in Las Vegas.

And five.

Holy shit.

Location number five.

1263 Hawk's View Court. Westlake Village, CA.

TWELVE

I STEADY MY BREATHING and look over at my mother, who's settled back into a motionless lump stretching the length of the couch.

"I'm going to go now," I tell her. Then I get on my knees next to the couch and lean in close. "Okay?"

"Okay," she mumbles.

"Are you going to be all right?"

"Aren't I always?"

I didn't expect to cry, but the tears filling my eyes pay my expectations no heed. Sometimes I hate my mother. Most times I'm just indifferent. But, once in a while, I love and pity Mom at the same time, and when that happens, it's gut-wrenching.

"You know you shouldn't drink when you're taking your pills," I say.

This elicits a slight widening of her eyes. "Don't tell me what to do. You have no idea what it's like. What it feels like." The sentences are slurred and blurred, but fortunately I'm fluent in her mumble speak.

"You're right. I don't."

"You know you're a burden, right, Pen?"

Burden. One of her favorite words.

"I know."

"A *burden*, that's what." She doesn't even bother to close her mouth now between insults. Words just ooze out like sludgy venom.

"Okay," I say. Seems like this would be a good time to insult her back, seeing as I'm walking through that door. But the memory of this moment—along with all other moments from my life—will be permanently etched in my brain, and I don't want this particular one to be of a fight.

Mom's face softens, and she closes her eyes. "You know I don't mean that, right?"

"I know, Mom."

A sigh, deep and full of sadness. "I don't know why I say things," she says, her voice now little more than a drunken whisper.

"I don't know either."

A pause. Ten seconds pass. Fifteen.

Then: "He's the only one I ever loved."

She's never said these words before.

"Who? Dad?"

My mother doesn't answer directly but confirms my guess when she speaks again. "I hate him for what he did."

I reach out to touch her arm, a small intimate gesture of support, but I drop my hand back to my side before making contact. Funny how empathy can weigh a thousand pounds while disdain floats, lighter than air.

"Me too, Mom."

Mom finally falls silent. I wait by her side for a full minute, then give her one last look, turn, and walk toward the front door.

As I reach for the knob, she calls out from the other room. "You get a card from him?"

I don't turn around. "Yeah."

"Wha'd it say?"

I don't even wrestle with how to answer. "The usual."

"Okay."

"Okay, then."

I lift my backpack, sling it over my right shoulder, and open the front door.

Mom calls out again. She has one last thing to say, two words delivered in the numbest of voices.

"Happy birthday."

THIRTEEN

THE FALL DOWN THE stairs when I was seven could have killed me. Instead, it broke me open.

When I finally returned home from the hospital, I was certain my brain was busted despite the doctor's assurances I'd heal *just fine, in time*. I felt certain because now when my mother said numbers, I saw colors. I don't remember much of life before the accident, but I did know my brain wasn't thinking the same way, which used to be more like a straight line but had become a thousand overlapping circles. I could suddenly remember every word spoken to me and all the words I saw on a page.

One day, a week after coming home from the hospital all those years ago, I tested myself. I pulled the family Bible off the shelf. I opened it to a random page before scanning it for a few moments, noting that every short chunk of writing had a number next to it. I remember thinking they were called *verses*.

After five seconds of this, I flipped to another page, repeated the process. Then I did it three more times. Five pages in total, five seconds per page. I shut the book, sat on the floor of my room, and closed my eyes.

What was the number on the third page I looked at? I asked myself.

Then I answered out loud, "Six fifty-eight."

A distinct chill ran all the way up my arms in that moment.

"And what were the words next to the little number three on the page?"

The answer came without hesitation because I didn't have to think. I just looked at the photograph in my brain, as easy as looking at the page itself. "O Lord, You brought my soul up from the grave; You have kept me alive, that I should not go down to the pit."

I grabbed the Bible to check if I was right, but I didn't have to. I was never more certain of being right about something in my life.

And yes, I had recited the verse perfectly.

I didn't know what any of it meant, but it was clear in that moment: I was a very different little girl than the one I'd been before the fall. There was fear and excitement in these discoveries. It was like I was Wonder Woman, figuring out my special powers for the first time.

I quizzed myself four more times that day, once for each remaining Bible page. Four more questions, four more correct answers.

I remember not wanting to tell my mother. I had these amazing new abilities, but they came from being pushed down the stairs. I didn't want her taking credit. The magic was mine alone.

Within a week, I discovered my final superpower: drawing like a real artist. Even more than the remembering, the drawing was the coolest superhero power I could have asked for. I wasn't just a memory freak who saw numbers as colors. I was artistically gifted. That's the kind of thing other people gravitate to. The visual.

But there were also some not-so-good side effects of my trauma. I soon realized even small groups of people now overwhelmed me, and grocery store trips with my mother were torture. And when I *was* with people, I never wanted to look at them, not in the face, because maybe they could figure out who I was now and do something to take my powers away.

But the worst side effect was having soupy memories of my before life. And the worst of the worst was not even remembering my father.

After my bones healed, I finally went back to school, and sitting in that second-grade class for the first time made me realize not only how different I'd become but how unlike any other kid I was. And rather than hide from that, I chose to embrace my new self. I didn't want to conceal my superpowers.

Turned out I liked being special.

As it also turned out, being special was a very lonely thing.

FOURTEEN

STANDING IN FRONT OF my house with the backpack slung over my shoulder, I take a moment to breathe, close my eyes, and check in with my father.

Hi, Dad.

Hiya, Pen Pen.

I'm leaving now.

I can see that. Aren't you rushing things a bit? You've been insulated your whole life, and now, what, you're just going away?

I feel myself nodding. *I wouldn't be if you hadn't left.*

Nah, little girl. That's too easy. Seems to me you been winding yourself up for twenty-one years, and now you can't store any more pent-up energy. You're craving the wild no matter what. But that doesn't mean you can't be thoughtful with how you go about things.

I know what I'm doing.

This makes him laugh, a rare thing in our conversations. *You're really never going to come back?* he asks. *Whatcha going to do when your little road trip is over?*

Just because I know what I'm doing doesn't mean I have all the answers yet.

Oh, well, sorry. I kinda thought that's exactly what it meant.

Now he's just pissing me off. *When I say I know what I'm doing,* I tell him, *it means I'm certain I want to leave. I know all this seems rash and like a big reaction to your letter, but maybe you're right, maybe I am wound up and need to get the hell out of here. Maybe you're just an excuse for me to leave, but I want to know what's out there. I want to find your notes, see what you were thinking back then. And find out what's so great about the wild that it's worth leaving your family for.*

I wait.

He never replies.

I open my eyes, start walking down the street, check my Casio. Just about 4:00 p.m.

As I walk I do a mental inventory of my possessions. My clothes: I'm wearing Jordache jeans, purple T-shirt, and well-scuffed Reebok sneakers. In my backpack are a few more shirts and pants, flannel pj's. I also have some other items: Some toiletries. An umbrella. A tattered copy of *The Princess Bride*—which I don't really need because I know every word, but there's a comfort in the physical pages.

And my purse, such a little thing, chicken-scratched brown with a zipper, containing a wallet, a house key, ChapStick, tampons, hair ties, and torn pages of magazines, mostly photos that grabbed me in a particular way. I also have some money of my own and the money I took (stole) from my mother. Ninety-six dollars in total.

Ninety-six. Leprechaun green.

No driver's license. Just a state ID card.

Are these enough things to start whatever journey this will become?

I don't know.

But it'll have to do. At least for now.

Step after step, I allow myself to be directionless, just for a little bit.

And I think, *What's this really about?*

To which I don't have an answer. Not really.

So I reframe the question: *What are you hoping to find?*

The sun leans in, presses heavily on my face.

My father, of course.

But no. That's not all of it, is it? There's something more. Something more intangible than lost notes written years ago.

Happiness.

Maybe I'll find happiness.

I think about happiness every now and then, just as I think about death. I picture myself smiling, having found happiness, *real* happiness, pure and flawless, distilled to its essence, not to be doubted, argued against, or diluted.

Perhaps you'll find death, my brain interjects.

Maybe.

I summon the vision of the airplane plummeting into the ocean, cringing at the horror.

But I can't see the future. I just have to walk toward it. Toward beautiful and ugly things. Wide-open skies and final breaths.

And I have a hunch the future will become the present at an alarming speed.

FIFTEEN

THE SUMMER AIR IS leaden and thick; I can nearly drink the humidity.

Sweat slickens my armpits, despite my antiperspirant. After a block on foot, I get to my familiar bus stop, knowing the schedule by heart. The unmistakable sound of a bus engine grows in the distance. I turn my head, and there it is, as if summoned.

Two minutes early.

The bus door opens, and a familiar face smiles at me.

Ugh. Nick.

I take this route to the institute whenever my mom can't drive, which is a lot of the time, so I know all the drivers. Nick is my least favorite. Skinny and toothy and with greasy hair perpetually pasted against his scalp. He always tries to flirt with me.

"Well, hey there, good lookin'," he says. "Wasn't expecting you."

"Hey." I flash my bus pass but keep my eyes to the ground.

"Where you headed?"

"Does it matter?"

"Suppose I'll find out when you get off." He lets out a fourth grader's chuckle.

I don't answer, mostly because Nick doesn't deserve a response. But also because I don't have a firm answer. Minneapolis? Might as well start making my way to the first note on the treasure map, I suppose. Some tree outside a Kmart. It sounds ridiculous even thinking about it, but I need to start somewhere.

This is a local bus and doesn't travel far, so wherever I get out, it won't be outside Eau Claire. I'll need to get to a bus station.

And I'll be needing more cash.

I sit next to an older woman, who tucks her arm in as I sit down. Like I have a contagious disease or something.

The bus groans and wheezes as it makes its rounds.

Fifteen minutes later it stops at the Oakwood Mall.

Yes, the mall.

Maybe this is where I'm supposed to get out first. The mall is just the kind of place where things happen, opportunities are found. And my stomach reminds me I'll need to eat soon—I could get a corn dog.

"Mall, huh?" Nick cracks an ugly smile as I whisk past. "Told ya I'd figure out where you were headed, didn't I? Next time maybe I'll join you." Then he shoots me a wink.

"You're a prick," I tell him, knowing I'll likely never see him again. "You've always been a prick."

The mall's entrance is a wall of shimmering dark glass, holding the reflection of the sky and hiding the contents inside. A vast sea of cars fills the parking lot, the asphalt dark and smooth, not even a year old. I pass through the automatic doors and find a steady stream of traffic inside, mostly women.

Noise everywhere. All the chatter, the shouting of little kids, the piped-in music, the electric hum of the lights.

I've been here three times before, each occasion with my mother. Once for new shoes, once to wait while Mom got her nails done, and the first time when the mall had its grand opening last year. October 15, 1986. There were hundreds of people that day, a speech by the mayor, and pink balloons for everyone. Some said the mall was *the very thing* Eau Claire needed to remain relevant. And I remember thinking what, aside from the dictionary definition, *relevant* even really meant.

I concluded being relevant meant you would still be talked about after you were gone. But really, once a person is dead, does it matter?

Of all the stores in the mall, the one I dislike most is JCPenney. On that grand opening day nine months ago, Mom confessed to me with a twisted grin that I had, in fact, been named after the store. That I'd been conceived in a dressing room of the Watertown JCPenney back in 1965 after a drunken road trip. It was the first time I heard that story, never having known the truth of where my name came from. In fact, I only ever asked my mother once why I was named Penny, back when I was ten. The answer she gave was delivered without hesitation or even a touch of sarcasm.

Because you're pretty much worthless.

So, yeah, that's Mom.

The mall floors gleam, and the entire place secretes a chemical smell, the good kind—manufactured cleanliness.

I stroll by the arcade, which offers an electronic symphony from within, a thousand instruments playing disparate pieces, and yet it's somehow kinda beautiful. The place is half-filled with teenage boys, all gangly and jerky, hitting buttons and yanking joysticks with reckless abandon. I imagine them doing the same thing during their first sexual experiences, working feverishly toward some unattainable high score.

I keep walking, past the Thom McAn, the Waldenbooks, the Gap, and Camelot Music. Toward the food court.

Minutes later I'm there, torn between Corn Daddy's and Burger King. I'm just about to decide when I spy a man, maybe forty, in a chair next to an easel. He's holding a pad of large white sketching sheets. A young woman—older than me, but not by a lot—sits on a stool maybe six feet in front of him, her hands on her knees, with perfect posture and a Super Bowl–sized smile.

I forget about the food for a moment and watch them.

It takes about ten minutes for the man to sketch this woman, and when he finishes, he rips the sheet from the easel and hands it to her.

The woman nods but does not smile, a shame because I wanted to see the expression again. Instead, her face wears creases of disappointment. She digs into her purse, pays the guy, and walks away.

The idea hits me at once.

Forget the food.

I just found a way to make some money.

SIXTEEN

I FEEL LIKE A creep running after her, but I'm too excited about my idea to let it stop me.

"Excuse me."

The woman turns, and this close to her, I'm struck by her beauty. Long and full chestnut hair, moss-green eyes, flawless skin. There's a timelessness about her that catches my breath, if just for a moment.

"Yes?"

"I saw you back there," I say, doing my damnedest not to stare at the ground. "Getting your picture drawn. You didn't seem happy with it."

"Who are you?" she asks.

"Penny Bly." I don't offer my hand.

"Okay, I guess what I meant was what do you want?"

"Can I see it? The picture?"

She plants her right hand on her hip. "Why?"

"I'm curious."

The woman stares me down for a few seconds, but by god, I hold

her gaze. Finally, she shrugs, says, "Whatever." Then she hands me the
rolled-up paper.

I unfurl it and see exactly what I expected: an over-the-top caricature, the woman drawn with a disproportionately large forehead, teeth
the size of tombstones, and a tiny little body (except for balloon-shaped
breasts bulging from her shirt). The caricaturist drew her leaping to hit
a tennis ball, and he wrote her name in a swirling script at the bottom
of the sheet.

Heather.

"I don't even know why I had it done," Heather says. "I'd seen him
there before, from time to time, and thought it might be a fun little gift
for my husband. A goofy thing he could put in his office. But—"

"But it's fucking terrible," I say.

"Well, I don't know I'd say—"

"It doesn't look anything like you. I know it's supposed to be
cartoony—that's the point. But even as a cartoon, it doesn't have a shred
of your essence."

"My essence?"

"Your frequency. The stuff that makes you *you.*"

"And how would you know what my essence is?"

There's no short explanation for this, so I don't try. "I have a talent
for it."

Heather tilts her head like a dog hearing a long-off siren. "You trying
to sell me something?"

"Yes," I tell her, my excitement growing. "You paid five dollars for
this." I recall the man's sign.

Heather nods. "So?"

I take a breath, try not to talk too fast. Sometimes I do that. "I want to draw you. I'll be fast, I promise. And if you don't think it's any good, it's free. But if you like it, really like it, you pay me what you think it's worth."

She looks around, as if hoping to spot a friend to pull her away from the conversation. "I don't know. I have more shopping to do and then an appointment."

"Keep shopping," I say. "Then meet me back here in fifteen minutes. I'll do my drawing on the back of this one."

Confusion spreads on her face.

"Don't you need me sitting in front of you or something?"

I shake my head. "I've memorized you."

This earns me a few rapid blinks and then a pause. "You're kinda weird, huh?"

I shrug. "I don't think that's for me to decide."

She then releases her hand from her hip along with seemingly half the tension her body was holding. "Fine, okay, I guess. Sure. Fifteen minutes. What do I have to lose?"

"Literally nothing."

"Now don't run away with that drawing. I might hate it, but it still cost me five bucks. Fifteen minutes. Right back here."

Why the hell would I run away with her drawing?

"Fifteen minutes," I confirm. "Right back here."

She turns to leave when I realize my plan is potentially doomed from the beginning.

"Heather," I call out.

She turns. "Yes?"

I nod at her purse, which looks like it could hold the world. "I need a pen."

SEVENTEEN

HEATHER'S PEN IS MEDIUM point. I prefer fine, but this will work.

I take the crappy cartoon and flip it over. The blank white page staring up at me is delicious.

I close my eyes and think of her, this Heather, and I picture her as someone who doesn't use that Super Bowl–smile as much as she should, maybe because someone once told her that's the way women move forward, get promoted, get the same opportunities as men. Don't smile or they won't take you seriously.

But that smile, or at least a version of it, is surely part of Heather's essence. Not the big smile the shitty cartoonist drew. Something softer, like the haze of an early-morning sun.

I open my eyes and let the blank canvas suck me into another world.

The dots.

It's all about the dots.

Sometimes I feel like a fraud about my artwork, because, really, I have nothing to do with it. At least not consciously.

When I draw someone, all I need to do is concentrate in just the right way, and when I do, little black imaginary dots start appearing on whatever canvas I'm using. It's kind of like those dots you get when you rub your eyes too hard, but, in the case of my drawings, they appear one at a time.

And all I have to do? Just poke each dot with my pen before it disappears. And they come fast, so I need to really pay attention, but if I keep up, an image gradually forms. An image that is nearly photographic in detail. I still don't get it.

Now.

Here they come.

I stop thinking of Heather altogether. My mind clears of all imagery, and I only focus on jabbing the tip of the pen on every dot I see before it disappears. Over and over, hundreds at first, then over a thousand.

I'm lost in my head as I sit on the cool and polished stone floor of the mall, crisscross applesauce outside a RadioShack, very nearly but not completely oblivious to the passersby.

I can vaguely sense them, and maybe there are even a few who've stopped to see what I'm doing.

I never really see the full picture until the end, and I know it's done when the dots stop appearing. I always wait, but only a few seconds. Four seconds is the longest it's ever taken for a dot to appear. If four seconds go by without a dot, I know my work is complete.

Time passes. I don't know how long.

Finally, the dots stop. I ink the final one, lean back, and absorb for the first time what my brain and left hand have conjured.

I see Heather, exactly as my mind snapshotted her. And in my picture, Heather's smile is not big and brash but restrained, really no more than what the Mona Lisa herself wore, a smile not of confidence but of complete vulnerability, as if Heather is allowing herself an occasion of something new, something exciting. Perhaps something a bit dangerous.

This is how I see her, this woman I met for all of a minute. On this page is Heather's essence, her frequency.

I look up and realize I've attracted a crowd of seven, all leaning over.

"Who is that?" a teen asks. I remember seeing him from the arcade.

"Heather," I reply, no more information to give. The small crowd makes me a little uneasy. Not so much that I don't like crowds, but I really don't like being the reason for one.

Heather walks up seconds later, finds me, stares down at the portrait. "Jesus Christ."

I struggle to make eye contact. "Do you like it?"

And there, just in the inside corners of Heather's eyes, tears, threatening to breach the lower lids, which they don't. But it's close. "I…I can't believe you just drew this."

She's happy. That's good.

"Would you consider it worth ten dollars?"

There's no hesitation. "Yes. Yes, I would." She digs into her purse, into her wallet. She hands me a twenty-dollar bill. "Keep it all."

I take the cash, flush with pride. I should have left Willow Brook years ago to pursue a commercial side to my art.

I hand Heather the picture.

"Thank you," she says. And it's the kind of thank-you a person means. Then she walks away, her pace slower than before. I keep my gaze on her until Heather turns the corner, thinking about the portrait hanging in the office of Heather's husband. I wonder if he sees the same essence in her as I do.

"Goddamn."

The voice startles me a bit. I turn and see a man about my age. Maybe that makes him more of a boy than a man.

"You're fucking good," he says.

I don't respond right away, taking him in instead. His shoulder-length dirty-blond hair is fine—not stringy—and parted in the middle so it sweeps along the sides of his face, cutting off the outside edges of each eye. He's got a whisper of a mustache that's not *quite* gross and skin as smooth as any I've ever seen. And his denim jacket (ripped in places, sewed in others), sports a Smiths iron-on patch about five degrees off-center.

"Um…thanks," I say.

He takes a step closer and is now firmly entrenched in my personal space.

I take a step back.

"I mean it," he says. "That shit was amazing. I was watching you the whole time and…I don't know. You were, like, in a trance or something."

"Okay."

"You in school for art?"

"No."

"You graduated already?"

"No."

He smiles.

And wow.

That smile.

"You're not a big talker, are you?" he asks.

I'm not, but right now I kind of wish I were. "I was just answering your questions."

"And I was just wondering where you took classes. I do some drawing myself, and I'm trying to get better."

"I've never taken classes for drawing."

"No shit? You're self-taught? Because portraits are a pain in the ass. The symmetry kills me."

"No shit," I tell him.

"I'm Travis," he says.

"I'm Penny."

"You do any teaching? Classes on sketch art?"

"No."

"You live around here?"

"I used to."

That smile again. "You're giving me nothing here. You must be a blast at a cocktail party."

"I've never been to a cocktail party."

"Big fucking surprise."

I have the sudden and distinct sense of failing some kind of social experiment, and though it doesn't matter with this person, not really, it matters in the wild. Out here I'm going to need to be an extrovert when it's important, no matter how much against my nature it is.

I need to try harder.

"Nice to meet you, Travis."

He thumbs the pocket edges of his jeans. "Yeah, you too. Look, seriously, I'm not hitting on you or anything. It's just that…" He lifts a hand and squeezes the back of his neck, while shifting his gaze to the ground. "Man, I love drawing. I fucking love it. The idea of getting paid for drawing is, like, I don't know." He looks up. "That would be awesome."

Awesome.

Is it awesome?

I consider it.

It is.

"That was the first time I've been paid for a drawing," I tell him. Then I reconsider. "Actually, it's the first time I've been paid for anything."

Now he laughs, just a short chuckle, and I can tell from the tone that he's not laughing at me.

"You want a corn dog?" he asks.

"More than anything."

And as we walk to the food court, I sneak a glance at Travis and think about the warning from my father about dragons in the wild.

Well, hell, Pen Pen. They're pretty much everywhere.

EIGHTEEN

DR. BROCK AND I came into each other's lives a decade ago.

I was eleven at the time, and nearly four years had passed since my fall down the stairs. Nearly four years of being the new Penny. The special Penny.

There was this place that studied the human brain, right in Eau Claire. The Willow Brook Institute for the Brain. Somehow they heard about me, and Dr. Brock invited my mom and me in for a consult. On our first visit, he told me they might be interested in learning how my mind works.

It was on my third visit that he told me I was a savant.

One of only seventy-five known in the world.

That moment, like all others, remains razor-sharp in my mind.

———

We were in Dr. Brock's office, just the two of us, my mother outside smoking Pall Malls.

I loved that Dr. Brock talked up to me, not down, and didn't view my abilities as someone would a circus act. In school I was a freak. At home I was a freak. There, in the doctor's office, this eleven-year-old was worthy of attention and respect.

Just before he told me, Dr. Brock took a deep breath, as adults do when they're being super serious. "Usually, a person we would consider a savant is born that way, and they often have mental disabilities. As rare as it is to be a savant, even more rare is a savant who became that way through an accident."

It wasn't an accident, I remember thinking.

Dr. Brock continued. "Is it okay if I give you a few tests?"

The idea of tests didn't sound like fun. "What kind?"

"Nothing too difficult, I promise. I'm going to give you a few math questions…it's okay if you get them wrong or if they sound too hard. Then I'm going to show you some pictures and ask how you feel about them, and finally I'll show you some pages from books and see if you can remember any of the words. How does that sound?"

"I'm not good at math."

"No? Would you say you can do math like other kids at school? No better, no worse?"

"Maybe worse."

"Okay, that's just fine. We can skip the math testing for now."

Half an hour later, we were done. I didn't feel so special when talking about the pictures he'd held up, and I kept thinking there was a right answer and a wrong answer to everything and about how frustrating it was not to know.

But I aced the memory stuff. He hadn't even made it hard, asking me to recite text from a kids' book instead of a dictionary or encyclopedia.

Easy peasy.

During the testing Dr. Brock held a steady face, and despite my memory recall, I felt like I kind of let him down. Like I wasn't actually that special, certainly not in a one-of-seventy-five-in-the-world kind of way.

"What else, Penny?" he then asked.

"What else what?"

"Well, we're certainly going to have many more visits together, assuming it's okay with your mom. So we'll have plenty of time to get to know each other. But for now, is there anything else that's been different since your accident? Anything at all that comes to mind?"

I didn't have to think long. "I see numbers as colors."

He blinked, processed, then asked, "What?"

"Say a number," I said.

"Okay, fifty-four."

"Fifty-four. Blue, but real dark, like the middle of the ocean. Almost black."

"I see," the doctor said after a few moments. "Well, I certainly want to talk more about that next time. But before we end here today, is there anything else you want me to know? Any other...*ability* that seems new after what happened a few years ago?"

What happened. It felt almost like I'd done something wrong, stolen a candy bar or cursed at my teacher.

"I can draw now," I said.

"Tell me more about that."

And I did, but I remember feeling like I didn't say any of the words right because they didn't sound like what I meant. There's always a big gap between thinking and talking, and sometimes I fall short.

"I can show you," I then said.

He'd looked at his watch. Bored people always looked at their watches. "We have about ten minutes left."

"That should be enough."

"All right, then." He flipped a page on his notebook and handed it to me. The blank page was lined, which wasn't my favorite—nothing beat a crisp blank page of depthless white—but it would do. "Pen or pencil?" he asked.

"Pen."

He handed over his pen, which was still warm from his fingers. "What do you want to draw?"

"I like faces."

"That's a good challenge. Faces are tough."

"Okay."

"Whose face do you want to draw?"

I scanned the room, spying a stack of magazines on a small table. I walked over and dug through to find one I wanted. A *Newsweek* dated August 22, 1977.

A pasty-faced man on the cover, looking off to the side. Blue button-down shirt open over a white undershirt. There was someone else's hand on his stomach and one on his shoulder, as if keeping him from flying away. And this man…what a goofy look on his face. Like cartoon-character goofy, as if he didn't have a care in the world.

I remember the words printed bold and large beneath the man's image.

The Sick World of Son of Sam

"This face," I said.

Dr. Brock furrowed his brow. "Why him?"

"Because he's interesting to me."

"Why?"

I looked back at the cover. "Because he's so sick, he made the cover of a magazine."

"Do you know who he is?"

"No."

Dr. Brock fell quiet for a second, looked at his watch again, then said, "Okay, then. Draw him." He pointed to the couch. "You want to sit there and draw? You could have the magazine on the table in front of you."

I went to the couch but didn't take the magazine with me. "I don't need it."

I looked down at the blank page and closed my eyes for a few seconds, dipping into that essential space of concentration.

The doctor might have said something, but if he did, I didn't hear him. I was fully focused on the paper.

C'mon, I thought. *Where are you?*

Maybe it was because the paper was lined, but it took longer this time. Twenty seconds, then thirty, and nothing. I just stared. And at nearly a full minute, just when I figured it wasn't going to happen and that I'd look like a failure in front of the doctor, it began.

One dot, then a second, and a third.

A tiny smile pulled at my lips as I began placing real ink dots on top of each imaginary one before they disappeared. They came and went fast, but by this time, I'd gotten good at keeping up.

It took less than the ten minutes remaining, and when the final dot came and went, I stared at my drawing and saw something in this sick man's face, this Son of Sam, like a desperate insecurity and fear that only a really good actor could cover with a smile.

I saw death on that man's face, but I didn't know whose. Or how many.

Then I stood, walked over, handed Dr. Brock the notebook. He gave me a tight smile as he turned it over.

The smile disappeared, replaced with an expression I could only label as wonder. I'd seen it before.

Most people said something about my drawings, about how great I was, how amazing, what a natural.

But Dr. Brock said nothing, and to me it felt like the biggest compliment in the world.

NINETEEN

TRAVIS SAYS HE NEEDS a smoke before a corn dog, that *that's* the correct order of things. He asks me to hang out with him as he does.

Okay.

Outside, the lights from the JCPenney sign hardly cast a glow, but true darkness will come before long, and the letters will shine like beacons. I look to my left, to the sunset, a special kind of orange-and-pink chaos today, but its beauty is wasted on the ugly gas station in the foreground.

Travis. Lighting a Camel, his head cocked, an ease about him, a lord of the lost. Maybe he's a sunset uglied by a gas station.

He takes his first puff, lets the smoke slide out through his flared nostrils, then sits on the curb outside the department store.

I follow suit.

"How old are you?" I ask.

Travis takes another drag, then lets it settle in and contaminate all his insides for a bit before freeing it. "Nineteen. You?"

"Twenty-one. Today, in fact."

"No shit? Today?"

"Yes."

"You should be out celebrating," he says. "Go to a bar or something. Hell, you can drink legally now."

"That's not really my thing."

Truth is, I've never had a drink or a smoke in my life. Maybe I'll start in the wild. Then again, I've seen what those things have done to my mother, and I sure as hell don't want to end up like her.

"So what *is* your thing?" Travis asks.

I scrunch my face and say the first thing that comes to my mind. "I'm running away from home."

He keeps an even expression for just over three seconds, after which he bursts out laughing. A genuine laugh, it seems, which grates on me. "You can't run away when you're twenty-one, you know that, right? Most people don't even live at home at our age."

For all the universe of knowledge in my brain, that simple fact never entered my consciousness. I've been living under someone else's roof all my life. I can't help but feel like a runaway.

I reach for his cigarette, and he releases it to my fingertips.

Screw it.

I bring it to my lips, the damp from his mouth on the paper—and inhale. The smoke attacks and my lungs recoil, and now I'm coughing until tears come, and Travis laughs again, damn him, but it's okay, okay because it's something new, and despite how bad this something new is, it's still better than the familiar.

When I recover, I hand the cigarette back. "I guess I'm not running away. I'm actually running *to* something."

Travis, the cigarette back in his mouth, says, "Oh, yeah? What's that?"

"My dad," I tell him, and with those two words comes a sharp pang of nausea, most likely from the cigarette. Also a reminder I need food.

"Where's he?" Travis asks.

"California. Maybe."

"You're gonna head all the way—"

"Can we not talk about this right now?"

Travis takes another drag and lets the smoke trickle from between his lips. Pretty lips. "Sure thing. You brought it up. Didn't mean to piss you off."

"You didn't. I just..." I shake my head. "He's the one I'm pissed off at. I'm so angry, but also...like, desperate to see him. I talk to him sometimes, in my head, and it's comforting. I swear I can hear his voice."

He flicks a dangling piece of ash to the curb. "When's the last time you saw him?"

"Thirteen years, eight months, and eight days."

"Wow, you keep count?"

"I can't help it."

He nods as if he understands. "That's a long time."

I'm tempted to take another hit from the cigarette but figure I might just puke if I do. Why do we chase things that hurt us?

"You ever love and hate someone at the same time?" I ask.

Travis waits a few seconds before answering, "I mostly just feel indifferent."

This might be the saddest thing I've ever heard.

It makes me want to talk to Dad.

So I close my eyes and call for him, loving and hating that I do.

TWENTY

HI, DAD.

Hiya, Pen Pen.

I'm talking to a guy.

Is that so? What's he like?

Not sure yet. But he likes my drawings.

Well, everyone does.

I suppose so. He also draws. So I guess we have that in common.

Do you like him?

I consider this. *I don't know. He's nice. Kind of sad. And maybe a little stupid or at least pretends to be.*

He pauses. *I see. Well, what does your gut tell you? When you look at this nice, stupid boy, what does your gut tell you about him?*

A fresh wave of cigarette smoke wafts into my nostrils. *There's more to him than what he shows the world.*

In a good way or a bad way?

Good, I think.

Well, then, that's something.

I gotta go.

Okay, Pen. Okay. Just one more thing.

Yes?

Be careful.

TWENTY-ONE

HERE'S A FACT: TOTAL memory recall is fucking exhausting.

I've built up my stamina for it over the years, but each day leaves me wiped out and ready for bed before prime-time TV is even in full swing.

And I sleep like I'm dead. Ten hours a night if I can manage. In that dark void, there are rarely dreams or imagery of any kind. Sleep is my brain's chance to shut down after so many hours of collecting, storing, and accessing data.

The yawn builds inside me, then lets itself out.

"You kinda spaced out for a minute there," Travis says.

"I need to eat," I say. "And then I need to sleep."

"Let me buy you dinner." He stomps his cigarette out on the ground. "Granted, the food court is no Sizzler, but it's the best I can do."

"Okay."

We head back into the mall and walk side by side until we reach the food court. It's busy at this hour, a steady hum of business, families having a night out. They all seem happy. I wonder what that's like.

Once, at a Bennigan's, my mother ordered a chocolate shake and asked them to put rum in it. When the waitress said they couldn't do that, Mom told the teenage girl to go fuck herself to the moon, whatever that meant.

There's no line at Corn Daddy's, so we beeline it over. The pimply teen behind the counter seems rightfully humiliated by his bright-striped uniform and Day-Glo hat, making almost no eye contact while he takes our order.

We take a seat with our own corn dogs and lemonades at a hard plastic table. The chairs are attached to the table by swinging metal arms, as if someone would certainly steal them otherwise.

I glance to my right. The caricature artist has gone for the day. I wonder how much he made. Enough to feed himself for a day?

"So, runaway, where are you staying tonight?" Travis asks.

"Haven't figured that out yet."

"You ever been on your own before?"

While I nibble at the corn crust of my dog, Travis dips his in a kiddie pool of ketchup, then lops a third of it off in one bite.

"First day," I say.

"And you got no plan?"

"Like I said, I'm going to find my father."

"That's not a plan," he says. "That's a *goal*. The plan is the moment-to-moment shit. Where you're gonna stay. How you're gonna eat. What do you do to make money. That stuff."

He's right. A plan versus a goal. He's totally right.

"I'm working on the plan. I sold that drawing for twenty bucks. I was thinking maybe I could make some more money doing that, and that would get me enough to head out west."

"So, what, you're gonna hide in the JCPenney, sleep there, then get to work competing with the cartoon guy tomorrow?"

"That's ridiculous."

"Really? I think it sounds awesome." He washes down half his lemonade, wipes his face with his arm. "I've always thought it would be great to spend the night in a closed mall. Go to the sporting goods store, grab some roller skates, and just haul ass all over the place."

I don't tell him so, but that does sound like fun.

"Do you live on your own?" I ask.

He looks down at the table, shaking his head. "Nah. Still with my folks."

"Why?"

When he looks up, he locks in tight with me. My chest tightens just a little.

"Never figured out the plan," he says.

"But you have a goal?"

"Go anywhere. Just get the hell out of here. I'm so fucking bored with everything."

I nod. "I get that. I've never even been out of this state since I was little."

"Wow, you are sheltered."

The word hits me, and I don't like it. It makes me feel like a caged animal or something. I open my mouth to argue before realizing he's described my life perfectly.

He looks at me for a few seconds, nodding his head, and something slightly dark comes over his face. A thought, a memory, maybe an intention.

The darkness suits him.

"So, after thirteen years, you just now decided to look for him?"

I take another bite. "Exactly."

"Well," he says, "sounds like you're braver than me."

"I don't think it's brave. It's just something I need to do."

He leans over the table. "But you're *doing* it. Most people don't end up doing the things they think they should be doing because it scares them. Look at me... I'm a high school dropout, living at home, and working for three fifty an hour at Pep Boys. I love to draw but have no idea what the hell I would ever do with it. You? You sold your art today. Do you know what a big deal that is?"

"So you said."

He shakes his head. "There's a reason they call it *starving artist*. You never hear about starving doctors or starving accountants. Point is, you've got a goal but no plan, and you're still doing it. You're leaving. You're going—"

"Into the wild."

"Yeah, that's right." He points his finger at me. "That's exactly fuckin' right. Into the wild."

In this moment I realize I like pleasing him, which is unusual not just because I barely know this guy but also because I don't care much about pleasing anyone except for Dr. Brock. And Travis and Dr. Brock are on opposite ends of the solar system, if not the entire galaxy.

He narrows his eyes. "You can stay with me tonight. I mean, if you want. At my folks' house... They're cool enough. Got a couch you can crash on."

Stay with him?

The idea of it instantly fills me with ice and fire, with neither of those two things blending into something warm and comfortable.

He fills in for my silence. "I swear I'm not a serial killer or anything."

"Exactly what a serial killer would say."

He laughs, then holds up his hands. "I mean, suit yourself. I was just offering."

I size him up again, wondering if my gut instinct is right. That he has more to offer the world than he shows.

Or if I should heed my father's advice: *Be careful.*

Travis polishes off his corn dog in a sizable gulp and then stands, almost losing his balance as he sweeps his leg up and over the attached seat of the table.

"All right then. Nice meeting you, Penny. Good luck out in the wild."

And then he just walks away.

It's so sudden, and god damn it if there's not a tiny bit of heartbreak in my chest. Could be I'm having a sense of being abandoned yet again. Or maybe that's reading too much into it—how could someone I barely know abandon me?

Nonetheless here I am, still eating half a corn dog and still needing a place to sleep. In a moment of reflex (that I prefer to label *logic*), I call out.

"Travis."

He turns.

"Fine," I say. "On your couch."

He takes a step toward me, smirks. "You're welcome."

There's this thing I'm guessing to be true about the wild.

The wild is where all the creatures live, the ones who grab you from the shadows, pull you into the cold and dark places where no one can hear you scream. I'm trusting that Travis isn't such a creature, a dragon, because what a horrible television cliché that would be. Spending my first night away from home only to fall victim to a nineteen-year-old with a wisp of a mustache and a look that actually makes me enjoy holding eye contact.

"Thank you," I say. Meaning it.

TWENTY-TWO

WE DRIVE THE FEW miles from the mall to his neighborhood in his red Volkswagen Scirocco (scirocco is a Mediterranean wind that comes from the Sahara, I recall from the *Encyclopedia Britannica*, and why would that be a good name for a car?) that has a tear in the passenger seat and a mesmerizing spiderweb crack in the windshield.

His parents' house is of the two-story variety, big empty driveway, and a lawn more green than brown. It's much nicer than the one I walked away from.

"My folks are out." He turns off the ignition and opens his door. "Good thing. Otherwise you'd end up answering all sorts of questions."

"What kinds of questions?"

"You know. Typical parent shit. All those little probing questions asked in an innocent voice, just so they can find out your life story."

I've never really thought about my life as a story, only as a series of events.

I wonder what genre my life story would be. Mystery, I suppose. With one profound moment of horror.

"C'mon," he says.

I get out, smell the night, sweet and heady. Cicadas chorus from a nearby tree, the collective hum peaking and dipping, an insect sine wave.

He leads me inside, and I smell stale cigarette smoke, just like my own house. It's the kind of smell that settles into the carpet, burrowing and festering, never to come out fully.

Travis beelines for the fridge and, despite the fact that we just ate, makes a sandwich and offers me one as well.

Sure, why not.

Then he grabs a two-liter Coke and a bag of Cheetos. "Let's go up to my room. I've got a TV."

"Where's the couch?" I ask.

"There's one in the living room, but the support's gone to shit. There's another one upstairs, in the loft area, pretty decent. What, you ready for bed already?"

"I'm really tired."

"Jesus, it's only..." He glances over at the microwave. "Eight thirty. Just a little TV. You'll feel better once you eat a bit more."

I take a moment to think about what I'm doing. I don't know this guy, and I'm spending the night in his house. Now he wants me to hang out in his room. Sounds like the setup for a slasher movie.

Still.

There's this thing.

I trust him, though I have no reason to. There's something safe about him. Not harmless, but safe. And my instincts tell me that, in the wild, instincts will be just as important as logic.

"Okay," I say. "But I might fall asleep watching."

"If and when that happens, I'll wake you up and take you to the couch."

Up the stairs, down a hallway, last room on the right. Travis opens the door, and now I smell pot, faint but unmistakable.

I hate the smell of pot.

My mother once had a boyfriend who smoked weed. His name was Randy, and he liked to hug me despite my constant insistence on not being touched. I called him *Handsy Randy*, but only to myself. Handsy Randy smoked pot, sometimes even in front of me, and all I could wonder was why anyone would intentionally destroy their brain cells when they're so hard to come by.

And now, because of the scent inside Travis's room, I have to admit I think a little less of him.

Still, that smile.

The room itself is an explosion, as if a Spencer Gifts vomited all over the walls and floors. A lava lamp sits on a cluttered desk, burping up a continuous stream of globs. Three street signs lean against the far wall: STOP, DO NOT ENTER, and DANGEROUS CURVES AHEAD. They certainly look real enough, so I suppose he stole them, and now I wonder if anyone got hurt or died because they didn't know to stop or because they weren't aware of the upcoming dangerous curves.

Crumpled clothes litter the deep-brown carpet. The bed, a twin like mine back home, looks quite accustomed to being unmade, the sheets and blankets twisted nearly to knots. A blacklight renders a Bob Marley poster into brilliant color; he looks very happy lighting a joint as the words *one love* seem to pulse under his chin.

My gaze settles on a hand-drawn movie poster for *Full Metal Jacket*. The singular image on the poster is a camouflaged soldier's helmet, bullets tucked inside a band stretched front to back, and the words *Born to Kill* handwritten next to a peace sign on the side. The drawing itself is a bit crude and would never be mistaken for the real thing, but there's talent behind the work.

"Did you do this?" I ask.

"Yeah, took me forever. But I like how it turned out. Did it in pencil."

"You're good," I tell him.

"I'm okay. No art genius or anything. But the movie itself is fucking rad," he says. "Just came out. Have you seen it?"

"No."

"You should. I'll go again if you want to go together."

I shake my head.

"There's not a *ton* a killing," Travis says, reading my mind. "Not as much as *Platoon* had. Hell, the whole first half of the movie, only one guy gets shot, but holy shit, what a moment."

I turn to face him. "I don't want to see people shot, not even in a movie." And now I spy the small knife collection displayed on a nightstand near his bed. I quickly count eleven—*eleven. Howard Johnson's orange sherbet*—knives, ranging from a tiny antique-looking blade to a full-size military knife, sheathed in leather.

Knives.

I've never had a bad cut in my life, but there's something about the sight of a blade that turns my guts to ice. I can't see a sharp knife without immediately imagining it slipping with ease into my stomach, just above the belly button. Deep, so deep. And cold, as if the blade was taken directly from a freezer before finding my intestines. If there's such a thing as reincarnation (and I doubt it), I figure in a past life maybe I was one of Jack the Ripper's victims.

Travis's TV is the same size as the one my mother has in her living room, which is to say small. He turns it on and twists the dial by a few rotations. Then he grabs the *TV Guide* on top of the set and thumbs through it.

"There's a movie called *Spring Break* at nine. Until then, maybe catch some of the All-Star game?"

"All-Star game?"

"Yeah. Baseball. You watch baseball?"

"No."

He shrugs. "Me neither, really. But I used to as a kid. Watching it makes me think of back then, I guess, in a good way."

"Okay."

He sits on his bed, and I find a place on the floor, my back against the wall with a pillow in between. I pick at my sandwich and take a handful of Cheetos. Both taste terrible and wonderful.

The baseball game plays, and sleeps tugs at me.

"*Stee-rike one,*" the announcer says.

Soon my eyes are closed, and I'm back to thinking about my dad, a common thing for me to do when all I want to do is sleep. For the millionth time, I wonder what kind of person would leave his family when their only child was in the hospital, and for the millionth time, I tell myself that will be my first question when I finally find him.

"*Was interesting to break down Wade Boggs's batting. As far as the count is concerned, he's scary.*"

I'm asleep before the movie even starts.

TWENTY-THREE

IN THE VOID THERE are images, a rare dream, and on a subconscious level, I'm concerned my brain isn't getting the rest it needs, instead being forced to work overtime. Worse, this is no fantastical dream with imagery bright and bold as all the numbers of the world, but rather this dream is a memory, *another fucking memory*, and not even in my sleep can I escape the trappings of this wondrous and cursed mind.

My father, there he is.

I don't remember much from my life before the fall down the stairs, so my memories of Dad aren't etched in steel but rather written in chalk on a well-used blackboard. Fuzzy, indistinct.

But in this dream, he's as clear as a movie star on a forty-foot screen: wiry and skinny, with ropy veins on long pale arms, white T-shirt and blue jeans, bare feet and a can of beer within arm's reach. He's on our front porch, and I decide I'm six in this dream, six and confused by love. Confused because I love my father and fear my mother, so what does that make the feelings my parents have for each other? Surely it can only be all love or all fear, nothing in between.

My dad holds his Gibson acoustic guitar in his lap, the setting sun occasionally reflecting off the instrument's shiny golden body as he rocks forward and back while he plays, shooting light beams into my face. He sings as he plays, something about a woman named Cecilia and how she's breaking his heart, but the song is too upbeat to be sad. He's good, I think, but in this dream, I'm only six, so what the hell do I know?

A smile pulls my face wide.

Then comes my mother, nearly barreling through the screen door, storming this pleasant dream like a boogeyman frothing to life from beneath a child's bed at midnight. Her words are muddled gobbledygook, but the tone is clear as can be: *You're worthless. You don't contribute. Stop singing and having fun when my life is so fucking hard.* And such.

Then she vanishes as quickly as she arrived, a vapor leaving a foul, acrid stench as a reminder of its intrusion.

Dad locks eyes with me, offers me a wink and a crooked smile.

Says, *We'll get it all figured out, Pen Pen.*

He always called me *Pen Pen.*

Things'll get better. She's just a little stressed. Fact is, might not hurt for your mother to see a doctor.

In this sepia dream, he leans in and makes his face more serious. *Seeing how angry she seems to get these days. Sometimes a person's brain acts differently than they want it to, and they make pills for things like that, but you know your mother. So stubborn.*

I'm about to tell him we'll find a way to get Mom to take some pills, anything that'll smooth out the constantly shifting tides of her emotions. Maybe I'll even suggest grinding up the drugs and slipping the powder into her food, her beer even, if it comes to that.

In this dream my father leans closer, poised to hear my grand ideas, but my mouth won't open, not even a stitch. All I can do is mumble incoherently through closed lips, which doesn't do a thing except make me mad, so mad and desperate that talking becomes shouting, which tips over into screaming, and how hot I am, so angry at my inability to say a single thing, because all I want to do is tell him not to leave, no matter what, *don't leave me alone with her*, because that might just about kill me.

Those muffled screams are so useless behind a closed mouth, and that alone is nearly the worst feeling in the world.

The *very* worst feeling is what happens next, when my father says, *Darling, I just can't understand you*, then sets his six-string down in its cradle, gets up, and walks not into the house, but off the porch into the front lawn, bare feet and all, then up the street directly toward the setting sun, as if he has an appointment with it, and that orange glare sucks him whole eventually, and I know he's gone, gone for good, and that's when I open my mouth again, and the words that come out are worthless because the person who needs to hear them is no longer there.

Please don't leave.

TWENTY-FOUR

I JOLT AWAKE.

The lights are still on, and the crusts of my sandwich weigh down the paper towel next to my face.

Wavy light, the television.

A man's voice, laughing, asking questions.

Travis is exactly where I saw him last, upright in bed, gazing directly at the screen, only now he holds a knife in his hands—a butterfly knife, I think it's called—the kind that can fold open and closed like a fan. He focuses on the tiny TV screen as he flicks his wrist, causing the blade of the knife to snap into place, and just as quickly, he uses a few more flicks of the wrist to close it. Over and over, like he's hypnotizing himself, and my gut clenches at the thought that with just one wrong move, his fingers will slice right off and clump neatly in his lap.

"Can you put that away?" I ask, rubbing my eyes.

Travis looks over, grabbing the knife after a swing of the blade, freezing it daggerlike in his right hand.

"You were snoring."

"Can you put the knife away?"

"Why?"

I sit up too fast and am rewarded with a dizzying head rush. "Because I don't like knives."

He smiles. "What, you scared?"

"I just don't like knives."

A pause, then a final flick of the wrist, and the knife folds itself neatly away. "Fine." He sets it on his night table. "You were out cold."

The head rush finally evaporates. "I thought you were going to wake me and take me to the couch."

"Sorry, got distracted."

"What're you watching?"

"*Letterman.*"

I've heard of Letterman but never watched him. I don't really get talk shows. I watched Carson once, and he was interviewing Burt Reynolds, and all I could think was *who cares?*

"Is he good?"

"You've *never* seen the show?"

I shake my head.

"Then you're, like, the only person. Holy shit, never seen *Letterman?* Can't believe it."

"I'm usually asleep at this hour."

He snaps his head toward the TV. "Well, you gotta check it out. I think after the commercial is stupid pet tricks."

Stupid pet tricks?

"Okay," I say. "A few minutes."

The next ten minutes come and go. Letterman's moderately funny, and I do kinda fall for his squeaky laugh, but the whole stupid pet thing?

"You didn't laugh once," Travis says, getting up to turn off the set.

"Was I supposed to?"

He takes a seat on the floor across from me, a crumpled pair of jeans and Van Halen album jacket separating us. "You know, I don't even think I've seen you smile."

"I'll smile when something makes me happy."

"And what makes you happy?"

I'm still dizzy with sleep. "Still trying to figure that out."

He keeps looking at me, not really in a creepy way, but not really in a harmless way either.

"You know, you're kinda fuckin' weird," he says. "No offense or anything."

"Special," I correct him.

"Huh?"

"I'm not weird. I'm special."

"Special how?"

I look up, catching his face, a face I've long since memorized, etched into my brain, with deep grooves. I think it's time to find out if this boy is a dragon.

"Can I draw you?"

TWENTY-FIVE

THE DOTS COME, AS they always do, and I wonder if there'll be a point in my life when they don't. Maybe there's a finite amount of them, and I could very well be depleting my future supply by drawing Travis.

I poke and poke at the paper with the pen, allowing my hand to simply follow directions, looking up at Travis every few moments, not because I have to but because I want to. I search for the part of him that the dots can see but few people can, his hidden frequency.

It's important to know if his inner essence is good.

And if it isn't, well, best to know that, too.

Minutes later I finish and take in the picture. Before me is an image of Travis boasting what could only be termed puppy-dog eyes. Not in an overly cute or cartoonish way, but rather in a way that makes him appear more boy than man, more vulnerable than certain, and more in need of acceptance than the Travis I've come to know over the past several hours.

"Here," I say, flipping the drawing around and showing it to him. "This is what I call a stupid Penny trick."

He reaches out and takes the page from me. "Holy fuck. This would have taken me hours and still looked like shit at the end of it. How do you draw so fast?"

I've been analyzed by cognitive researchers for over ten years who have tried to answer that same question. I tell him the truth. "I don't know. It just comes to me."

He keeps staring. "I mean…"

"So you like it?"

"Yeah. Yeah, I do. I mean, Jesus. It's me, but it's…I dunno. A different version of me or something."

"It's how my subconscious sees you."

He flicks his gaze to me. "Meaning what?"

Deep breath. "Meaning it's how my brain sees you, and maybe it's able to see the *you* that you hide from the world. Sometimes that hidden part is a little different than the way you see yourself."

He looks at the drawing again. "I look like I'm about to cry or something."

"Do you feel sad?" I ask.

He doesn't answer, though maybe his silence is answer enough. "I mean, if…like, if *you* went on *Letterman* and did this, drew him, can you imagine? You'd be famous."

Famous, that word again. As much as I don't like attention, his excitement makes me visualize being on the Letterman show. After all, if stupid pets can make it there, surely I can. And maybe Letterman would like my drawing, really like it, and he'd hold it to the camera, and the audience would gasp.

Then, as fast as the fantasy enters my mind, so does my mother's voice.

You know why I named you Penny? 'Cause you're pretty much worthless.

And the fantasy vanishes, leaving me back here. With who I am.

Penny Bly, brilliantly gifted, good for nothing.

"Tell me everything," Travis says.

"What do you mean?"

He puts the picture on the floor, placing it with care, then scoots closer to me. His eyes seem to glow, beautiful, but in a wolf-beautiful kind of way.

"You said you're special, and I believe it. I want to know everything about you."

I suck in a breath. "That could take a little time."

He smiles. "Sometimes I think all I got is time."

"What about sleeping?"

He nods. "You're right, I'm sorry. I can show you the couch. Do you want to sleep?"

Want is a tricky word. So closely tied to *need*, but not the same.

"No."

TWENTY-SIX

I TELL HIM EVERYTHING, and it might be the most words I've ever spoken without stopping.

Thirty minutes pass, then an hour. I tell Travis about my fall down the stairs, a trauma that could have killed me but ended up breaking open my consciousness. About how my father left the family that same time, never even bothering to visit me in the hospital.

I tell him I see numbers as colors, and he says, "A hundred and fifty-seven," and I say, "Avocado skin. *Ripe* avocado skin."

He smokes pot and laughs as I talk, giggling like he just discovered a trunk of gold doubloons.

I show Travis my treasure map and how I want to go to each location en route to California, even though the odds are long that there'll be any notes in bottles to recover.

Finally, I explain to him what a savant is, explaining my abilities are drawing and remembering things, and nothing else really useful beyond that. He giggles more, this boy, saying something about me being a superhero, and I say no, I'm more quirky than heroic. I can't stop a bullet or see through walls, but I can tell you what I had for dinner every day for the past five years.

At one point Travis slouches to the ground, making me think he's fallen asleep. But out of the haze of smoke, he says, "I have a cousin who's autistic."

"Okay."

"That's what you are, right? Autistic?"

"Not that anyone's ever told me."

He's silent for a moment. "So what are you?"

This could be a top-five stupid question. "I'm Penny."

"No, I mean, what condition do you have?"

I reply with a question of my own. "What condition do you have?"

He thinks on it for a minute before saying, "I'm a smart kid who can't stop doing dumb things."

I nod to myself. "I'm a genius potentially making the worst decision of her life."

He laughs, which turns into a coughing fit. "I'd kill to have what you have."

Despite all the people who have analyzed me over the course of my life, no one has ever said these specific words to me. This stoned kid I met just hours before fills me with more confidence than I've ever had. Maybe I was destined to meet him just to have this moment. To actually *feel* special, rather than just being told I am.

With closed eyes and a half grin, Travis mumbles about how *this is it*. That he'll go with me to find the notes, to find my dad, and between my talents and his street smarts, we'll figure out how to score some cash along the way. We'll be a traveling circus—see the magic drawing lady who can recite volumes of Shakespeare!

Looking at him, I doubt he'll remember much of anything he's said in the morning.

He falls asleep, snoring softly.

I leave his room and find the couch, a two-seater upholstered in corduroy that'll certainly leave indented stripes on my face.

Next to the couch is a side table, and on the table is a phone, which suddenly seems to shine like a beacon.

I pick up the receiver and dial.

TWENTY-SEVEN

"IT'S ME."

I wait for a response, but there's only silence, which makes me nervous. Why the hell am I nervous?

Finally: "Penny? It's the middle of the night. Are you okay?"

Dr. Brock's voice isn't the steady and reassuring one I've come to expect from him. It's tired and confused.

"You told me I could call anytime," I say. "Your exact words were 'you can call me anytime, day or night.' So that's anytime, really. And right now is part of anytime. So I'm calling. Hello."

"I did say that. You're right. But you haven't answered my question. Are you okay?"

"Sure."

"Are you at home or the institute?"

"Neither. I called to tell you I've left both places, and I don't intend on returning."

A pause. Then: "What?"

"I've left."

"Wait, hang on. You left? Did you tell anyone? Your mom? Dr. Cheong?"

"I'm telling you. You can let them know if you want."

There's rustling in the background, and I imagine him sitting upright in bed and scrambling to turn on the light.

"Penny, where exactly are you?"

"At a guy's house. But not like that. I'm just staying here tonight."

"And then what?"

This is more difficult than I calculated. "I'm going to find my father."

An exhale, the angry kind. "How on earth are you going to do that? Do you know where he is?"

"I have a zip code. California."

"A zip code? I can't imagine that's helpful."

"We took a road trip when I was six. We left each other notes. On the way to California, I'm going to look for the notes. I know it sounds crazy. More silly than crazy, maybe. But it's just something I want to do." I consider this, then revise. "Have to do."

"You're right. It does sound crazy. A fool's errand."

Heat builds in my chest. "Good thing I'm not asking your permission," I say.

"Your mother must be worried sick not knowing where you are," he says.

I almost laugh but don't. He knows my mother. "Come on."

"Okay, okay," he says. "But I will tell her. She needs to know. And clearly you're calling me for a reason, so if you're looking for some kind of validation, you're not going to get it from me. You don't seem to be thinking this through."

This is when anger wraps its long bony fingers around me and shakes me into an angry hornets' nest.

"*Think?*" I say—well, maybe shout. "You're telling me I don't know how to *think?* Of all the things I'm capable of, thinking is at the top of the list."

"I know, Penny. I just—"

"And why? Why can't I go find him? Since I was seven, I've just done as I've been told, sitting around, *thinking,* and never actually doing anything. I don't *do* anything, don't you get that? I'm so special, so I'm told, but what good is it doing me talking to psychologists in that antiseptic building every day? Or trying to take care of a mother who doesn't care about anything? I'm so fucking tired of being rational."

"It's precisely because you're so special that I'm concerned for you. You have tremendous value to the world."

These words, these specific words, open my eyes to a very hard and sudden truth. "And yet I have no value to myself."

Dr. Brock exhales again, but not the angry kind this time. Sad, maybe.

"No…no…I hope that's not true," he says. "You are…priceless. But as I've told you for years, your abilities came to you through trauma, and they can go away through trauma. Just…if something were to happen to you, God forbid. At the institute we could shield you from something happening. Out there, wherever you are, I can't protect you."

And I think, *Maybe losing my abilities wouldn't be such a bad thing.*

"You left me, remember?" I say. "So you're not in any position to protect me. And it's not just…finding my father. I'm twenty-one. I'm ready for something different. To take control of my life. To make decisions for myself. Like you said, it's not like I was going to stay at the institute forever."

"I understand that, and we've discussed it. A few more years and—"

"No more years. Not one more day."

Now I picture him running his hand through his hair. He does that when he gets frustrated. "This is all my fault," he says. "I shouldn't have just left you."

"You're right," I reply. "You shouldn't have. But maybe it was supposed to happen like this. Maybe you needed to move on so I could."

"Penny, Penny..."

"What?"

"Do you have a plan?"

That question. "I have a goal."

"What about money? How are you going to make a living on your own?"

The worst questions are the ones you should have an answer for but don't. "I'll figure it out."

"Okay," he says. "Let me ask you something else."

"What?"

He pauses. "Are you scared?"

I answer truthfully because, aside from my phantom father, Dr. Brock's the one person to whom I can.

"A little. But also excited."

"And there's no way I can convince you to come home?"

"Do you think that's what best for me?"

Another pause, this one lengthy. "I don't know. Maybe you need some time on your own. But yes. I'm worried about you, and you should come home."

He's never expressed worry for me before.

"I have to go," I say.

A long sigh. "Okay," Dr. Brock says. "Promise to call me again? Even just to check in for a few minutes every now and then?"

THE FATHER SHE WENT TO FIND

"I will."

"Good."

I hang up. Exhausted. Confused. Brittle.

This is when the tears come.

And how I hate every damn one of them.

TWENTY-EIGHT

I'M ON THE COUCH, chasing sleep, yet it eludes me. There's just enough moonlight to make out the outline of a grandfather clock on the other side of the room, and the deep operatic bass of the seconds chunking away creates in me a sudden and aching loneliness. Since my injury, my life's been unusual but, for the most part, routine. Rare are the unpredictable moments.

But that's all gone now. Everything from here on out will be unpredictable.

Unpredictability might just be the thing that scares me most.

But.

No.

I'm not going back.

I'll embrace this loneliness, embrace the unfamiliar. No matter how hard it gets, how desperately I crave normalcy, I vow, right here and now, to celebrate the unknown.

Eyes closed, I will sleep to come but am only rewarded by the ticking of that goddamned grandfather clock, its metronomic beats a slow and steady march forward, ever forward, to a fate I cannot possibly know.

Finally, finally, as sleep grasps me, my mind conjures another vision of death. Not the airplane falling out of the sky this time. And not knives ripping open my belly, nor dragons biting me clean through.

I'm underwater, having decided to see how long I can hold my breath, and I guess wrong.

My passing is simple, bloodless, and almost peaceful.

TWENTY-NINE

July 15, 1987
Wednesday

SUNLIGHT CREEPS ONTO MY face, slowly. I keep my eyes closed, try to ignore it, then remember where I am. Travis's house.

I sit up, look around. No movement. I strain my ears but hear nothing other than some birds outside.

I stand, stretch, find a bathroom. The top of the toilet seat has one of those carpeted lids. Gross. Worse, the seat itself is padded and has dozens of cracks in its shiny, spongy vinyl. It wheezes as I lower onto it.

Still, I could've slept at a bus station last night. I'm grateful to be here.

I wash my hands, then look in the mirror. Sure enough, corduroy stripes on the left side of my face. After an attempt to comb my hair with my fingers, I look at my watch. Nine in the morning. I figure I got four, maybe five hours of sleep. Not enough.

When I step out of the bathroom, I hear voices downstairs, one of them attached to Travis. The other, feminine. His mother?

I head downstairs, recommitting to embrace the unfamiliar despite my instinct to hide under a blanket.

The smell of bacon helps to lure me.

Seconds later I make my way to the kitchen. Travis is sitting at the round wooden kitchen table, in the same clothes from last night, and from ten feet away, I can smell the pot on him, which tells me something about his relationship with his parents.

He's shoving food into his mouth, which reminds me of how hungry I am.

Travis looks up and sees me. "Hey."

A woman turns from the stove to face me. Her face wears disappointment. "Hello," she says.

"Hi."

No smile. "I'm Marion Shepard, Travis's mother. This is my house, though I'm sure you already knew that."

She has the same eye color as Travis, but on her it's not so mesmerizing. My gaze dips to the floor. "Thank you for letting me sleep on the couch upstairs."

"You slept on the couch, dear?"

"Yes."

She assumes I spent the night with Travis. In his bed.

"I'd address you by your name if you told it to me," Marion says.

I decide to lock eye contact, difficult as it can be for me. Sometimes I'd do this with my mother. Lock in tight, despite my raging hunger to look away, to hide within the gaze of inanimate objects. But I discovered if I could manage to hold someone's eye contact long enough, really hold it, it was like staring at the sun or holding your breath underwater. At some point, the pain goes away, and there's this remarkable peacefulness, even though you're still dying.

"Penny. Penny Bly."

"Well, Penny. Are you homeless?"

Travis chokes on a wad of bacon. "Jesus, *fuck*, Mom. The hell kind of question is that?"

"A valid one." Marion's tone remains calm as a midnight lake. "And don't use language like that around me."

"I suppose I am homeless," I say. "I had a home until yesterday, and I left it."

Marion's hands find their way to her hips, and she takes a single step forward, peering at me as she does. "That's quite a bold move."

"She's hella smart," Travis says. "And can draw like...I dunno. Way better than me, that's for sure. Name any famous painter. That's who she can draw like. Better, even."

"Vermeer," I say. I always like to think I have an ability to capture realism in the same spirt as Johannes Vermeer. Of course, I can't do all the cool stuff with light and shading because I only use ink, not paint.

"I see," Marion says. "Well, I'm sure your parents are very proud."

Travis keeps talking with his mouth full. "I'm going with her."

Marion snaps her head to him. "Going where?"

He hesitates, then spits the words out in a burst of courage. "We're driving to California."

"*What?*"

"Calm down. It's just for like, I don't know. A couple of weeks or something."

The woman's jaw twitches with tension. "I don't think you know what you're talking about. You have work."

"I can take some days off."

"*Two weeks?* You won't have a job left when you come back." A crack in her voice. The slightest fissure of panic.

He pushes back in his chair. "Well, hell, then. Maybe I won't come back at all."

"Don't say that. Travis...you can't just... Where will you stay?"

Travis shrugs. "Motels, I guess."

Now she turns to me. "This was your idea, wasn't it? You just met him and convinced him to leave home, didn't you? Just like you did."

"No, it was *my* idea," Travis says, a growl behind his words. "Give me some credit for something, god damn it."

"Do not talk to me like that," Marion snaps. Then she walks right up to me, close enough that I can smell her perfume over the smell of Travis's smoky clothes. It's a cheap scent she's wearing, a thousand flowers mashed together without thought.

"I'm not your mother, so you're not my problem. But..." She leans in close, whispers, "He *can't* be on his own. He's not...not capable."

"Mom, what're you saying?" Travis stands. "Quit whispering."

"I'm going to find my father," I tell her. "I need transportation to do that, which your son offered me. I didn't ask him. He offered. But I'm going to California with or without him."

Travis bursts into the conversation. "Goddamned right I'm going. I'm her manager. We'll sell her drawings."

I look at him. "Manager?"

Marion barks a laugh. "Ha. You couldn't manage your way out of a paper bag."

And there, that comment, so close to something my own mother would say... Maybe Travis needs to be out in the world just as much as I do, if for no other reason than not to be at home.

Travis and his mother look at each other and say nothing, a thousand memories of perhaps this very stance filling the gap between their faces.

Travis breaks the silence first. "Screw this. We're leaving." He looks at me. "Get your stuff. Meet you in the car."

My eagerness to leave Marion's sight is greater than the lure of bacon, but just barely. I go upstairs, gather my stuff, and head to the car. The outside morning heat feels good for about three seconds, then starts to grow stifling.

Some shouting inside, but I can't make it out. A few seconds later, Travis barrels through the front door, a duffel bag in his right hand. Marion appears at the door just as it shuts behind him. She throws it open.

"Come back, sweetie! I'm sorry about what I said. Just please come back."

My dream returns in an instant. The image of my father disappearing down the street, with me screaming for him to return, only to have my words as useless as Styrofoam bullets.

As I slide into Travis's passenger seat, I think about how ironic it is that I'm riding shotgun with this person, another man who has deemed it perfectly fine to leave his pleading loved ones behind.

But no.

This isn't about Travis.

It can't be.

Whatever happens next, whatever I look like on the other side of this journey, whether I come home in tears or build an entirely new life somewhere else, whether I find my father or just traces of his ghost, I have to keep one thing in mind at all times.

This is about me.

And no one else.

THIRTY

"HOW MUCH CASH DO you have?"

I'm sitting in the passenger seat of Travis's car, suddenly wishing I knew how to drive.

"I left my house with eighty-seven dollars," I answer him. "Then I got twenty for my drawing."

He glances over. "Any credit cards?"

"No."

"Hmm."

"How about you?"

Travis shrugs. "I've got a card with a three-hundred-dollar limit, with maybe half that available. As for cash? I dunno. Maybe twenty bucks. So we're gonna have to figure out money so we can get a motel rather than sleep in the car. Plus food and gas."

Motel? How would that work? Would we share a room?

Travis makes his way to the interstate, then heads west.

"I feel like all I do is think," I say, looking out the window. "But this trip, I've put hardly any thought into it."

He turns, smiles.

That smile.

"That's good. Maybe this'll teach you how to be spontaneous. Shit, I spent three minutes throwing clothes into a duffel bag. I'm so not prepared for this at all." And with that he starts laughing, a lovely, infectious laugh. "And it feels fucking great. But still, we need *some* kind of preparation. Like a plan in case we get separated."

"Why would we get separated?"

"I dunno. That's why you have to plan for it." He speeds up and whisks around a car. "Last year I went to England with a buddy for a couple of weeks. Only time I've been out of the country. On the third day, he boarded a train and thought I was behind him. I thought we were waiting for the *next* train, so we got separated. But we'd agreed if we got split up, we'd both call my mom and tell her where we were. It worked like a charm. We met up in a pub in Birmingham."

"Good idea," I say. "What's your home phone number?"

He tells me. "I'm guessing you don't need to write it down."

"No."

We settle into silence for a few minutes. Travis coaxes the car up to seventy.

"Minneapolis," he says, nodding to himself.

"Minneapolis what?"

"Last night you said the first place on your dad's little treasure map is in Minneapolis, right? So that's where we go first."

I sink back into my seat. "It's so stupid," I mutter. "There's no chance any of the notes are even still around. And even if they are, so what? What could they possibly say? He wrote them to a six-year-old."

"Or he wrote them to a much older Penny, hoping you'd find them one day." He glances over. "Hell, I dunno, maybe he knew he was going to leave you and used the notes to explain why."

"That's a terrible thing to say."

"Not trying to be terrible. Just speculating is all."

I hate the idea of my father having planned for a whole year to leave me.

"Besides," Travis adds, "a guy I went to high school with moved to Minneapolis. We're in touch every now and then."

"What, you want to visit him?"

He keeps his gaze fixed dead ahead. "He's…I don't know the right word for it. Connected."

"Connected?"

"You know. His family…they aren't totally on the up and up. My friend's not a big shot or anything, but he told me once that he clears a thousand bucks a week."

"Doing what?"

"That's the question you never ask a guy like that."

"So something illegal," I say.

He shrugs. "It's a good assumption he's not writing children's books."

"And why would we want to visit this person?"

Travis takes his time in answering. "Look, I know he lends money. Sure, he charges some crazy-ass interest rate, but maybe he can cut us a deal since we're friends."

"So you want to borrow money from a criminal?"

All I get is a meager shrug.

"I thought we were going find a way to sell my drawings," I say. "And you were going to be my *manager*."

"As your manager, I can tell you I don't have the slightest fucking clue how to get started with that. You can't just keep going to malls and selling portraits. I'm sure you're supposed to have a license for that. I mean, sure, we'll eventually get it figured out, maybe talk to an art gallery or something. But in the meantime, we need more cash, and unless you want to beg on a street corner..."

I think of the movie *The Godfather*, wondering if Travis's friend looks like one of those characters.

"I'm not sure your friend is the best way to get money," I say.

"You have a better one?"

Facing reality, I know our cash on hand will buy us a couple of days at most. It'll take longer than that to get to California, especially if we go looking for the notes.

"No," I concede.

"Look," he says. "There's nothing to worry about. I've actually talked to him about borrowing money before, when I was thinking about getting my own place. I never did it, but he was cool with the idea. I figure, what, five hundred bucks? That should be enough. You find your dad, we'll figure out how to make some quick cash with your drawings in California, and then I'll repay him on the way back."

Way back.

"I'm not sure I'm returning," I tell him.

"Well, I'd have to come back to repay him. He's probably not the kind of guy who accepts wire transfers. And he's certainly not the kind of guy you stiff."

I don't want to decide on this, not yet.

I turn and scan the back seat, where I spy a *Thomas Guide* for Wisconsin and Minnesota on the floor. I reach over, pick it up, and thumb through the pages.

"About ninety miles to Minneapolis," I say. "I'm not saying we should meet with your friend, but I suppose we can check the Kmart on the extremely unlikely chance we find my dad's note. Hour and a half to get there."

"Oh, it won't take me that long."

"I'm in no rush."

"It's not about getting there fast," he says. "It's just about *going* fast."

Then he rolls down his window and tells me to do the same. Hot, thick air whips inside the car, creating both a loud whooshing and an imbalance of pressure. My hair incessantly attacks my face. I pull it back, tie it up, and suddenly the wind feels nice.

Funny, for all my life, I've never liked being in a car with the windows down. It always felt too overwhelming.

But now, there's freedom in the chaos. A sense of finding joy in something new. Of embracing my lack of control.

I settle back and breathe in the world.

But my brain, as it always does, wants to distract me. Asks me questions. Protests my decisions. Tries to coax me back to the safety of everything I left behind.

I disengage by counting cars.

Get up to four hundred and thirty-two before boredom wins, and I focus on the sky because there's nothing to count in it during daytime, and sometimes it's best to simply focus on nothingness.

It never lasts for long.

THIRTY-ONE

TRAVIS WEAVES THE CAR through downtown Minneapolis, then pulls over at a pay phone next to a row of storefronts.

"Lemme call my friend. See if he can meet."

"We didn't agree on meeting him," I say.

"Okay. Let's have a meeting. Manager to client. Should we meet with my friend and borrow money?"

"I don't know."

"Well," he says, "I say yes. Absolutely yes. And that beats out *I don't know.*"

I start to argue, but I have nothing. Maybe this is like driving with the windows down: embracing the chaos. I can't control everything, and even when I try, it doesn't mean I'm right.

"Fine," I tell him.

He walks to the pay phone, and I get out of the car to stretch my legs.

The air is meatier here. More exhaust, more noise, more sweat. I've been to Minneapolis a few times, but not enough to feel comfortable.

I look over at the store next to me and realize it's an art gallery. The old-fashioned sign above the gallery door stands in stark contrast to the art displayed in the windows, a dizzying array of colors splashed across multiple canvases on display, the predominant ones being lipstick red, Smurf blue, and nuclear yellow. One artist's works, I recognize. Keith Haring, his shapes so simple and so recognizable, all squished together in a beautiful maze.

He seems like someone who might know happiness, I think.

I allow myself a daydream about seeing one of my drawings in the gallery display. *An original Penny Bly!*

The dream dissolves when Travis's voice enters my brain.

"All set. We're going to meet, but not until tonight. He's busy all day."

I turn. He looks both cute and stupid in the moment, his eyebrows raised like a dog waiting for the ball to be thrown.

I wonder what his lips taste like.

Coconut, I decide, for no particular reason.

"Did he say he'd lend you money?"

"Yeah," Travis says. "Well, actually, he said, 'I'll see what I can do,' but I'm sure he will."

"We can figure out how to get money another way."

He shakes his head. "Look, it's gonna be fine, Pen. Don't be such a stress case."

Pen. The only other person who's ever called me that is Dad.

"If you say so." I walk away from him and head to the display window of the art gallery, placing my right palm on the glass. "I sure would like to have a gallery like this someday."

His voice dribbles from behind. "I can't hear you."

"I'm talking to myself," I say, keeping my gaze on the glass, then lower my voice so I'm my only audience. "I wouldn't have to remember anything. I wouldn't have to take tests. I would just draw, all day long. And people would come. They'd come. Even celebrities, maybe. And it wouldn't be twenty dollars a portrait. It'd be two hundred. Maybe more. And that's all I would have to do for the rest of my life. Just follow the dots."

And in this moment, I decide this just might be the thing to make me happy.

I turn, see Travis leaning against the car.

"What's the address?" I ask.

"Huh?"

"Your friend. What's his address?"

Travis smiles and taps the side of his head, clearly excited that he memorized something. I wonder briefly what it must be like to have to work to memorize something, then decide it must be like enduring a rash.

"Eighty-one Fifth Avenue South. Downtown."

The number gives my gut a little squeeze.

Eighty-one.

Dull gray, the color of rotten meat.

THIRTY-TWO

MIDAFTERNOON, AND I'M STANDING outside Travis's car in the parking lot of the Minneapolis Kmart indicated on the treasure map.

Treasure map.

God damn it. I *am* a little girl.

Travis lights a cigarette, and the smoke wafts my way. For once I don't hate it. Smells like change.

I look down at the piece of paper in my hand, the one with my father's handwriting all over it, and I know immediately there will be no note to find. We're in the southwest corner of the lot, and there is no oak tree. Or tree of any kind.

Anything could have happened over the years. Could be they expanded the parking lot, cut down all the trees. Or my dad was confused and wrote down the wrong information. Or maybe...

Just maybe...

He's fucking with me.

Some elaborate plan to get me to chase my past, only to find out nothing is real.

"What's the call, Columbo?"

I look over at Travis, and he looks serious. Maybe it's the breeze whipping his hair over his left eye. Suits him.

"Wild goose chase," I say.

"You sure? We can keep looking."

"There's nothing here." I take a few steps out onto the empty asphalt, wondering if I've ever actually been here before. The memory I had of the road trip is fragmented and incomplete and certainly contained nothing of a Kmart.

"Sorry," Travis says.

"It's okay. I don't know what I was expecting anyway."

He takes a drag, frees the butt to the ground, grinds it dead with his shoe. "I don't think you were expecting as much as hoping."

I walk back to the car, then peer at him over the top. "He left when I was in a fucking coma, and I don't think I can ever really come to terms with that. The seven-year-old girl in me still clings to him, and maybe that's just biology. What's messed up is he only writes to me once a year. A couple of sentences *once a year*. I should be throwing those birthday cards away unread. Instead? I cling to them like a life preserver. They keep me going. And here I think, okay, there are more words from him. *Notes* from him. And if I can find these notes, it'll be like, I don't know, cocaine to a junkie. I need his words. I'm *addicted* to his words." I settle into silence, picturing his face from my memory. It doesn't look like a mean face. He looks…soft.

"I can't claim to understand," Travis says. "My every waking moment is spent hoping for fewer words from my parents." He looks at me—my, there is sadness. "Guess I don't know what's worse."

I open the car door, then slide back in, and this time the heat doesn't feel stifling. It melts me all the same, but I feel as if I've earned a little taste of hell.

"Sometimes I think I'm on a quest just to prove he even existed at all."

THIRTY-THREE

ELEVEN MINUTES AFTER 8:00 p.m. Travis eases the car to the curb in downtown Minneapolis and looks up at the building next to us.

"I don't understand," he says. "It's a comedy club. Why would he ask to meet here?"

I crane my neck and look at the building. The address checks out with what Travis told me. Sure enough, the unlit neon sign in the window says ROASTERS COMEDY CLUB.

"Is your friend funny?" I ask.

"I never thought so."

"You sure this is the place?"

"Hell, I'm never sure of anything," he says. "But there's only one way to find out." Travis slips his car keys under the sun visor and opens his door.

"Wait," I tell him.

He shuts the door again, and the car's interior resumes its heady reek of this boy and his world. "What?"

I say nothing.

He must realize I need to collect my thoughts (and how many there are of those) because he stays quiet except for the soft drumming of his fingers along his knee.

I look out my window to the other side of the street and, really, into the beyond of everything. There's nothing linear about my future anymore, nothing predictable, and it's kind of hitting me all in this moment. I don't think I've been honest with myself about how fucking scary being out on my own really is.

Still.

Still, there's something special about this night. This place, this moment. An *inflection* point. Borrowing money from Travis's friend seems like a no-turning-back kind of thing, and all our energy will be focused on forward momentum afterward. We'll seek out the treasure map notes on the way to California. Then I'll find my father. Maybe start a new life there, become an artist. Maybe even a famous one, open that gallery.

Tonight could be the catalyst for my success, something that I'll recount in interviews years in the future.

Well, it all started one night when we met a gangster in a comedy club.

I smile at my hazy reflection in the window. I am, perhaps, on the verge of something wonderful.

I turn to Travis. "I'm going to kiss you now," I say.

"What?"

"I just wanted you to know. It would be wrong to surprise you."

His eyebrows inch up a fraction. "That's not usually how it works," he says. "Usually, you just lean in and do it."

I bite my bottom lip, just to fill it with sensation. "Okay."

"Okay."

I lean in and do it.

I kiss him not because I'm falling for him (though maybe I am, in an after-school special kind of way) but because this person is part of the chaos, and I have a sudden desire to know what chaos tastes like.

Turns out, not like coconut at all.

THIRTY-FOUR

TRAVIS OPENS THE DOOR to the club, even though a sign in the window says doors open at 9:00 p.m.

"I've never been in a comedy club before," I say, following him inside.

"Imagine my surprise," he mutters.

There are muffled voices somewhere in the distance. Otherwise, the place is dead.

His steps are tentative, and so are mine. Maybe because the place is poorly lit. Or because it smells of cigarettes and booze. Or because it's so damn quiet. I feel desperation in here.

We continue down a hallway filled with framed pictures of comedians. I focus on one of a man with very big hair.

ROASTERS…*thanks for the laughs! Richard Lewis*

We enter a large room. The show room. A small stage sits in the back corner, a fake brick wall behind it. The rest of the room is mostly filled with small tables, each with either two or four chairs. The ceiling is low enough to trigger a hazy sense of claustrophobia.

To my left, a bar.

There's a man sitting there, a drink on the bar top in front of him. Travis sees him, too.

"Leo?" he calls out.

The man looks over. Not really a man. In between man and boy, like Travis. Short black hair. Pale skin. Leather jacket. Unlike Travis, this person is big. A mix of muscle and fat that looks both impressive and intimidating on a young person but, I'm guessing, won't age well.

"Travis!" he calls out. A smile sweeps across his face, and, well, it's rather ugly. "Dude, it's been fucking forever." He pushes himself off the barstool and gives Travis a hug, which Travis didn't seem to be expecting.

They release.

"You a little lit, Leo?"

Leo looks directly at me and starts laughing. Sloppy, foolish laughter. "Maybe a little, brother. Maybe a little. Got an early start tonight, I guess."

"This is Penny," Travis says.

Leo looks me over, and it's borderline gross. "Hey."

"Hey."

He directs us to one of the tables with four chairs. "You want something? My family owns this club. You can have whatever I can find from behind the bar."

"Beer," Travis says. I decide to ask for the same.

Leo grabs two bottles and pops the tops. He brings those over to the table, then darts back and grabs a bottle of tequila and his half-finished drink. He tops his off and sits across from us.

"Travis Shepard, as I live and breathe," he says. Then Leo turns to me. "This dude was a fuckin' riot in high school, you know that?"

"No, I didn't know that." I take a sip of my beer. Disgusting.

Then Leo digs a vial out of his front pocket and wags it in front of us. "Want some coke? I need to pep up a little."

I don't know why I'm stunned to see it. Maybe it's because I've never seen cocaine before—where would I have? But I think it's something deeper than that. I think the sight of that white powder is my official welcome to the real world. A *you're not in Kansas anymore* moment.

"No," I say.

He turns to Travis. "How 'bout it, brother?"

Travis hesitates, and I'm a little saddened by it. He eventually says, "I don't think so."

"You ever have it?"

"No."

"Aw, shit, man. You have to try it. It's like…I'm not good with words. I don't know. It's like something." He sits back, reflects, then says, "It's just fuckin' happiness, man. Just happiness."

The word hits me.

Happiness.

Is that all it takes?

What an easy solution that would be.

But no. I'm not going to believe happiness comes in that little vial. I think happiness only comes after struggle.

"I don't know," Travis says. "I'm pretty happy with my weed."

"No one smokes pot anymore, man. What is this, the sixties? Dude, you gotta try this." Leo takes the top off the vial, taps a bit of the coke on the back of his left hand, and snorts. When he opens his eyes, it's like he just surfaced after nearly drowning. "*Whoa.*"

Travis squirms and I say nothing. I'm not here to be his mother. No matter what, I'm looking out for myself first. He can do what he wants.

And yet I'm disappointed when he agrees.

"Just…I don't know. Like a tiny bit," Travis says.

"That's my boy," Leo says. Travis reaches his own hand out, and Leo taps a small amount onto it. But not a negligible amount.

Travis snorts and then shakes his head like a dog fresh out of a swimming pool. He waits, says nothing, then, "Jesus, that's instant."

"Right? Want more?"

"No," Travis says with zero hesitation. "That's enough for me."

The two of them then largely ignore me as they launch into reliving their high school years, which hardly sound worth having lived the first time. Leo continues to slur his words, and a fresh sheen of sweat glazes his forehead, but his energy levels remain peaked.

Travis, for his part, hardly touches his beer, but he starts talking a mile a minute. It takes some time, but at the earliest lull in the conversation, I ask about borrowing money.

"Yeah, man," Leo says to me. "I got you. I got you. Cash flowing in like rivers to me. I can lend you guys some. Business is *good*."

"So, you run the club?" I ask.

"Nah, I don't do much with the club. That's my dad and his buddies. Truth is, I do lots of different things. I'm a real entrepreneur. A little import-export action. A little distribution. Some personal security. Banking. But mostly, I run a collection agency. See, you both want to borrow some cash. That's when I turn into a banker. Then, if you don't pay me back with interest, I turn into a collector."

"I see," I say.

Leo swivels his head to Travis. "But that's not going to happen, is it? You'll pay me back, right?"

"Yeah, man. Of course."

"Word," Leo says. "How much you need?"

Travis squeezes the back of his neck, and now he's sweating. "I was thinking five hundred."

Leo bursts into laughter. "Five hundred? Oh, shit, dog, you *are* a high roller." He downs the rest of his drink, pours more from the bottle. "Nobody coming to see me needs five hundred. They need five grand. Ten grand. Not really worth my time to do five hundred."

"But that's all we need," I say.

Now he looks at me, that smile becoming creepier by the second. "Maybe it's all you need but can't be all you want. Got to dream a little bigger, sweetheart." Suddenly, the smile evaporates, and Leo's eyelids droop a little more. "My minimum is a thousand for fifty points. Due in thirty days."

"Points?" I ask.

"His cost," Travis says. "We borrow a grand, we pay back fifteen hundred." Then, to Leo, he asks, "Don't you have a friend's discount or something?"

Leo turns. "That *is* the friend's discount."

Travis takes a deep breath, then finally downs a large gulp of his beer. "Okay, okay. A grand at fifty points."

"That's my man," Leo says.

"How are we going to earn that money back?" I ask Travis. "We have to earn it back somehow. And within thirty days."

Travis leans in and smiles in the happiest, dopiest way imaginable. "You're smarter than all of us combined. I'm sure you'll figure it out."

"If I knew how to make that kind of money, we wouldn't be here."

Leo takes another drink, and I'm trying to figure out how long he can possibly keep it up. Then I decide I don't care as long as we get the money.

"This falls under the category of your problem, not mine," he says.

"So we're good?" Travis says. "You can get us the cash?"

Leo looks down at the table. "Well, technically, my pops approves all loans, and the money is up in his office, so we'll just go up there and get it. It's a formality. I basically run all loan operations."

"The comedy club has loan operations?" I ask.

Travis places his hand on my forearm. "Just…don't."

Don't? I want to say. *Don't ask about all the illegitimate business tied to the person we're borrowing money from?* But I don't say anything because I've seen movies about the mob, and it always seemed the people who talked the most were the first to be killed.

"It's all good," Leo says. "Follow me."

And we do. As we walk out of the main room, I whisper to Travis, "You doing okay?"

He turns to me. "Heart is pounding, but I feel fucking great."

"Let's just get the money and get out of here, okay? I don't like this place."

"Yeah, yeah. No problem. All good."

Leo leads us up stairs that creak and groan at our trespass. I can never walk a flight of stairs without imagining myself tumbling down them.

We head into an office, at which point I hear a muffled conversation. Leo crosses the room and knocks on a closed door.

"What is it?" someone calls out.

"Pops, quick transaction," Leo says into the door.

A second of silence. Then: "Aw, Jesus Christ. Okay, quick. I'm in a meetin' here."

Leo opens the door and tells us to come inside.

To be honest, it's the last thing I want to do.

THIRTY-FIVE

HI, DAD.

Hiya, Pen Pen. Whatcha doing?

Remember that nice, stupid boy?

Yeah. Travis, right?

Right.

What about him?

We need money for our trip to come find you. So we're borrowing some from a friend of his. We're in this comedy club in Minneapolis, and it's a little scary.

A pause. Did I lose him?

Scary how?

He's charging us five hundred dollars to borrow a thousand.

I see. So he's a loan shark.

Among other things.

Those aren't the people you want to be around, Penny.

I know, I know. But we're here, and we're walking into another office to meet his dad. To get the money.

And you don't feel safe there?

I have this microconversation as I walk the fifteen feet to the doorway. *I don't know. There's just a bad energy here. I want to leave.*

So leave, sweetie.

It's not that easy.

His tone becomes a bit edgier in my head. *See, that's the thing, Pen Pen. And it's hard to appreciate this at your age, but the truth is, it is easy. So easy. You just do what you want and get on with things.*

The advice is so basic, I would never have thought of it in a thousand years.

Still.

We need the money.

I walk into the next room.

Sorry, I gotta go.

What's going on, Pen? Are you—

And then...

THIRTY-SIX

THE CIGAR SMOKE HITS me first. There's only a thin haze of it in the room, but the stench packs a wallop.

This office. It's dark. Not pitch-black or anything, but the only illumination comes from a small lamp sitting on a wooden desk. There are three windows, but all the blinds are drawn.

A man sits at the desk, facing us as we walk inside. He's a bull of a person: bald and bulky, his face all jowls. His white button-down shirt strains to contain him. I'm guessing this is Papa Leo.

Behind him stands someone else. This man is much fitter, a bit younger. Lean and muscular, his hair worn military style. Jeans and black T-shirt for him.

Leo walks in first, followed by Travis and me. And as soon as my body passes the doorway, my gaze catches movement.

Two other people. Both men. I didn't notice them at first, as dark as the room is. They were sitting in chairs facing Leo's dad, but they rise and walk away from us, to yet another door on the other end of the office, then disappear behind it. I don't catch their faces; they don't catch ours. But my brain records their similar builds, jet-black hair, and boots. Each wears boots made from, I think, snakeskin.

"Forgive my friends," Papa Leo says to us. "They don't mean to be rude, but they're a little shy. Prefer not to be meeting new people right now." He turns his attention to Leo. "You gonna introduce me to your friends or what?"

"Yeah, yeah," Leo says. "This is Travis and Penny. Went to high school with Travis. Penny, I just met." Then Leo looks at us. "Meet my pops."

"Arthur," the man says. He picks up a cigar from a metal ashtray and takes a puff, then releases a white plume of smoke toward the ceiling. No smoke detectors in here, I note.

Arthur nods at Travis. "Same high school, huh? You graduate with somethin' better than two-point-fuckin'-oh? Because that's what this dipshit here managed."

"I did okay," Travis said.

"Oh, yeah? How okay? Specifically."

Travis clears his throat. "Three-point-four."

Arthur leans forward. "Good for you. You see that? This kid applied himself. You goin' to college now or what?"

"No," Travis says. "Still, uh…figuring out what I want to do."

Arthur nods, a look of mild disappointment washing over his face. "I suppose I could tell you the whole *when I was your age* shit, but I think we both know neither of us cares. I will say college *is* a good thing, however."

"Okay."

The man standing behind Arthur says nothing. Still as concrete, but taking in everything. He scares me most.

Now Arthur rests his gaze on me, and there's something about his attention that makes my skin itch. "And what's your story, sweetheart?"

I look at him, proud of myself for keeping eye contact. "I don't understand why everyone keeps calling me *sweetheart*."

This earns a smirk. "What do you prefer?"

"Penny. My name is Penny."

"Okay, Penny." Arthur leans back again. "I was just trying to make conversation, but now I don't give a shit." To Leo: "Why are they here?"

"They need to borrow a large," Leo says.

"That's it? You interrupt a very important meeting for a large?"

Leo shifts his weight, back and forth. "You said all transactions had to go through you."

"Jesus fucking Christ," Arthur says. "You're drunk or high, aren't you? The fuck with you? I swear to god, I'm gonna make you see someone. A counselor, whatever the fuck. You got a problem, and your problems are our problems, okay?"

Silence.

"*Okay?*"

"Yeah, yeah," Leo says. I imagine him trying to figure out how to appear sober before realizing it's impossible. "I'm sorry. Seriously."

"Come here," Arthur says.

Leo walks behind the desk, and Arthur sits up and reaches a massive, meaty hand to grab Leo behind the neck. I picture him slamming Leo's head against the top of the desk, splitting his skull open. Instead, Arthur pulls him down close and kisses him on the forehead. "I fuckin' worry about you, you know that?"

Leo closes his eyes and nods. "I know, Pops."

Arthur gives him a mild smack on the head, then digs into his front pocket and pulls out a roll of cash secured with a rubber band.

I don't know how much is in that roll, but I'm quite certain I've never seen that much money in my life.

Arthur takes the band off, stands, and strolls my way as he counts off hundred-dollar bills. "Don't even have to open the safe for this one," he says.

He stands a foot away from me, and I think he's purposefully trying to be close. To get in my space. He's got a powerful musk. Smoke, sweat, and brute force.

He reaches up and offers me the money. I'm expecting him to pull it away as I go to grab it, but he doesn't. He sticks his hands in his pockets, eyes me up and down, and says, "So, Penny, what're you going to do with all that money?"

"I'm going to find my father."

"That so? And where's he at?"

"California. I think."

"And is this the kind of father who wants to be found?"

"I don't know," I say. "He left a long time ago."

"Well, if you don't mind me saying, he sounds like a real piece of shit." He pulls his right hand out of his pocket and wags a finger at me. It's a harmless gesture but also menacing, mostly because I can imagine him doing this with other people before he "teaches them a lesson."

"I ain't no saint," he says. "God fuckin' knows that. But you never leave your family. No matter what. So you and your friend here, you go find your daddy and tell him from me that he's a piece of shit. And then make *him* pay back the money and interest. You got that, sweethear... Penny?"

"Okay," I say.

Just like that, it's over. Arthur returns to his desk, and the silent man goes to fetch the other two to resume whatever business they were conducting. Leo pulls us out of the office, and I hand the money to Travis, who slides it into his front pocket.

"You're my manager," I whisper. "Make sure the money lasts."

Leo tells us to sit down in the room next to the office. Tells Travis he needs to walk him though the *terms and conditions* of the loan. Now that the true business is being conducted, I become a bit player, ignored by the men.

Seconds later, I'm distracted by the fact that I can actually make out some of the conversation in the office next door. Between Arthur and the men with snakeskin boots. I don't even think Travis or Leo are aware I'm listening—they're too engaged with each other.

Arthur is the easiest to hear, but I have to still my mind to make out his words.

"*You know we do good business together. For a long time. Your boss and I go back. We've been very happy with his product. But I'm not telling you where she is.*"

Some muffled voices. Maybe accented?

Then, more clearly: "*We know where she is. We found her. We're not asking permission. We are informing you, as a courtesy.*"

Arthur's voice rises, and neither Travis nor Leo seems to be paying attention to anyone but each other.

"*As a motherfucking courtesy? I don't believe you. You tell me what you think you know.*"

A pause in the conversation, and I'm riveted. I wish I were back in that room because it's a lot more interesting than out here.

One of the snakeskin men speaks, I think the same one as before. He does have an accent, but that makes his enunciation more careful, more precise. Easier to understand.

She is the current owner of the Out to Lunch Diner in Willmar, Minnesota. We have visited her. Now we are going back to execute her. As we said, this visit is a courtesy to you.

I stop breathing. Stop doing anything that might interfere with my listening.

Willmar.

He pronounced it *Weel-mar.*

Just then Leo flashes his attention to me, and I'm not sure if he heard what I did. "That's enough business," he says. "Let's celebrate with a drink downstairs."

I start to protest, as does Travis, but Leo insists. He is very focused on suddenly moving us away from his father's conversation.

We head back downstairs, back to the club area. To the same table we sat at earlier. Another round of beers for us and tequila for him.

Five minutes into the drink and conversation, I'm bored to tears and yearning to hear what's going on upstairs.

Execute her?

Who is "she"?

What did she do?

And…are they serious? Are they really going to kill some woman who runs a diner?

I want to know more. I want to know everything. And I don't want to be down here, in this dingy club. There's a sadness here, which is ironic since this is where people come to laugh. Maybe when the club is full, maybe when the drinks are flowing and the comic on the stage has everyone in stitches, the mood of the place changes. But right now it feels desperate, like an old woman getting her third facelift to cling to a past she can never reclaim.

I'm about to tell Travis I'm ready to leave when the shooting starts.

THIRTY-SEVEN

I DON'T REALIZE I'M hearing gunshots, not at first. Five popping noises come from upstairs. Sounds like muffled firecrackers.

But Leo.

He understands right away.

"Fuck!" he screams, and never has a person sobered up faster.

"What's going on?" Travis says.

But Leo doesn't even answer. He jumps to his feet, pulls a gun from an ankle holster under his sweats, and runs out of the main room and back up the stairs.

Screaming.

Then another shot. Seconds pass. Another shot.

I'm frozen, staring toward where Leo's disappeared up those stairs.

I don't know what's happening, but in my soul, I know Leo is dead. Dead on those stairs. The first shot collapsed him, and the second was at close range to the skull. Finishing him.

What do I do?

My legs move without me asking them to, and seconds later I'm near the bottom of the stairs, too afraid to go up them but somehow needing to be close. I don't know why. Maybe it's because I think I can help, even though I can't. Maybe it's like those people who willingly run into burning buildings to save a cat.

But I'm no hero.

Maybe it's because I don't have a good history with stairs.

But here I am, willingly closer to the violence than I was moments ago.

This is a part of me I've never discovered until now.

In the face of terror, it turns out I want to taste it.

Shouting. Rapid staccato commands.

Then I hear them coming down the stairs, their footfalls fast but controlled, a rhythm of urgency.

I pull back into the shadows, but there's no real hiding. If they head anywhere but out the front door of the club, I'm the first person they'll see.

They'll shoot me, probably in the head.

Funny, I think, that's a death fantasy I've never had. Shot in the head by gangsters in a comedy club.

The intrusive thought vanishes as the men blur from the bottom of the stairs and, to my infinite luck, out the club's front door, vanishing into the night.

The last thing I see is their snakeskin boots slithering away.

THIRTY-EIGHT

THERE'S AN OPPRESSIVE SILENCE. I don't move, not for at least ten seconds.

Just as I'm about to go back to Travis, I hear a brutal gurgling from the stairwell.

Choking. Then more gurgling.

There's no way I'm going up there. I've tasted enough terror.

I run back into the main club, and Travis is gone.

"Travis?" I call out. My voice seems as loud as an entire football stadium cheering.

Our drinks are on the table, where we left them moments ago, never to be touched by us again.

No reply from Travis.

I run behind the bar and find what I'm looking for in a matter of seconds.

A phone.

I grab the receiver and dial 911.

"What's your emergency?"

I lower my voice, as if that makes a difference. "Roasters Comedy Club. Gunshots. I think people are hurt. Maybe dead."

I hang up immediately.

Now it's my turn to run out the front of the club, get out of here. Find Travis—he's probably in the car waiting for me.

As I pass the staircase, I can't help myself.

I turn and look up.

It's dark, nearly pitch.

But I think I see something. A form, a lump, near the top of the steps.

Somebody is dead or dying up there, just twenty feet away, and there's not a thing I can do about it.

There be dragons.

I race out the front door and am nearly blinded by the low summer-evening sun, hearing my father in my head. I reply to him with the first thing that comes to mind.

There be fucking dragons.

THIRTY-NINE

TRAVIS'S CAR.

He must be in there, waiting for me.

I rush over, open the passenger door. Empty. The inside of the car still smells of him.

Cops. They'll be coming any moment. I haven't done anything wrong except borrow money from a mobster, but I don't want to be here when they show up. I don't want any part of this.

I scan the street. It's pretty quiet but not empty. I have no idea if anyone else heard the gunshots. No clue if anyone is alive in that club.

I call out nearly as loudly as I can. "Travis?"

No answer.

Then it hits me, and when it does, my skin tightens in anger.

Travis left me.

He just left me inside that club.

He probably ran out a back door and, for all I know, is still running. Arms and legs pumping, cocaine coursing through his bloodstream. Didn't take a single second to make sure I was okay. He just *left*.

Screw this.

I have to take care of myself, and that means getting out of here. Right now.

I could leave on foot, but I need Travis's car. He left me behind, and now I'm going to steal his car and drive it to California alone. Serves him right.

I run around to the driver's side, then climb in.

It's foreign to me, sitting behind a steering wheel; I've never driven a car in my life. Not even in an empty mall parking lot on a Sunday morning. I've asked a few times, but my mother was always opposed to the idea, saying I'd surely kill us. Ironic, considering how many times *she's* driven full of booze and pills.

I reach up and pull down the visor, knowing Travis put the keys there. They fall to my lap like candy from a piñata.

Deep breath. I can do this.

I can instantly conjure any one of thousands of memories of watching others drive, teach myself the mechanics. I'm guessing that will only do me so much good.

I twist the key, start the car, then tap the gas gently and ease it onto the street.

Another car blares its horn at me as it races by, narrowly missing plowing into me.

Oh, right.

Mirrors. Check the mirrors.

The car moves forward in fits and starts. After two blocks I pull over, collect myself, and sweep my gaze again for Travis.

No Travis, but I hear sirens in the distance, growing louder.

Off I go, sputtering for a bit and then growing steadier. There's some traffic, not much, and I give everyone a wide berth. I roam the streets of Minneapolis randomly, partly for practice but also because I don't know where I am. Seven cars have honked at me so far.

Driving, I'm learning, isn't complex. Like most things, it can be learned. Within thirty minutes of starting the ignition, my driving confidence grows. More or less.

I see a sign: INTERSTATE 394 WEST.

Three ninety-four. Hawaiian sunrise.

That feels positive, but not as much as the second part of that sign. West.

I take the on-ramp, laughing outright at my ability to make this machine go so fast. Laughing because it feels better than screaming.

I was just in a club where people were murdered.

But I can't focus on that now. I need every ounce of my focus on driving.

West.

I'll just keep going west.

All the way into the razor-thin morning.

FORTY

IT HITS ME.

The sudden and violent jolt of All That Just Happened. Disorienting, disgusting, forceful, like someone waking you up by spitting in your face and then punching you in the stomach.

I've been on Interstate 394 for seventy-two minutes, the whole time my primary focus on keeping the car at a steady speed and between the lines. After twenty minutes on the interstate, I feel myself relaxing as the adrenaline drains from my system, replaced with fatigue. That settles in my bones nicely at first, but soon sleep begins yanking at me in a very demanding way. I knew I'd have to rest at some point, but I just became so intent on getting as far away from Minneapolis as I could. I made it nearly an hour longer.

Then, in that seventy-second minute of my journey west, I have that spit-in-your-face and punch-you-in-the-stomach moment.

I hear the gunshots all over again. Listen to the gurgling of a man dying in darkness.

That *really happened*.

It's real in a way I've never experienced reality before, as visceral as being buried alive, trying to move but being paralyzed, trying to scream but being voiceless, the panic, the fear, the undeniable truth of it all, and the complete inability to change the past.

This. All. Happened.

Seventy-two minutes ago.

These thoughts send my body into a full and sudden seize, snatching my breath, ripping into my chest, all while I'm driving at fifty-five miles per hour.

I feel the claws of panic then and there, and I am somehow just able to pull the car over to the side of the highway. I turn off the engine and then put both my hands back on the steering wheel, squeezing it as if it's the only thing keeping me from hurtling into the void.

I try to breathe, but each sip of air only serves to further seal my lungs.

Pain, hot fire through my body. If someone suddenly wrapped me fully in plastic wrap, I wouldn't know any different; the blazing sense of suffocation is overwhelming.

And I can't do anything about it. Can't do anything except let the panic have its way with me.

If I'm lucky, it'll stop soon, like a cat tired of playing with a dead mouse.

I close my eyes and, for a moment, steady my breathing. Not a lot, but it's something.

But the small victory is interrupted by lights behind my eyelids.

I open my eyes and look into the rearview mirror, seeing the unmistakable red wash of police car lights.

FORTY-ONE

IT'S WEIRD. IT'S A single red light, not the rooftop rack of swirling red and blue lights. My mind interrupts with a memory of watching *Starsky & Hutch*, how they'd slap that magnetic light on top of their car when they decided to go for the chase.

The silhouette of a man grows closer.

A rap of knuckles on my window. I crank it down with a shaking left hand.

I stare into a blinding flashlight beam, reminded of the annual cognitive tests I did at Willow Brook. The doctors always wanted to look at my pupil movements while I recited memorized book passages.

The first thing I notice is there's no uniform on this person. Just regular street clothes.

The second thing I notice—which happens a half second later, even in the limited light available—is that I recognize this man.

He was the silent one standing behind Arthur's desk at the comedy club, all those miles and nightmares ago.

"Hello, sweetheart."

FORTY-TWO

"I KNOW YOU," I say. It's all I can think of.

"I know you do." He sweeps his flashlight beam inside the interior of the car. "Your boyfriend ditched you."

"He's not my boyfriend."

"That's all you got to say? You don't have any questions for me?"

I squint against the flashlight beam. "Are you really a cop?"

"Sure I am. Technically off duty."

"What's your name?"

"Is that important?"

I swallow. "Otherwise, I'll have to call you *sweetheart*."

He grins. "Officer Bain."

I can hear my heart pounding in my head but try as hard as I can to appear calm. "What happened...back there?"

He leans in farther. "A real fuckin' shitshow is what happened. It was ugly. Ugly and bloody."

"But what exactly—"

"You think I'm going to tell you that?" I hate how soft and smooth his voice is, like this night was nothing out of the ordinary.

"Why…how did you find me?"

"Followed you," he says. "Have been for some time. I was going to pull you over back in the city, then saw you were headed in the same direction as me. Fact is, we're not far from where I live now. Just came to Minneapolis for a little meeting that ended up going all sorts of sideways."

"I don't understand," I say.

"You don't know how to drive, do you?" He straightens for a moment, stretches, and I'm head level with his crotch. Then his face returns in the open window. "I followed you at a distance the whole time, wondering at what point you were going to kill yourself or someone else. Best entertainment I've had in a while."

"I don't understand what you want. Are you even allowed to pull me over? Off duty?"

Any trace of his grin disappears. "I can do whatever the fuck I want. You think you've had a bad night? A substantial portion of my income has three holes in his chest right now. I followed you because I need to make sure you're not going to say anything to anyone about what happened tonight. You saw me there, and that's a problem."

"I swear I won't—"

"Swear to who? God?"

"I don't believe in a god."

"Then swear to who?"

I've never thought about this before. Is there anyone in the world worthy of such a pledge?

"I swear to myself," I say.

This gets a laugh. I'd be annoyed were I not too busy wondering what he plans to do with me.

"You have a license?" he asks.

"No."

"Big surprise. Get me the registration for the car."

"It's not my car."

"That wasn't what I asked. Get me the fucking registration." He coughs, then spits to the side. "I'm collecting names."

"Fine. Okay." I reach up and turn on the interior light, which is aided by Officer Bain's wavering flashlight beam. I check the visors and the center console first, finding nothing but cigarettes, fast-food wrappers, and a half dozen cassette tapes. Then I open the glove box, realizing it's the most likely place for the registration to be, but the first thing I spy is a gun.

A gun.

Travis has a gun in his car.

I'm both happy and horrified see it.

FORTY-THREE

I SAT IN FRONT of that gun all the way from Eau Claire to Minneapolis, two feet away, never knowing it was there.

I know one thing for sure. I can't let Bain know it's here.

"Find it?"

I put a hand over the weapon as I rummage, finding a few official-looking paper scraps and pulling them out, then close the glove box.

"Here," I say, handing Bain the pieces of paper through the open window. "Maybe it's in there."

He takes them from me. "Take the keys out of the ignition and hand them to me."

I do.

"Wait in the car." Bain walks back to his unmarked car and sits inside for a few minutes, the swirling red light continuing to hypnotize me.

Three cars speed by in this time. I'm tempted to get out and flag the next one down, but, really, what good would it do?

I flick my gaze to the rearview and see the silhouette of Bain in his car, then lean back over to the glove box, open it, and grab the gun.

It's heavy. So beautifully heavy. I turn it over, and the black metal absorbs the dim glow from the car's dome light.

Movement in the rearview. Bain's getting out of his car. Rather than put the gun back in the glove box, I slide it beneath my seat, where it jams against what feels like a century of discarded fast-food wrappers.

Bain's head invades my space again. "Car's registered to Nicolas Shepard. Who's that?"

"I'm guessing Travis's dad."

"Okay. And Travis was the guy with you in the club?"

"Yes."

"He live at home?"

I nod.

"And now tell me your full name and date of birth."

I do.

Why do I?

I guess because I'm scared, but that doesn't feel like a good enough reason in the moment.

He scribbles the info down on a small notepad, puts his pen and paper in his pocket, then rests his forearms on the bottom of the opening and leans his head in. "Okay, so here's the deal. You know how I'm not going into detail about what happened back in the club or why I was there?"

I nod.

"Well, that's good news for you. The easiest thing to do would be to tell you the whole story for the fun of it and then shoot you in the fuckin' head, then go over to Travis's house and do the same. But I'm not gonna do that because, well, while I wouldn't call myself a *good* person, I'm not a monster."

"Okay."

"Yeah, okay," he says. "But I need you to get a hold of Travis and tell him what I'm telling you, which is to forget everything you saw tonight. Everything you know."

I almost tell him forgetting is an impossible thing for me. Almost.

"You got that?" he asks.

"I got it."

"Because if anything comes out that connects me to what happened back there, I will find you both and kill you. I don't wanna, but I will. Understand this is not an empty threat. Understand I am highly capable of extreme violence."

"I understand."

He cranes his neck and stares down an oncoming car, then speaks again after it whizzes by. "I barely got out alive myself. Those fuckin' guys. Zero respect. Don't like what they hear, so they just start shooting."

"Please don't say anything else," I tell him.

"Oh, yeah. Right. Okay."

"Actually," I add, "and I suppose I can find out about this in the newspaper, so it's not a secret. Did...Leo...?"

Bain nods. "Right in the gut. Kind of wound that kills you slowly but mostly certainly kills you. Fucking brutal pain. Nearly tripped over him tryin' to come down the stairs."

I absorb the words. I figured as much about Leo, but hearing the truth is a whole blanket full of smother. Not that I cared for him. Didn't care for him at all, really. But he's dead, and that fact transcends my opinion of him.

"Okay," I say.

Silence falls between us. Bain seems lost in his head, and all I want is to leave.

"So, I guess, thank you?" I say. "I'll go now and find Travis, tell him what you said."

He's not even looking at me, but he's still right here in my face, his head halfway in my car.

"Yeah, thing is," he says, staring blankly past me, "you're not going quite yet."

FORTY-FOUR

"IT'S A GODDAMNED SHAME," he continues. "I was going to Minneapolis for this meeting and then planned to head home. And this meeting? Standard shit, easy peasy. Half hour, tops. And then…well, you were there. Not good. Ruined my fuckin' night."

My skin slowly starts to crawl, starting with my forearms, up to my chest, and then down to my thighs. I just want to leave. All I want is to leave. And I hate how he's taking his time telling me what he wants.

"Thing is," he says, "my evening got all sorts of screwed up. Not just because of what happened in the club. Then I had to follow you. And sure, you and me were headed in the same direction, but this whole fuckup of a night ruined my plans for when I got back home."

He wants me to ask what his plans were.

I say nothing.

"See, Penny, all I really wanted to end my evening were a couple of late-night beers and a blow job."

The word settles over me like a blanket made of steel wool. The asshole is grinning. And looking right at me.

"I got this neighbor," he says. "Not much to look at and a little old, but always ready to go whenever I want. It's a kick. I just pick up the phone, and nearly every time, she's at my door in a matter of minutes. It's like Domino's for my dick."

There's that feeling in my stomach again. A sharp blade slicing.

I finally speak. "Why are you telling me this?"

"Because nothing in life is free," he says. "That's the thing about me. I've been known to be lenient when I pull speeders over. I can be a nice guy." Bain's gaze is suddenly oppressive and unforgiving. "And I'm being lenient with you, letting you live and all. But it's not free. I figure you owe me what I was planning on getting tonight otherwise. Five minutes, and you're on your way."

I feel a gag coming on. "Just so we're clear, you want oral sex in exchange for letting me go."

"Well, when you say it like that, it kinda loses its sexiness." He winks. He fucking *winks*. "But only a little."

"But you said you live near here. You could be home soon. You could still call your neighbor."

He smiles, but I imagine him growling. "I don't want her anymore. I want your mouth, so young and perfect."

Maybe it's because I've already used up a lifetime of fear this evening, but I'm surprised by a sudden calmness that settles over me. I don't feel powerless, as I probably should. I'm better than this bastard. *So* much better. And because I am, he won't win. Somehow, I'll figure this all out.

Or maybe that's just my brain injecting a defense mechanism to keep me from screaming in terror.

"Maybe I'll tell your boss about this," I say.

Now Bain leans in even more, and I pull back. "First, you don't know what department I'm with," he says, "and I sure as fuck didn't give you my real name. Second, even if you knew everything about me, you still wouldn't say shit. And it's not because I'd hunt you down, which I would. You wouldn't say anything because *nobody* ever ends up saying anything. Girls like you, they always do as they're told because they got something to lose. You were at the club tonight, borrowing money from a loan shark. A loan shark who died minutes later, and then you up and ran away. You've got trouble. It's written all over your face." Bain twists his head and sniffs the interior of the car. "Hell, I even *smell* it on you." He grins again, just for a flash, then settles into a dead-eyed stare. "Now the question is this: Are you willing to lose your freedom by refusing me? Simple yes or no question, Penny. Simple yes or no."

I question whether this is really happening. Maybe I died when I fell down those stairs, and everything since then has been one long dream, which is now turning into a nightmare.

But I smell him.

Dreams don't smell.

"Maybe I'll just bite it off," I say.

He shrugs. "You can try. But if I feel even a single tooth on my skin, I'll take out my utility tools from my car and remove every last one of them."

I don't respond. I'm too busy imagining a rusty pair of pliers and Bain's forearm flexing as he goes to work on me.

He must be interpreting my silence as acquiescence. Or he doesn't have the patience to wait for an answer.

"So this is what's going to happen," he says. "Drive to the next exit, then pull into the parking lot of the video store there. It's closed; the lot'll be empty. I'll follow behind." He stands, gives a little stretch, but keeps locked in on me. "Maybe you decide to keep driving, not take the exit. Maybe you think I'll change my mind and head home, that you're not worth the effort." Now the smile, so practiced. "Tell you something, Penny Bly, you keep driving, and it's gonna trigger my instinct to chase you something fierce. And how I'll be tempted because—and this is the god's honest truth—the chase is better than the kill. Not always, but most times. But I won't. You'll just keep driving, safe and sound for now. But starting tomorrow, you're gonna wonder when the hammer is going to fall. And fall it will, right into that pretty little skull of yours. And you won't even see it coming." He turns his head and spits on the ground. "And I'll go home and still call my neighbor. I'll fall asleep with a smile on my face, and you'll be looking over your shoulder until you're unable to do anything ever again."

I lower my gaze, amazed I've held it this long. Process his words, search my brain for information that can help, find nothing.

"Ninety" I say, speaking mostly to the steering wheel.

"What's that?"

"Your IQ, I'm guessing. Ninety or less. Certainly not more."

Bain hooks his thumbs in his pants pockets, looks right, and tracks another oncoming car. "Oh, yeah?"

"Based mostly on how you talk and your craving for sexual power. Obviously, that's not a scientific assessment, but I'm fairly confident in my conclusion."

"That so? Ninety or less?"

I nod. "Very likely less."

"And I suppose you have a high IQ, then? Otherwise, not really sure why you'd bring it up in the first place."

"One ninety-eight. As of March third."

The smile isn't there anymore, and Bain's next words are spoken with ease and confidence.

"That's a difference of one hundred eight points," he says. "Pretty fast math for a dumbass like me." Once more he leans in. "Well, then. Surely, you've figured a way out of this situation. All those smarts and all. You figured out a way?"

I say nothing. Instead, I roll up the window, start the car, and ease off the shoulder.

As I drive, I finally answer him, with only my ears to hear the two words.

"I will."

FORTY-FIVE

THERE'S THIS MEMORY, ONE from the time before every memory of mine became etched in permanence, one of the very few that exist. I must've been no more than five and was at park with Dad. Just the two of us. The park was dotted with rusty swings, a cracked and faded seesaw, looming metal monkey bars, and a spinning merry-go-round that had likely flung more than a few passengers to the ground. I remember the equipment clearly because even at that age I thought it depressing. Looking back, it may have been my first grasping of irony, that these things designed to bring children joy only made me sad.

But it was time alone with my father, and that did bring me joy, so rather than play on the equipment while he watched, I sat next to him on a bench and told him I just wanted to be with him. He smiled, put his arm around me, said that was a fine idea.

So we sat there, mostly in silence, the sun starting to dip. No one else was around; the park and the moment were ours.

I remember how it felt to be there alone with him, like we were the last two people in the world, and how safe that made me feel.

That everything would be okay, with no proof at all to support such a belief.

And perhaps that was the only time I felt that pure and flawless happiness, felt it without questioning it, and perhaps I'll only find it ever again in my father's presence.

If I live to see that day.

Dad's not here to protect me now.

Now?

Now I'm sitting next to a different kind of man altogether, here, in the dinge of Travis's car, the cabin light off, parked in an empty lot in front of a dry cleaner's, a sewing store, and a movie rental store (LIVING ON VIDEO—BRING HOLLYWOOD TO YOUR HOME!).

Bain trailed me on the interstate, likely nodding in knowing approval when I, indeed, turned off at the exit and parked as instructed. I hoped the short drive would give me enough time to figure out how to get out of this. I came to no conclusion, making me doubt the misplaced confidence from before, that a seventy-eight-point IQ advantage would more than compensate for a predator twice my size, who's likely armed. I hoped a battle of wits would prove decisive, negating the need for a battle of brute strength.

Yet here Bain is, sitting in the passenger seat, his polyester slacks slipped down around his knees, his tighty-whities the only thing separating me from a future of constant nightmares.

"Don't worry," he says. "It'll be over quick if you know what you're doing."

I think about my father on that bench from that day long ago. About what advice he'd give if he saw me right now. What would he say?

I close my eyes and decide to find out.

FORTY-SIX

HI, DAD.

Hiya, Pen Pen.

Things are bad. Things are really bad.

I know, sweetie. And lemme tell you, it just shatters my heart, plain and simple.

I appreciate not having to bring him up to speed on the night's events, considering he's only in my head. But I hope he can tap into a piece of my consciousness that'll reveal a solution to this problem.

What do I do?

He doesn't answer straightaway. Rather, the phantom voice expresses dismay at not being there for me in this monumental time of need, which then leads to a grander apology at not being there since I was seven.

Okay, okay, Dad, I get it. Save your apologies for when I'm standing in front of you. I need to know what to do. Right now.

Bain smells like deodorant overpowered by a day's worth of sweat, sickly sweet, more decay than musk.

Well, hell, Pen Pen. Woulda thought that was obvious, but I suppose we know your brain and my brain operate in very different ways.

I squeeze my eyes shut even tighter in frustration.

Obvious? Whatever it is, it's not obvious to me. And I don't have much time.

Silence, silence.

Only one thing to do, darlin'.

And that is?

Silence, silence.

Then: *Easy peasy. You gotta kill him.*

FORTY-SEVEN

"WHAT?"

I'm barely aware I just said this out loud.

Dad's voice continues.

Doesn't matter he's a cop, though who knows if that's even true. He's scum. He doesn't deserve to breathe the same stale air inside this car as you, much less be able to defile you.

"I can't do that," I say.

Now Bain's voice is in my right ear. "The hell you talking about?"

You can, Pen. He abuses girls all the time. You wouldn't just be protecting yourself, you'd be saving dozens of 'em. Some he probably rapes. Maybe even kills, far as you know.

"That doesn't make it right," I tell him. I keep my eyes closed and visualize my father next to me on the bench from years ago. I swear I can smell him, and he bears the scent of cedarwood. Strong. Fresh. Fortified. Permanent.

"You nuts or something?" Bain asks. "I don't have all night here."

Love, you already know this, but maybe your brain's a little beaten up.

You've experienced more horror tonight than most folks have in a lifetime, so I get that your processing might be a little slow, so let me lay it out for you. First off, he'll probably want more from you than he's said. And second, if you refuse what he wants, I'm certain he'll kill you. Maybe he's planning on doing that anyway. Maybe he's done it before. Preys on young women, drifters and such. Your only hope is to strike first. Strike first and strike hard.

In my mind a cloud passes over the sun at the park, shadowing Dad's face, but somehow his eyes gleam even brighter as he looks directly at me.

Sorry, honey. You gotta kill him.

"I can't," I say. "There has to be another option."

"God damn it, quit wasting time," Bain says. "This is happening right *now*."

Sure you can. We're all capable of violence when faced with our own mortality. And you must've been thinking this all along because why else would you have put Travis's gun under your seat?

"No," I tell him. "No, no, no. I don't know why I did that."

And that's when you use that brain of yours. After the killing. Getting rid of the evidence. You can get away with it. I'm certain of that.

"C'mon, slut. Right now, or you're gonna be sorry."

Bain's right here, but he is so far away.

I'm not a killer.

I can't believe I even have to have that thought.

There *has* to be another way.

Maybe I can reason with Bain. I need to at least try. Talk with him just a little more. Tell him more about me and make me human to him, not just a target.

I open my eyes and turn. Bain looks so suddenly small and pitiful sitting here, red-faced, pants around his ankles.

"I'm going to tell you a story," I say. "It's about what happened to me as a kid and how—"

Bain lunges.

In an instant, his hands are around my throat.

I can't breathe.

I can't fucking breathe.

FORTY-EIGHT

IT ALL HAPPENS SO fast.

Him, sweat and strength. His hands gripping, angry, so angry.

Me, my eyes bulging yet seeing only fog, my mouth open but no air going in or scream coming out. The back of my head presses hard against the door, the pain acute but not as much as the fear.

His face on mine, a forced kiss with bloodlust behind it, a jackal's first taste of its kill.

"I changed my mind. I decided I want more than just your mouth."

Just as Dad warned.

Me, feeling a slight easing of his grip, sucking in beautiful stale air, exhaling a glob of spit on his face. Knowing I can scream or beg but doing neither because it'll do no good. The helplessness. The fucking helplessness is the worst part of all.

His right hand, releasing its grip long enough to punch me in the stomach.

"Goddamned whore."

Me, gasping like fresh catch thrashing and dying on the deck of a trawler. Feeling myself weakening. Fast. Too fast.

Both his hands off my neck, one now pinning my right shoulder and the other reaching for the snap on my jeans. His stench so rank, so present.

Me, wondering in the most distant way what it'll feel like to die, a thought I've had so many times before.

Dad, somewhere deep in my brain and still on that park bench, saying, *You know what to do.*

Bain, opening the top of my jeans with a skill that suggests I'm far from his first victim, trying to work his fingers lower.

Me, playing it forward in my mind, seeing my body in a dumpster. Found a week later. The coroner pronouncing me a Jane Doe and that I was raped repeatedly before being strangled to death. No one knowing I was special, one of seventy-five, sentenced to become decomposing meat buried in an unmarked grave.

Bain, getting stronger. Impossibly stronger.

Me, all my energy commanded to my legs, forcing them closed, knowing they can't withstand his power very long. Hearing my father again, this time just an echo, distant and fading, but the message intact.

You know what to do.

Bain, laughing.

Oh my god, he is laughing.

Me, left hand free, at least free enough. Reaching under the seat, but the angle is wrong. Wrist unable to bend enough.

Bain. "It didn't have to be this way."

Me, gasping for words. "Just let me up a little. I can hardly do anything like this."

Bain, pausing, considering, then finally obeying, because maybe he likes the idea of me pretending to be into it. "Don't try anything funny, now."

Me, free for a few more inches, just enough. Angling my wrist again, my hand finding the handle of the gun. Pulling it free from the floor-boards like Excalibur from the stone. It's beautiful. How can it be so beautiful? Metal and plastic and wood, that's all.

Bain, his eyes narrowed at first, then jolting wide with realization. "I said not to do anything funny. Now give me the gun, and I won't hurt you too much."

But it's late. It's too late.

Me, taking sloppy aim because that's the only kind I have.

Him, lunging.

Me, firing.

The blast, deafening.

Him, dying instantly. His skull shattered open.

Me, in another world, another life, one of safety and security and very much shielded from the wild, barely registering my own words.

"Now, was that funny?"

FORTY-NINE

THE HEADY SMELL OF gunpowder.

My ears continue to ring as I stare at Bain's body. Deep in the recesses of my consciousness, Dad's voice.

Atta girl.

"No, no." I'm not to be congratulated.

I nearly stumble to my knees as I burst out of the car before slamming the door behind me. Cracked asphalt of the parking lot beneath my feet. Lights from the video store sign washing the scene in a soft blue.

Except the lights from the store and the moon, there's only darkness.

Ahead, up a small grade a quarter mile away, the interstate. I consider it for a full thirty seconds. No cars pass.

The only sounds are my own labored breaths.

I reach up and touch my neck, finding it tender but nothing worse. I'll probably have bruises.

I steady my breathing, then turn back to Travis's car. With all my willpower, I manage to open the driver's door.

The cabin light illuminates.

Look at it. You have to look at it.

The body.

Bain's slumped over, and what's left of his head is between his knees, as if assuming a crash position.

Keep looking. Know this is real. You need to deal with this.

I'll have to drive away with Travis's car, with Bain inside. I need to get as far away from here as possible and take as much evidence with me as I can. It's the most logical thing to do.

But logic, turns out, has its limits. There are only so many steps one can plan out, so many actual steps one can take, before emotion dominates all thought processes. This is what happens now, with no warning or request for permission. Emotion swallows logic with the suffocating hopelessness of a mouse traveling down a snake's trachea.

Before doing anything else, I sit in this video store parking lot.

Crisscross applesauce, hunched over my legs.

And I cry.

Cry harder than I ever have before, except maybe the moment I was told my father had gone away, and that was fourteen years ago.

Fourteen.

Deep purple, squished blueberries.

"Stop," I say. "Just stop. *Just stop.* I don't fucking care about colors anymore."

But my brain doesn't listen. It'll keep doing as it has always done since I was a little girl, for better or worse.

I keep sobbing, almost not even caring if someone finds me like this. Almost hoping I'll be caught so I never have to make another decision again.

Almost.

Minutes pass.

No one finds me.

The tears eventually come to an end, and I know it's time to push the emotion down.

Now more than ever, I need to start using my brain again.

FIFTY

FIRST THINGS FIRST.

I stand, wipe the tears off my cheeks, and suck in the night air.

Then I walk over to Bain's car.

After using the bottom of my shirt to open the door, I peer inside, the front seats illuminated from the cabin lights above. It looks like a normal car except for the police radio. Did he use it to call his police station after I handed him Travis's registration? What if he called into some dispatcher and said he was conducting a routine traffic stop and gave them info about Travis's car?

I don't know.

I have no idea if Bain called anyone on that radio. If he did, that's beyond my control.

I look for the small notepad he used to write down my name. It's not here, which means it's probably still in his pocket.

I get out and shut the door, making sure my fingers touch nothing.

Back to Travis's car.

I suck in a breath and ease back into the driver's seat, then roll down my window. I'll be needing as much fresh air as the world can give me.

My plan?

No idea.

I'll have to ditch Travis's car, most certainly. I'll be stranding myself in the process, but the car is too much of a liability. If Bain used his radio and called in Travis's plates and registration, cops far and wide will be looking for it when Bain fails to turn up. As tempted as I am to steal new license plates and spray-paint the car a different color, it's not worth the risk. Better to be on foot.

I start the ignition and make my way back onto the highway, fighting against shaking hands and a shortness of breath. It's all I can do to keep the car at the speed limit and in the right lane.

The stench from Bain creeps, punishing me.

I'm still heading west, and it's only a few minutes before the answer to *where west?* dawns on me.

Minnesota.

The land of ten thousand lakes.

Yes.

That's it. That's what I need.

A lake.

FIFTY-ONE

THE LINE ON THE gas tank indicator edges into the red.

I need to find a large body of water soon.

I pull over at the next exit and drive to a gas station. It's closed, but that's not why I'm here. I turn on the overhead light and grab the *Thomas Guide* from the back.

As I bring the hefty book of maps back to the front seat, I can't *not* look at Bain.

The head.

Oh, god, the head.

My stomach flips as I pull my gaze away and try to focus, flipping through the maps of the Minnesota guidebook until I find the page showing my approximate location. I know I just passed through Litchfield, and the next few towns west are Grove City, Atwater, and...

Holy shit.

Willmar.

The name seems to glow on the map, and that's probably because it's seared into my mind. I haven't seen the name of that city in print anywhere, but I did hear it spoken by a man wearing snakeskin boots.

She is the current owner of the Out to Lunch Diner in Willmar, Minnesota. We have visited her. Now we are going back to execute her. As we said, this visit is a courtesy to you.

The two men in the comedy club, the men with accents. They're going to Willmar to kill some woman, and Arthur told them not to. That disagreement got both Arthur and his son killed.

Best I can figure, Willmar is twenty miles due west of here on the same interstate I'm on now.

I close my eyes and speak to the night. "I need you."

I'm right here. Have been the whole time.

"I'm going to dump the car and the body in a lake."

Seems reasonable, Dad says.

"And there's this woman in Willmar. The men from the club shooting said they're going to kill her. She's near the lake I have in mind. I have... I think I have the opportunity to warn her."

It's a sign, right?

He's right. It's a cosmically twisted sign. Here I am next to a dead cop whose body I need to get rid of. And yet, due west and only twenty miles away is a woman I can save. At least warn.

Maybe it's a chance at redemption, if such a thing exists.

"I don't want to get involved. What if the men come after me?"

He's quiet for a bit. Then Dad says, *Yup, that's a risk. Long and short of it, I suppose it depends on what kind of person you want to be, Pen Pen.*

"You mean a good person or a bad person?"

Not sure it's that black-and-white, but sure.

I've never spent much time considering whether I'm a good or bad person. I guess I haven't really done enough of anything to warrant a verdict. But the idea of being a bad person is massively disappointing.

"I'm scared," I say.

You have every right to be. For many reasons. But say the men were after you and someone else had a chance to give you a heads-up. Wouldn't you be grateful for that?

"Yes."

Well, then.

"Well, then."

Things aren't going to be easy again for some time, I suspect. Maybe never. But you know how to face down challenges. I think you've proven that. Make the right choice, even…especially…if it's the hardest thing to do.

And his voice fades to nothing, leaving me to pore over the map.

I home in on Willmar and all the many surrounding bodies of water.

I search for one that's large and not directly in the heart of the town itself. One immediately jumps out at me.

"Solomon Lake," I whisper.

I can make it.

Just another twenty minutes or so of driving this horror show on wheels. I can make it to Solomon Lake, ditch the car, then walk into town. Just a couple of miles, it looks like.

I start the car and keep going west, wondering if anything I intend to do will actually play out.

God damn it.

I hope so.

FIFTY-TWO

THERE'S ONLY ONE ENTRY site on the east side of Solomon Lake. The last thing I need is to run into another person, but thankfully the small parking lot is empty. No campers, no late-night teens making out in their car. Just a dirt lot and a single concrete boat ramp.

I coax the car halfway down the boat ramp, put it into park, and get out. The aroma of the lake water washes over me, a heady mix of algae and mud. Moisture hangs heavy in the air. The headlight beams don't travel far past the shoreline, swallowed by the lonely and vast stretch of black water beyond.

This'll do.

The universe is out here, watching, waiting to see what I plan to do next. This is the big one. The point of no return.

I can explain why I was at the scene of a multiple homicide in Minneapolis, though I might not be believed.

I can explain why I ran from that scene and illegally drove a car for more than an hour, though I might not be believed.

I can argue I killed a cop out of pure self-defense, that he was going to rape and kill me. The same cop who was also at the comedy club crime scene. It's all true, of course, though I might not be believed.

If I do this, however, this thing right now...well, there's no explaining it. No argument solid enough to convince anyone I'm innocent. I may as well plead guilty if caught, just for the sake of ease.

But I've already made up my mind. I will not wrestle any longer with this decision.

What I *do* wrestle with is the math. The angle of the ramp. The speed of the car. The resistance of the water. If I just let the car roll down the ramp in neutral, its nose might hit bottom and leave its tail end exposed to the first boater of the morning. But if the car is traveling at speed, decent speed, it might carry itself far enough into the lake to sink in a deeper area. A few extra feet of water could buy me a day or two.

I've seen it in movies. The guy who puts the brick on the gas pedal, making the car speed straight ahead. But I don't have a brick, and I know the movies are full of inconsistencies within the physical universe. A brick would fall off as soon as the car jolted forward. I need something like a sandbag, a thing large and heavy enough to cover the gas pedal.

I glance back to the car, grimacing at a sudden idea.

But no. I'd never be able to carry Bain's deadweight from one side of the car to the other. And if I could, there's no way of ensuring his foot would stay on the pedal.

So, on this summer night, full of the dark and fantastic and horrible, I take my faux-leather backpack out of the back seat and place it on the boat launch. Then I strip naked, as if preparing myself for a sacrifice.

Maybe I am.

I fold my clothes and lay them beside the backpack before placing my shoes neatly on top.

All my worldly possessions, right there, in those two square feet.

Then I get back into the car, the upholstery scratchy on the bottom of my thighs, and slowly ease the car up to the top of the launch.

The engine hums.

Then I remember.

The guns. There're two of them in the car, one belonging to Travis and the other to Bain. I decide to let them sink. I don't want anything to do with guns for the rest of my life.

What about my fingerprints? They're all over the car.

I get out, grab my shirt, and wipe down what I can. I'm guessing (hoping?) prints won't last long underwater. Not that it really matters. Someone will discover the car, maybe tomorrow, maybe a week from now. This car with the corpse of a police officer will be traced back to Travis's family, a family with a missing son who was last seen with Penny Bly. There is no fool-proofing this crime scene without burying the corpse somewhere else, which I'm simply not physically capable of doing.

Physics dictates the car will float farther into the lake if the windows are closed. It also tells me I'll be less able to open my door with the weight of the water pressing against it.

I toss my shirt back to the boat ramp, then roll down my window just to the point I imagine I can squirm through.

Okay, I'm ready.

Am I ready?

Wait.

Fuck.

The notepad. Bain wrote my name and date of birth on the notepad. It's in his pocket.

What follows next is almost unimaginable. The notepad is in his right pocket, and it's much harder to slip out than I would have thought. Death makes everything more difficult, and I gag and retch as his cooling blood smears against my right arm.

Finally, I free it.

Turn on the overhead light, then find the page with my name and Travis's name. Rip the small page out, crumple it up, and swallow it.

Deep breath.

Be calm, but be quick.

I strap on my seat belt, knowing my body will bear marks from it later.

Keeping my foot on the brake, I shift the car into drive.

A few seconds pass as I look forward, then move my gaze to the dead man.

"All you had to do was be someone decent. But you couldn't do that, so this is where you end up."

This is the extent of the eulogy.

One deep breath.

Then I floor it.

FIFTY-THREE

I MANAGE TO GET the car to thirty before it hits the water.

BOOSH!

Even with the ramp's minimal slope, the impact into the lake is fierce. I strain against the seat belt, which does its job of keeping me from slamming into the steering column.

For three seconds the car does what I hoped. It seems to float, driven by momentum. In that tiny slice of time and calm, I picture myself remaining in here with Bain, descending into the darkness of this watery grave. First would come horror, and then there'd be peace, and how disquieting a combination that is.

Water starts pouring in through my half-open window. It isn't heart-stoppingly cold, but it's cold enough to jolt me into action.

Off with my belt, out through the window. This is it. I have to push against the heavy torrent of lake water pouring in—which is harder than I expected—but by the time I'm free, the car still isn't fully submerged.

Some water makes its way into my mouth, but I'm able to keep from swallowing it. I imagine a thousand bacteria attaching to the inside of my cheeks, and I spit them out as soon as my face breaches the surface.

I wish I'd taken swim lessons.

But still I manage the short distance back to shore by dog-paddling. Soon, my bare feet meet the grooved concrete of the submerged ramp, and it feels like freedom. At least temporary freedom.

I stand upright, naked to the night, and walk up to shore.

Exhausted.

I'm so exhausted from life.

When I turn, the car has finally gone under, and that's when I realize I didn't think about the lights. The headlights are still on, giving off a murky underwater glow, like a giant mass of bioluminescent sea organisms. The lights finally steady as the car hits bottom, which I'm guessing is maybe fifteen feet deep, certainly no more. In blazing daylight, the shape of the car could very well be visible from the surface in that shallow of water.

I tilt my head back and look to the sky, grateful for the nearly full moon, the only light guiding my way.

I grab my clothes, put them on over my wet skin. I won't be dry anytime soon, but the early-morning air is warm enough.

Last, I reach down, grab my backpack, sling it over my shoulder. Then, guided by this moonlight, I walk, first to the dirt parking lot and then to the road that guided me here.

South, back to the highway.

I don't even know where to find this woman to warn her.

The Out to Lunch Diner? Somewhere in Willmar, but could be on the outskirts, miles from here.

You'll figure it out, a quiet and calming voice in my head says. This could very well be a lie, and the one person who can always tell if Penny Bly is lying is Penny Bly.

You'll figure it out.

This surely sounds very much like a lie.

A lie dipped in hope and coated in sweet, sweet ignorance.

FIFTY-FOUR

THE MOTEL IS ON the southwest corner of where I exited the interstate a lifetime ago.

The sign above the one-story roof struggles to shine. STAR*LITE INN.

Just seeing the sign makes me realize how completely exhausted I am. I'm lured by the idea of a bed. Even for just a few hours, until daybreak. Just a little rest.

The door triggers an electronic chime as I walk into the small cluttered reception area. Of course, it's a risk stopping only a few miles from where I got rid of Bain, but it's either this or spending the rest of the night in the woods. This is the longest I've ever gone without sleep.

Quite a day of firsts.

The clock above the faded-wood reception desk reads 1:05 a.m.

The reception area feels tired and lonely, evidenced by the automatic-drip coffee maker next to the door. Rusted on the front, half a pot (likely cold) in a mineral-stained glass carafe, and an index card taped above with $0.25 handwritten on it.

"Hello?"

I wait after calling out, but no one comes. So I try again.

Still nothing.

I'm just about to crash in the single recliner chair next to a rack of local-attraction brochures when a woman emerges from the back office, rubbing sleep from her eyes.

I'm guessing her to be a hard-earned forty.

"Help you?"

I try my best to appear alert and normal, even though my wet hair smells like lake water. "I'd like a room for the night."

"Night's pretty much over. Checkout is at ten a.m."

"That's fine," I say.

The woman—Eileen, according to the crooked name tag pinned through her denim blouse—squints and scans me.

"We don't tolerate prostitution or drugs here. Just like Mrs. Reagan says. Just say no."

"I'm not part of anything like that."

Eileen shrugs. She doesn't believe me. "Just saying, a pretty young thing wanders in here after midnight. I've seen it before, but I suppose it's none of my business."

"How much is the room?"

"Thirty-five. Thirty-seven if you want HBO turned on. Forty for both HBO and Skinemax."

"Skinemax?"

"You know, Cinemax. The porny version of HBO. Lots of people pay extra for it."

"I don't need that."

Eileen pulls out a registration card and starts circling things. "Tell you what, for an even fifty, I'll throw in a second night. In case you need more sleep than you think."

I don't think I'll be needing a second night. Plan is to find this woman in the morning, warn her about the Snakeskin Boys, then figure out how to keep heading west without a car.

But still, she's giving me a good deal. And if it turns out I do need to lie low tomorrow, best to have place to do it in.

"Fine."

Eileen slides the registration card over. "Fill this out, and I need ID and payment."

Here's where I need to sound convincing. "I don't have any ID."

"'Course you don't. And you drove here?"

"No." I search my brain for more lies. "A friend dropped me off."

"Sure they did." Eileen looks me up and down again, then wags the pen like a scolding schoolteacher. "Like I said, no whoring or drugs. Not here."

Eileen is testing my nerves, which are nearly nonexistent at this point. I say, "Do I look like a whore or a junkie?"

"Trust me, they come in all types, and I've seen every one of 'em." She lets out a sigh that says, *I'm going against my better judgment here,* then slides the pen over next to the card. "Fill this out the best you can and pay up."

I take the pen and quickly spot the first and most troubling part of the registration card.

First name, last name.

This'll have to be another lie, of course.

But also a chance at rebirth.

In this broken-down motel, I can be anyone in the world.

I've always liked the Bly name, mostly because of the famous (and unrelated) Nellie Bly. Nellie was notable for many things but was best known for traveling around the world in seventy-two days in 1889. She did it just to see if it was possible, attempting to turn the fictional *Around the World in Eighty Days* into a reality. Nellie Bly was a woman who *really* went into the wild. Twenty-five thousand miles around the world and came out the other side all the stronger for it.

Shit.

I've traveled maybe two hundred miles and am rapidly crumbling to dust.

I write *Nellie* as my first name.

And last name?

I think about all the female characters from all the books I've read, and it takes only a few seconds to come up with *Drew*, for the handful of Nancy Drew mysteries I read while at Willow Brook. Nancy Drew wasn't just a woman solving crimes. She was a woman in power. In control.

A woman in charge of the direction of her life.

I write the name down.

Nellie Drew.

Yes, I think. *That'll do.*

A bogus address and signature later, I hand the card back over.

"Fifty-four twenty-three, with the government's take," Eileen says, reading the card. "*Nellie.*"

I pay, get my change, my key, and one last sideways glance from Eileen.

Outside, I head down a long row of uneven planks, hazy incandescent bulbs lighting the way.

Room ten, a bleak affair, but the door has a lock, and the room has four walls and a bed. Sink and toilet. A TV with no HBO or Skinemax. Fifty-four dollars of luxury, far as I'm concerned.

I'm tempted by the shower, wanting just to wash the lake away. Even more tempted by the bed.

Pen down, lights off. I crawl into bed with the weary victory of summiting Everest yet having lost all my friends along the way.

I close my eyes, try to shut off my mind.

But my mind. My wondrous mind.

Just like the world, it just keeps spinning madly on.

FIFTY-FIVE

I WAKE ONLY AN hour later with a ferocious urge to pee. I make it halfway to the toilet before *the remembering,* and each memory comes unannounced and with tremendous, brutal force.

Leo and Travis snorting coke.

Arthur telling me my dad's a piece of shit.

Arguing on the other side of the office door.

Gunshots. Screaming.

Gurgling.

Travis, gone.

Bain.

It'll be over quick if you know what you're doing.

Chunks of skull on the passenger seat.

Naked on the boat ramp.

In this dark and foreign room, it occurs to me this jolt will be a daily occurrence for the rest of my life. Those few seconds every day upon waking, consciousness fresh and clean from sleep. The seconds before memories storm the gates of my mind.

I might end up wishing never to sleep again just to avoid the whole waking-up part.

After the bathroom, I stumble back to bed, back to the scratchy sheets damp with sweat.

Lower my lids.

But when sleep does not come immediately, I try to distract myself into a fantasy, something to keep me from looping the horror movie of the past twelve hours in my brain. I think and think but come up with nothing. Then, just as I'm about to turn on the TV for distraction, it comes to me. A fantasy so unrealistic, it just might do.

I play the absurd scenario out in my mind.

I'm on the Letterman show. They found out about my special abilities and asked me on as a guest. Not even in a stupid-human-tricks segment but as a bona fide guest. Sitting right next to Dave.

I can see it so clearly.

Walking into the TV studio. An assistant meets me and says how *thrilled* they are to have me. Then, after a stint in the hair-and-makeup room, I'm as pretty as ever but also older looking. Sophisticated. Like I could throw a successful cocktail party were that suddenly required.

I see it all, and it's wondrous.

There I am, sitting in the greenroom, all nerves and excitement. Popping M&M's. A different assistant—headphones and mic—dips in to tell me, *Two minutes.* And yet another person comes in a minute later to escort me behind the stage. Music playing, wild and frenetic, coming back from commercial.

Then Dave's voice.

Our next guest is one of the most gifted people in the world. Well, one of seventy-five. She has a photographic memory and can draw such realistic portraits, you'd think you were looking at a photo. Jeez Louise. Oh, and did

I mention she's only twenty-one? Ladies and gentlemen, please welcome the lovely and talented Penny Bly!

The music starts up (curiously, the *Jeopardy!* theme song in this fantasy). I'm softly pushed onto the stage, my stomach awhirl.

But the applause. So much applause, and I've never heard that before. Not ever for me.

This fantasy continues before I finally fall back asleep. Through the interview, the probing questions, the answers that make Dave laugh, that squeaky cackle, and how I kinda die when I hear it. And of course I draw him, right then and there, in just a few minutes, really, and the camera does a close-up of the result, and the audience gasps as Dave says, *Good god, that's amazing.*

And how I cling to this dream, sure as the scratchy blanket and thin sheet damp with my rank sweat clings to me. My fantasy and reality duel this night, each gaining ground before yielding it once again to the other. And so it goes for a countless amount of time because, in this state, I refuse to let my brain tally the seconds, as it would have unabated. This tug-of-war, what I want my life to be and how it is, happiness and despair, a zero-sum game in which I'm still rendered brittle bones and decaying flesh at the end because that's what becomes of us all, no matter how special someone is, no matter if you're one in seventy-five or a dime a dozen.

The beautiful and aching injustice of everything mattering in the now and nothing mattering in the forever.

In the end exhaustion wins, and I sleep. My last thought before unconsciousness is about all that applause. So unlikely, fantasy or not. Nearly impossible to imagine.

So much applause, and I've never heard that before.

Not ever for me.

FIFTY-SIX

July 16, 1987
Thursday

I OPEN MY EYES.

Still dark.

What time is it?

It seems like I just used the bathroom, so I slept what, maybe another hour?

If that's the case, I need more sleep. It's not even light out yet.

I shove my head under the pillow and will myself back to unconsciousness, but then—*BAM!*—come the memories.

Day one of the rest of my life.

Fuck.

I toss and turn for what feels like forever, but it's still not growing light outside. Maybe the world ended when I was asleep. What a relief that would be.

I finally get out of bed, needing to pee again. I go to the bathroom, then do my business, and on the way back to bed, I spy the digital clock on the VCR, which is nestled in a small stand housing the TV.

9:02

That doesn't make any sense. It would be full sunshine at nine in the morning. So the clock is wrong.

Or...

I walk over to the window, open the curtain, and stare out at the dark parking lot. The motel's sign is lit, as it was earlier, along with the weak lighting over the outside corridors. The light nearest to my room has a couple of moths bumbling over one another, again and again.

Or maybe it's nine at night.

The idea of it is so disorienting, it's hard to wrap my mind around it, an unfamiliar feeling. Nine p.m. That would mean I slept for nearly twenty hours.

I throw on clothes, run my fingers through my hair, grab my purse, and stumble back down to the lobby.

This time Eileen's at the front desk, her hands wrapped around a paperback. She looks up to me and offers a thin smirk.

"Well, Miss Drew. You must've been pretty tired. We knocked for housekeeping to come in, but you never answered. Door was locked, so we figured you were in there. Guess it's a good thing you paid for that second night." She looks me over. "Same clothes as last night, I see."

"What time is it?" I ask.

Eileen holds out a hand and points to the clock on the wall. Sure enough, just after nine.

Well. Twenty hours, then.

Perhaps that's for the best, but every hour that passes is another hour closer to Bain's body being discovered.

Oh, shit.

The woman in danger. The owner of the diner.

I was going to warn her. It was literally the first thing I was going to do in the morning. She could be dead now. Dead because I didn't set an alarm.

"Do you know a diner called Out to Lunch?" I ask.

Eileen smirks in an annoying way. "Um, yeah, you mean the one right next door?"

"It's here? Part of the motel?"

"Not part of the motel. But yeah, it's next door. It's nothing much, but then again nothing here is."

She returns to her book as I'm still processing.

"A woman runs it, right?" I ask. "She owns it or something?"

Eileen looks pained to have to answer me. "You're talking about Fia. Yes, she owns it. Probably there right now. Place closes at ten."

"Fia, you said?"

"Yeah. It's short for something, I think. Mexicans like nicknames."

Snakeskin Boys had an accent. Were they Mexican as well?

"Okay." I turn away from Eileen, saying nothing more, and take two steps over to the coffee maker. I reach into my purse, to my wallet, where I rummage for a quarter. As I do, the TV at the other end of the room plays the rapid-fire cadence of a local reporter.

"*Thanks, Jim. I'm here at Roasters Comedy Club in downtown Minneapolis, where last night police arrived at a grisly scene.*"

My whole body freezes.

"*Responding to an anonymous nine-one-one call, police discovered two bodies, both apparently victims of bullet wounds.*"

In the back of my mind, I think, *Two bodies. Arthur and Leo.*

"*One of the deceased is Arthur Clayton,*" the reporter continues, "*the club owner rumored to be tied to organized crime. The other victim is thought, but not confirmed, to be Arthur's son, Leo. Authorities are establishing a hotline looking for any information and are particularly interested in the identity and whereabouts of the anonymous tipster, who is thought to be female. We'll be playing that nine-one-one audio as soon as it becomes available to us. If anyone has any information—*"

I listen for another minute, then decide against the coffee.

Caffeine has nothing on panic.

FIFTY-SEVEN

I RETURN TO MY room, lock the door, and turn on the television. I stay with the local NBC news for a while longer, then change to CBS, then ABC. CBS has some coverage; ABC, none. The Star*Lite has a few channels of free cable, including CNN. I tune in, looking for anything about Roasters Comedy Club but instead find Larry King asking David Lee Roth about his first solo album after leaving Van Halen.

Back to NBC, cut to commercial. Upon the return, weather.

I shut it off and stare into the fading image on the screen. As it dissolves, I try to organize my thoughts but find it impossible to untangle all the swirling questions and emotions into anything giving me a straight path forward.

I should've gone to the police after the shooting.

I shouldn't have run.

But what would I have told them? That I saw the backs of a couple of guys in snakeskin boots? That I was there to borrow money from a loan shark? That the guy I was with snorted some coke?

Ruminating on this does no good. The decision's been made, and there is no undeciding it because of the other—much larger—problem.

I think of Bain, his hair drifting like a sea anemone in the tomb of Travis's car, the shallow grave in Solomon Lake.

Bain is the biggest problem of all.

Time is what I need. Time to put a lot more distance between me and that lake.

Maybe I'll go farther than California.

Mexico, if I can figure that out.

One step at a time.

I need to get to that diner. Find this Fia person and warn her.

But before that, I have a sudden urge to make two calls. If Fia is still alive, I doubt a few more minutes will be the difference between life and death.

I reach over, lift the phone receiver, and dial the number I memorized the moment it was given to me.

FIFTY-EIGHT

"HELLO?"

I close my eyes. "Hello, Mrs. Shepard. This is Penny Bly."

"Who?"

"Penny. I...I stayed at your house—"

"Yes, of course." I hear the panic creep into Marion Shepard's voice. "What's wrong? Did something happen to Travis?"

"No, nothing like that." Although maybe. "Has he called you?"

"He's not with you?"

"No."

Marion's rapid breathing bursts through the phone line. "No. No one's called me. You two just left my house without so much as a goodbye, and now you're telling me he's missing?"

I search in the darkness behind my eyelids for words that'll keep Marion from freaking out completely. "He's not missing," I tell her. "We just got separated is all. In Minneapolis."

"How the hell did that happen?"

If only I told her the truth.

"It's a long story. Just some miscommunication. But your son had a plan in case that happened, and he said to call you and tell you where I am. So, if he calls—*when* he calls—tell him I'm at the Star*Lite Inn in Willmar. That's Minnesota."

"What are you doing there?"

"Waiting for Travis."

Marion pauses, and I picture her squeezing the phone handle until her knuckles blossom white. "You won't understand this because you're a stupid little girl. But that is *my boy*. The boy I raised the best I could for nineteen years. You come into my life, steal him from me, then tell me he's missing? You have no idea what that does to a mother."

"No," I say. "You're right. I don't."

"God damn it all."

"He's fine, Mrs. Shepard. I'm sure he's fine. We just got separated for a bit is all. Star*Lite Inn in Willmar. He'll be calling real soon, I'm sure."

I don't wait to hear the response, knowing that since Marion already hates me, I won't fracture our relationship by hanging up without a goodbye. So I do.

It's not how I wanted the call to go.

I hoped Travis had already called his mother.

But he hasn't.

Travis presumably ran like hell out of the club that night. Didn't take his car. Didn't check in on me. He just ran.

That makes him a coward, and I hold a little bit of hate for him over that.

Yet I desperately hope he's okay.

Such are feelings.

I'll wait one more day, max. If there's no word from him, I'll keep moving. It's already a risk telling Marion where I am; I can't stay at this motel indefinitely.

Okay.

One more call.

FIFTY-NINE

"IT'S ME. HELLO."

Dr. Brock lets out a heavy sigh. "Penny, I'm so glad to hear from you. I know you haven't been gone long, but I've been worried sick."

"Well, I'm still alive." *Barely.*

"Yes, of course you are. I didn't mean to imply you can't take care of yourself. But…we're all worried here. And your mother came down to the institute and gave Dr. Cheong an earful, saying we drove you away."

"That might be the most concern she's ever expressed for me."

He exhales the softest of chuckles, a placeholder more than anything. "Where are you?"

"I'd rather not say."

"Why?"

Why?

The world spins as a billion whys go unanswered.

"I don't know… I just think it's for the best."

He clears his throat. "Are you okay?"

"No," I say.

"What happened? Last you told me, you were with some boy. Did he...do something?"

"No. Nothing like that."

"Then what?"

"There...there was an incident." I don't close my eyes this time, like I did during the call with Marion. I stare directly into the crumbling plaster of the motel room wall, losing focus within the textures.

"What do you—"

"Just let me talk, okay?"

"Okay. Of course. Go on."

I pause, thinking about everything all at once and what a mess it is trying to find the thread of logic I need. Maybe that's why I'm calling Dr. Brock. For *his* logic. I trust him but have no idea how deeply that trust can be tested.

Still.

He's the closest thing to a father I've had since the age of eleven, and at some point, a person just has to let go and believe.

So, then...I choose to let go.

I start talking, telling Dr. Brock everything.

Everything. Even about Bain.

Funny thing.

It takes less than ten minutes.

When I'm done, I don't feel relief. The knot in my stomach has grown to a noose, and all I want is for Dr. Brock to say something. Anything. But he's silent for nearly a full minute.

I begin to cry, not so much from fear but from sheer mental exhaustion, my body needing some kind of outlet. If not tears, then surely it would be vomit.

When he finally speaks, he doesn't tell me things will be okay. And he doesn't tell me to go to the police.

"This is a lot to absorb," he says. "I'm trying my best to understand everything you just told me, but I'm struggling."

"What would *you* do?"

"Jesus, Penny. This is a tough situation for empathy. What would *I* do? I don't think I have the foggiest idea."

In my telling of the events, I broke down my reasoning for calling the police after the club shooting but not waiting for them to arrive. There's no point rehashing that. But the simple fact remains I killed a cop and have no way of proving it was self-defense other than my word.

"Everything you told me, it's exactly how it happened? You didn't leave anything out?"

My shoulders slump. "As if I could forget."

I can almost hear him thinking. "Listen to me," he says. "What I would do is irrelevant because you and I are very different. You have talents I don't have. Have you thought about how those talents could serve you now?"

Another tear spills down my cheek. "That's the thing," I tell him. "My fucking *talents* mean nothing out here. Away from home. Away from the institute."

"I'm sure that's not true."

"As far as I can tell, it is. I'm nothing more than a wild animal, just trying to get through the day without getting eaten by something bigger and hungrier."

"You could come home," he says.

"You know I can't."

"You have no car. Not much cash. And you're stranded at some motel, the location of which you won't even share with me."

"I won't be here much longer."

I keep staring at one particular crack in the wall, picturing it opening wider and wider until it's large enough for me to crawl through. Maybe there's a different reality on the other side, and how sublime that would be.

"I need to make a phone call or two about this," he says.

"What? No. You can't tell anyone what I just told you."

"Penny, I'll be discreet, I promise. You are…a known entity. People will listen."

"What does that mean?"

"It means, for the time we've been together, you've piqued the interest of others. Others who might be able to help you more than I can."

"No one else can know."

His voice takes on an edge. "I don't need to share the exact details with them, but I don't have any other ideas. Will you allow me to do this?"

Here I am, failing all the lessons I learned from Nancy Drew. I told Marion Shepard my location and Dr. Brock all the details of the past two days. Truth is, now I just need help.

"Okay," I say.

"Just lie low for a day or so, then call me back. I'll hopefully have some information then."

Lie low, I think. *What does that even mean?*

"Fine." I hang up, keep looking at that crack in the wall, losing myself deeper in it, wondering if I've just made a terrible mistake. What if Dr. Brock betrays me and calls the police? If our situations were reversed, isn't that what I would do?

I don't know.

I just don't know.

"Fuck," I say to that crack in the wall.

It doesn't reply.

SIXTY

I WALK ACROSS THE motel parking lot to the diner, its exterior consisting of dirty windows and checkerboard tiles, as if trying very hard to be era authentic but instead coming across like a cheap replica. The sign—in that 1950s swoopy script—reads OUT TO LUNCH.

After opening the glass door, I'm greeted by a smell that threatens to make me swoon.

Bacon. Corn bread. Grease. Fries. Burgers.

Minutes ago the idea of food didn't even cross my mind, but now I don't think I can even wait long enough to place an order. Having a burger in this place is almost worth the risk of the Snakeskin Boys walking in shooting while I'm eating.

"Sit wherever you want," a voice calls out. "Shouldn't have any trouble finding a spot."

I look over and see the woman attached to the voice. She's crouched in front of an old jukebox, its front frame open and wires spilling out on the floor like intestines. "You know how much I spent on this thing?" the woman says. "And even when it works, I make maybe three bucks a week in dimes. And now it *doesn't* work, so it's just something that'll sit here and take up space until I can afford to fix it. Some advice? Don't go into the restaurant business."

"I wasn't planning on it," I say.

This must be Fia.

I look around. Not a single other customer. No sounds of sizzling bacon or flipping burgers. Did I actually smell food cooking, or was I so hungry, I simply imagined it?

I turn and look back out the windows, into the night.

All is quiet.

I walk over to the long counter at the back of the diner. I pull out a heavy chrome stool topped with cherry-red vinyl padding, which wheezes as I sit. The counter is cool, white linoleum well stained by time and grease.

The woman remains wrist deep in jukebox guts.

"Is it always this dead?" I ask.

"This close to closing time, yeah."

"I need to eat something."

She pokes her head out. "Well, that *is* why most people come here."

I get my first good look at her. Her accent—while minor—is obvious. She's slight of build with full ink-black hair that cascades to her midback. Her caramel face holds small eyes, a button nose, and not a single wrinkle I can see from this distance.

"You're not Mexican," I say.

The woman stands and faces me from across the room. "That's a hell of a thing to say."

"The hotel manager implied you were Mexican. But you're from Nicaragua."

"And why would you think that?"

I point at the flag on the wall behind her. "That's the Nicaraguan flag."

"You've been there?"

"No. I haven't really been anywhere."

"You just happen to know the flag?"

"I know the flag of every country in the world."

The woman smiles, her teeth movie-star quality. "Is that so?"

"Yes."

"Quite a party trick."

I think about that. "I really wouldn't know."

The woman leaves the machine in its dying state, walks over, and slips behind the counter, then grabs an apron. "So you said you need to eat."

"Yes."

She ties it on, slides me a menu. "If you keep it to breakfast items, I only have to turn on one part of the grill. But you're the customer."

Doesn't take long to scan the menu and decide. "I'll have the Fonzi, eggs over easy, bacon, white toast, and an extra side of hash browns."

"You got it. To drink?"

"You have any vodka?" The words just come out of my mouth. I've never had vodka in my life. But this would be the day to start.

"No liquor license, honey."

Probably for the best. "Strawberry milkshake?"

"You got it."

She turns and gets to work.

This woman is the reason I'm even in Willmar. There were a lot of lakes I could have driven Travis's car into, but I chose one in Willmar because I wanted to warn this very person.

I decide to wait until I've eaten.

My stomach growls as bacon hisses against the surface of the grill, and to distract myself, I study Fia. Think about what she might look like if I drew her. I can't know what the dots have in store for a portrait of Fia, but I can at least guess.

I think the dots would render Fia's hair even fuller than it is tonight, and a bit longer. It would flow, a thick black mane, and I decide Fia is outdoors in this mental image, a light wind against her face.

The shading would be more intricate than usual, and perhaps that's because Fia has a darker skin tone than most of my other subjects.

And then there are her eyes.

They aren't looking forward in my mental drawing. They're looking just a touch to her right, gazing at something beyond her. Her eyes are bold, wide, and dark, rife with emotion, and that emotion is fear. I have no basis to justify this conclusion, but I think fear and Fia are well acquainted.

The drawing would show Fia's eyebrows raised in alarm, her lips parted at the beginning of a warning, her jaw tight and tense. It's as if Fia's looking at an oncoming tsunami wave and caught in the process of both screaming a warning and running for her life.

Fia drops off the milkshake on the counter in front of me. "Food will be right up," she says.

I sip the milkshake and decide it's the greatest thing I've ever tasted.

Less than a minute later, she returns with plates in each hand.

"Breakfast of champions. At ten o'clock at night."

I don't hesitate.

The egg bleeds its yolk all over the toast with my first cut, which is dizzying in its beauty. The first bite is perfect, and somehow the second is impossibly better. At the first taste of bacon, I see a heaven I never believed existed.

In less than five minutes, my plate is empty. For a moment, just a brief moment, I have an overwhelming sense that everything will be all right. That this will all work out, somehow, some way.

But the high of bacon, like drugs, always wears off. I'm still left wondering, *Now what the hell do I do?*

I look up.

Fia's watching me as she wipes down the countertop. "Someone was hungry."

"Yeah." I let out a little burp. "I was."

"Get you anything else? I'm closing up here in about five minutes."

There's still half a milkshake left. I don't think I can have any more. Then I do. "You're Fia, right?"

Her hand freezes in midwipe. "Who's asking?"

"I'm Nellie."

"I don't know who you are."

"But you *are* Fia, right?"

Now her hands go to her hips, and while she tries her best to look fierce, I see the fear on her face that I saw in my mental drawing of her. I'm the tsunami.

"You want to tell me what the hell you want?" she says.

I tell her the truth because it's easiest. "I'm trying to save your life."

SIXTY-ONE

FIA'S VOICE IS CALM but firm. "I get crazies in here all the time. You don't fit the mold, not exactly, but I'm guessing you're on the crazy spectrum."

"I'm not crazy. I'm unique."

"Whatever. I don't know what you want or how you know who I am, but my life doesn't need saving."

This isn't going the way I expected. But what was I expecting?

"It does need saving," I say. "And I'm just here to warn you. Nothing more than that."

Her gaze shifts past me and to the front doors, as if she's expecting the grim reaper to walk in. Maybe he will.

She shifts her attention back to me. "Warn me about what?"

And I tell her. Not in huge detail because I want to limit how much she knows about me. But I make it very clear that I overheard a conversation in which two men with Hispanic accents and snakeskin boots talked about executing a diner owner in Willmar. A diner with the same name as the one I'm sitting in.

The color drains from her face as I talk, and when I'm done, she sums up her feelings succinctly. "Fuck me."

"So you are Fia."

"Yes, yes. Of course I'm fucking Fia. *Dios.* I knew it was them."

"Who?"

She doesn't answer at first. Instead, Fia walks away, back around the counter, reaches down, emerges with a shotgun. Rather than aim it, she rests it on the countertop, barrel pointing at my chest. Her finger isn't on the trigger, but it's within flirting distance.

"A few days ago, two men came in here," she says. "*Latinos.* I don't get many of those, at least not ones dressed nice. Snakeskin boots. They ordered coffee, black, nothing else. Then they left without saying anything, but I got a feeling about them. Are you with them?"

"What? No."

"I've had eyes in the back of my head since then. And now you show up, just happening to have overheard a conversation. I'm supposed to think you tracked me down based on that?"

I feel the same strange and unlikely calm in the face of possible violence that I experienced in the car with Bain.

"A lot of things have happened to me in the past two days," I tell her. "Finding you is the least crazy of them."

"I don't believe you."

"I'm just trying to help." I eye the shotgun, and as I do, a thought hits me. "This sounds weird, I know, but statistically I'm likely the smartest person you've ever met or will meet. I don't know how, but maybe I can help you. And then maybe you can help me."

"Oh, so now there's a price to your generosity? Well, I'm not buying. I don't know anything about you, and I'm not looking to start." Fia inches her fingers up the stock of the shotgun. "Diner's closed. Forget the tab. Just get the fuck out."

"I'm trying to tell you these guys are coming to kill you. It's a miracle they haven't already."

"*Leave.*"

I stand, take a breath, walk back a few steps. She is laser focused on me.

"Listen," I say. "I'm staying here. At the motel. And I'll be here all day tomorrow. Room ten. I believe I just saved your life, and I need help. I think you owe me. So come get me in case you change your mind."

I turn and pass through the diner doors, with a tickling anticipation of being shot in the back.

But I make it outside safely.

Yet there is no safety. Not really.

Even all that diner food can't weigh down the well of anxiety in my gut.

SIXTY-TWO

I'M PRAYING FOR SLEEP to come, but it's been hours of crushing wakefulness. Between the massive meal and the fact I slept all day, I've been wide awake since coming back to the room after the diner. There's been a horrible loneliness to these hours, which I've spent in the dark with nothing but my thoughts. But I haven't let myself break.

I *will not* break, no matter what.

I've done a horrible thing but only because I had to.

I need to remind myself:

I'm a good person.

I'm a good person.

I'm a good person.

I repeat these words, over and over, under the hot and scratchy sheets.

I finally drift off, and this time there are no dreams of being on *Letterman.*

Instead, my mind decides to offer yet another vision of death.

In this one, I meet my end choking on hot sand.

SIXTY-THREE

July 17, 1987
Friday

I WAKE MIDMORNING, AND when I rise, there's no sense of feeling refreshed. The unsettling pit in my stomach remains. I'll need food again at some point, though the idea of eating holds no lure.

My skin itches from all the dried lake water and nightmare sweat.

Worst of all are the memories. Those can't be sated with food or washed away by a hot shower. They are forever things, parasites attached to my brain, feasting on their host until all parties involved eventually die.

I try my best to think of other things, but it's like trying to do math while being eaten by a shark.

I start the water of the motel shower, which sputters at first, choking out liquid the color of weak coffee. After a few seconds, the stream becomes steady, mostly translucent, and warm.

I strip, disgusted from days of grime. Stepping into the shower, I let the water pour over me, and I adjust the temperature to the hottest setting I can stand, as if I can scald away the past.

Cheap soap and watery shampoo. They both feel good.

Afterward I brush my teeth and dig a fresh change of clothes from my bag. Then I turn on the TV before flipping through the channels, looking for any news about either the comedy club shooting or a missing cop. I find neither, just soap operas and talk shows, all full of people yelling at each other.

Next stop is the motel office.

Eileen looks up briefly when I come in but soon returns to her paperwork.

"Checkout was an hour ago," she says. "Or did your Spidey senses tell you I'd be okay with you ignoring that?"

I ease up to the small counter. "I need another night."

"Well, then, good for you we're not sold out. You know, I could do a weekly rate if you're planning on being here longer."

I fish my wallet out and pay for another night. "No. I'm definitely leaving tomorrow."

Eileen shrugs, takes the bills, gives me change.

"Have there been any calls for me?" I ask.

When she looks at me, I'm convinced I'm right about her. There's a subtle rot to the woman.

"Nope."

Then I realize my mistake. If Travis called, he wouldn't have been looking for Nellie Drew.

"How about Penny?"

"What?"

"Did anyone call looking for someone named Penny?"

Eileen smirks, and it's the closest to joy I've seen her wear. "What a surprise, you registered under a fake name."

"Did they, or didn't they?"

"No, dear. No one called looking for a Penny, a Nellie, or a partridge in a pear tree. We don't get many calls here. Fact is, most of our guests don't want to be found. I assumed that was your case, but maybe not."

"I'm not hiding."

The smirk morphs into an ugly smile. "And I'm Lady Di."

I turn and leave, angry at being just another one of the motel's parade of forgotten. Worse, it's stupid that I even care. But part of me wants to grab Eileen by the shoulders and tell the woman my story. Convince her I'm not just another down-on-their-luck con looking for an anonymous hole-in-the-wall to hide out for a few days.

I'm okay telling Eileen my real first name; since I've already told Fia, my anonymity in this location is already blown. I've allowed myself the assumption that Bain's body is yet to be discovered, and if I leave first thing tomorrow morning, I can put some distance between myself and anyone coming and asking about me.

Tomorrow morning.

Bright and early.

I'll call a cab to take me to a bus station.

I think about money. It's becoming an issue.

Damn it, Travis, not only did you run from me, but you took Leo's money with you.

There's a gas station a bit farther down the road, its signage reading KUM & GO. I know the chain; there'll be cheap snack food to buy there.

I walk over, soaking in the sunshine and summer air after so many hours in the motel room. My long wet hair slowly dries against my back and shoulders. The sporadic hum of cars on the nearby interstate sounds like giant insects sweeping through the area.

I don't waste time in the Kum & Go, keeping my gaze on the ground as much as I can. Doritos, Cheetos, a few bottles of Coke, a jar of Planters peanuts, and, as a treat, a package of Little Debbie's.

The cashier rings me up, and fortunately his interest in me seems to be as much as mine in him. Only seven words are exchanged between us.

Back to the room, where the smell of sadness and eternal days greets me. It's like the room has some kind of energy field where all the despair and desperation of previous guests have soaked into the cracked walls and stained carpet, waiting to overpower the next Star*Lite customer.

I sit on the bed and, despite not being hungry, pick at the Cheetos while polishing off one of the Cokes. It provides the predictable experience of tasting amazing and making me feel like shit.

I'm only here in the hope Travis shows up, which he likely won't. In the meantime, I have no idea what I'm going to do all day.

Fidget, most likely.

Worry.

Pace.

Try to will time to reverse course.

For the sake of distraction, I watch TV, which serves to pass a couple of hours while making me feel as bad as the Cheetos. Talk shows stuffed with angry, shouting people, on nearly every channel. I ponder the attraction of these shows, then decide everyone wants an opportunity to watch someone worse off than themselves.

I make it through a full episode of *Donahue* before deciding none of those miserable guests would change places with me.

I'm about to take a walk when the phone rings, nearly causing me to jump.

"Hello?"

"This is the front office." Eileen.

"Yes?"

"There's a man here asking for a Penny Bly. Figured that was you but didn't want to presume."

My chest tightens. "What does he look like?"

A pause. I picture Eileen giving the person the once-over she gave me a dozen times.

"Skinny and hungry, like a stray dog."

Travis.

"Be right there," I say, then hang up.

Not even those depressing talk shows can dampen my suddenly uplifted spirits.

SIXTY-FOUR

TRAVIS LOOKS EVEN WORSE than me.

He's wearing the same clothes from the night of the shooting, and when I hug him, it's clear he's in dire need of a shower.

"Jesus, Penny," he says. "I'm sorry. I'm so sorry."

As I release his hug, I catch Eileen eyeballing us.

"Come with me," I say and lead him to the parking lot. It's midafternoon, and despite the intensity of the sun, the heat is invigorating.

I turn and face Travis. He really does look like a stray dog.

"You just left me," I tell him. "You left, and I was in that club all alone."

Travis reaches out and touches my arm.

I pull away.

"I know," he says. "I don't know what I was thinking. I mean…I was high and…not even sure if what was happening was even real. You left the table, and I thought you were leaving. So I freaked out, I guess, then ran out a back door."

"I thought you'd go to the car."

"I was scared. That coke…I don't know. It really fucked with my head. I just started running and running."

Now Travis grabs both my shoulders, and when I weakly try to squirm away, he doesn't let me. "Penny, I'm so sorry. I really am. I feel like I'm a coward, but really, I didn't know what to do. I've never been so scared in my life. Do you even know what happened?"

"Snakeskin Boys shot Arthur and Leo."

"Snakeskin Boys?"

"Yeah," I say. "The guys who hid during our meeting. I don't suppose you overheard their conversation right after we met with Arthur, did you? When we were in the office next door?"

"No. I don't think so. Leo was talking to me then. Wait, are…is Leo okay?"

"Dead," I say, probably too matter-of-factly.

"Jesus Christ." He massages his temples. "How do you know all this?"

"It was on the news. What happened to you? Where did you go?"

"Not so long a story, but I need to eat. Can we just sit somewhere and eat and talk? If I don't get food, I'm gonna pass out."

I nod to my left, to the Out to Lunch Diner.

"I know the owner there. We're not on the best of terms, and I should probably leave her alone. But she's an amazing cook."

Travis follows my gaze and takes in the sight of Fia's restaurant. "Fuck yeah," he says.

SIXTY-FIVE

FIA'S WORKING ALONE INSIDE the diner. I'm starting to think Fia and Eileen are some kind of Star Trek androids who can work twenty-four hours a day.

There are four other customers, none of them wearing snakeskin. We grab a booth in the back near the jukebox, which is silent for the moment.

Fia walks over with two menus and drops them on the laminated table.

"You're still here?" she says to me.

"Apparently. And so are you. I thought you might have left town after what I told you."

"Thought about it," she says. "Not such an easy thing to do. Also still unsure whether or not you're full of shit."

"I'm not. Why would I be?"

"I have no idea," Fia says. "But I'm keeping eyes in the back of my head and my shotgun close."

"What is happening here?" Travis asks.

Fia pivots to face him. "Your girl came in here and started ranting about boogeymen."

"That's not what I—"

"She's not my girl," Travis says, "and I need food. Sorry, can I just order something? I feel like my brain can't even function."

"Fine," Fia says.

As Travis scans the menu, Fia and I lock gazes. There's such defiance in her face, but also traces of the fear I saw before. Why hasn't she run away?

Travis makes a decision. "I'll have the Matlock burger. Bacon. Cheese. The works. Two orders of fries. And…" He flips the menu over. "Holy shit. Chocolate shake. The largest size you have."

Fia doesn't write anything down.

"And what about you?" she asks me.

I'm still full from the convenience store garbage, but I figure this might be my last chance to eat for the day.

"Club sandwich," I say. "How come that doesn't have a TV character name?"

Fia grabs the menus off the table. "I guess I ran out of ideas." Then she turns and walks away.

"What's going on with the two of you?" Travis asks.

"I'll tell you later. First, tell me what happened to you."

He presses himself back against the booth. "It's all kinda fuzzy. I think my brain overloaded or something. Like…I remember most of what happened in the club, but the shooting… It's like hearing those shots short-circuited my brain. Tell you what, I'm never doing coke again."

"Good plan."

"Leo's dead, for real?"

"I think so. It's been on the news."

Travis leans over the table. "The news?"

"Yes, the news. What do you expect? It was a shooting at a comedy club."

"Did they say anything about us?"

"Not that I know of," I say. "Where did you go?"

Travis looks over to the grill, nearly salivating. "I was out of my mind. I remember running out of the club and looking back, seeing you weren't behind me. I thought about circling around and getting my car but decided I couldn't drive away. That would be abandoning you."

"You did abandon me."

"I didn't... I mean...I wasn't trying to. That's why I left the car. Plus, I wasn't exactly in a condition to drive. So I ran. Just kept running. Thought my heart was gonna explode, but it didn't stop me. At some point, like a half hour later, I came to my senses a little. As scared as I was, I doubled back to the club. There were cop cars there, a fire truck, ambulance. All lights flashing. And my car was gone. I hoped you had taken it, but I had no idea."

"But you knew I didn't know how to drive."

Travis looks down. "I also knew you were smart as shit, could probably figure it out."

"Good thing you were right about that."

When he lifts his head, I think I see a trace of tears in his eyes. "Where did *you* go?"

"We're talking about you right now," I tell him. "What happened next?"

He holds up a hand. "I'm so fuckin' tired," he says. "Let me eat a bit first."

"Fine." We wait in silence. When Fia comes over with plates in her hands a few minutes later, I see on Travis's face how I must have looked when coming into this diner and watching the food arrive. Like a jackal, frenzied from the kill.

I nibble on my food while Travis tears into his. He finishes his burger and one plate of fries before I eat half my club sandwich. When he slows down, he starts dipping fries from his second plate one at a time into his milkshake.

"That's disgusting."

He continues with closed eyes. "This is the single greatest meal I've had in my life."

When he finishes, he pushes the plate away, leans back, grabs his belly. "I'm gonna puke."

"Hold it in." I push my own plate away. "Where did you go after you saw I'd taken your car?"

Travis sits up and continues. He tells me how he found a YMCA in downtown Minneapolis. With nothing but his wallet and the clothes he was wearing, he booked a room for fifteen dollars a night. He ended up staying two nights.

"I didn't know what else to do," he says. "I was worried about you. Didn't know where my car was. Didn't want to go home." He wags a finger at me. "And then, after forever, I remembered our conversation about calling my mom if we got separated. Can you believe that? I don't know why it took me so long to remember that."

"So you called her," I say.

"I did. And let me tell you, she was freaking out after you told her I was missing."

"I didn't say that."

"When I heard you had called, I was so happy. So fucking happy."

And how that hits my heart, right in the middle.

Travis wipes a solitary tear from his eye. "I hitched a ride here as soon as I could. A trucker. Pretty much left me alone the whole ride." He smiles, and there's such vulnerability in it. "I'm so happy to see you. I barely know you, but I feel like we've been to war together or something."

"Something."

He nods. "And I don't have a clue what to do or where to go next. But we're back together at least. And we have my car, so that gives us some options."

I lower my gaze to the table. "About your car…"

"What about it?"

I catch movement in my peripheral vision, look over, and spot Fia looking out the front windows of the diner. Looking intently, as if waiting for danger to arrive. Waiting for the worst.

I wonder if that's how I'll spend the rest of my life.

Anticipating doom.

Or maybe hoping for it.

Just to get it all over with.

SIXTY-SIX

HI, DAD.

Hiya, Pen Pen.

I did what you said to do. With the cop.

I know.

It was awful.

I know.

I wasn't going to, but then he attacked me.

You had to, darlin'. I know that doesn't make it any easier, but you had to.

I stare at Travis's empty plate as I talk to my dad. Travis probably figures I'm just zoning out.

How do I live the rest of my life with it? With those images?

Not exactly sure. I suppose it has something to do with knowing you still have a life to live.

I guess so.

Uh-huh.

But Travis—the boy I've been telling you about—he wants to know what happened to his car, and I don't think I'm ready to tell him the truth. Maybe I won't ever be.

Dad goes silent for a bit.

Then he says, *I guess you lie.*

I exhale, feeling my shoulders slump.

I won't ever be the same person again, I tell him.

No, sweetie, no, you won't. And you know what?

What?

Neither will I.

Then I close my eyes, ending the conversation.

I have no idea what he meant by that.

And that's okay.

SIXTY-SEVEN

I TELL TRAVIS THE car was stolen from the motel parking lot. That I left the keys inside and it was gone when I woke in the morning. He expresses understandable surprise that anyone would be interested in that shit car but doesn't question my story.

I feel bad about lying to him, but the truth would've been way worse.

So I shift the conversation to tell him something truthful, specifically what happened after he left the comedy club. That I didn't want to leave the car there in case the whole area became a crime scene, so I taught myself a jolting lesson on how to drive.

"I can't believe you didn't get pulled over by a cop," he says.

I try not to blink. "Yeah, I was lucky."

"My parents are going to fucking kill me," he says. "They bought me that car."

"They're not your biggest problem right now. If the police find out we were at that club, they'll want to question us. I'm worried if our names are connected to what happened there, the Snakeskin Boys will come looking for us as well."

I haven't yet disclosed that the Snakeskin Boys could be on their way to this very diner to pay a visit to Fia.

"I know."

I reveal a bit more information. "There's a man. He was my therapist for the past ten years. A mentor, really. He's trying to find a way to help me. Help *us*." My conversation with Dr. Brock seems a thousand years ago. "I'm supposed to call him tomorrow morning to see if he was able to figure anything out."

"How much did you tell him?"

"Everything," I say. "It's okay. We can trust him."

"I don't even know him."

I search his sad, desperate eyes. "And I hardly know you. But this is where we are. We need help."

Travis looks like he's about to say something else, nods instead. "So much for your big journey to find your father."

"I'm not giving that up."

"You're still headed west?"

"If I give up looking for him, everything that's happened in the past few days will have been in vain."

"In vain?" Travis lowers his voice, though no one is nearby. "What happened at the club was going to happen with or without us. We were just bystanders. There's no shame in giving up your quest. At least postponing it."

Of course, Travis doesn't know about Bain. The idea of giving up after what happened in that car is unacceptable. "No. I'll keep going."

He shifts in his seat. "Without my car, I can't even be your transportation anymore. I don't even know what I have to offer."

He seems no more than ten years old in this moment.

"Do you want to keep going with me?"

"Yes," he says.

"Good. Because I'd like you to come."

He cracks a shy smile, and it's just right. "I'd like that."

"And you're the one with all the money. If there's anything good about what happened, it's that you don't have to pay Leo back now."

"That's cold," he says.

"Doesn't make it any less true."

Outside the diner, Travis turns to me.

"So, now what?"

"Now we lie low in the room until tomorrow morning. I'll call my therapist and see if he has any solutions. If not, we figure out how to keep moving."

Travis pulls his wallet from his back pocket and counts the bills. "I can get my own room. I'm guessing it's not expensive."

"Depends on if you want Skinemax or not," I say.

"Huh?"

"Doesn't matter. Just stay in my room. Might as well save the money."

"You sure?"

"I'm sure."

I say this not with excitement but with logic mixed with trepidation. And, okay, a little excitement. I don't want to be alone. After what happened with Bain, it could be a long time until I feel safe again. If ever.

In the room we talk a little more but not much. Fatigue creeps over both of us. I look at him as he watches TV, remembering him stoned that night in his bedroom, giggling and laughing and extolling the virtues of David Letterman. I remember his excitement at leaving his house, heading with me into the wild. But most of all, when I look at him, I remember kissing him right before we went inside the club and how he didn't taste like coconut at all.

We're such different people, but now we only have each other. Our collective plans were dismembered only one day into our journey, and together, here, in this sad little motel room, we're both no longer who we once were. Whether that's ultimately a good thing or a bad thing will only be revealed in time.

Travis sleeps on the floor.

SIXTY-EIGHT

July 18, 1987
Saturday

WHEN THE KNOCKING COMES, I open my eyes to daylight streaming through the edges of the curtains. The pumpkin-orange digital readout of the nightstand clock reads 9:33 a.m.

Who the hell is knocking?

And, damn it, I didn't want to sleep in. I wanted to call Dr. Brock first thing.

The call will have to wait, at least until I find out who's at the door.

The knocking stops for a few seconds, then starts again, the sound digging into me.

I make my way on soft feet to the door. Travis is sprawled on the floor, dead asleep, a bedsheet wrapped around him so tight, it looks like he's being eaten by a snake.

It must be housekeeping, though I put the DO NOT DISTURB sign up last night. But what if it isn't? What if it's the cops? Or worse, the Snakeskin Boys?

I hold my breath as I peer into the peephole. There I see the partially illuminated figure of Fia, her face and head distorted by the fish-eye lens.

"Yes?" I say through the door.

"It's Fia."

"I see that."

"Can you open the door?"

"What do you want?"

"*Please*, I need to come in. *Rápido*."

But I hesitate. "You told me to get the fuck out of your diner the other night. Shotgun and all."

"And then you came back into my place the next day and ordered a club sandwich. Look, you said you needed help. Maybe I can help you after all, but I'm walking away in three seconds if you don't open the door."

I peer out again. She's looking left and right, over and over.

I open the door.

Fia rushes inside, shuts the door. Locks it.

And in that moment, I know.

I just know.

The Snakeskin Boys are here.

SIXTY-NINE

FIA LOOKS DOWN AT Travis, who starts to stir.

"Chocolate shake, two orders of fries," she says.

Travis looks up at Fia with half asleep eyes.

"Oh, lady from the diner," he says, then turns to me. "You order room service or something?"

I ignore him and put my attention back on Fia. "Why are you here?"

She takes a few steps toward my bed. "I need to know if I should be afraid of you," she says.

I blink. "Me? What did I do?"

"I need to know you're not with them."

"With who?" Travis asks.

"You think I'm a potential threat, and then you willingly came to my room?" I ask Fia.

Travis stands, his pale and skinny frame clothed only in a pair of green-checkered boxer shorts. "Seriously, what the fuck are you two talking about?"

Fia's expression hardens. "My name is Fia, not *lady*, and I'm not talking to you." Back to me, she says, "My culture is a very superstitious one. I believe in shit that makes no logical sense, but it's worked out for me over the years. I believe in instinct, and my instinct tells me you're a good person. Am I right?"

I consider this. "I suppose. But your instincts obviously didn't tell you to run after I told you to."

"What kind of help do you need?" she asks.

"Well, like you, I need to disappear," I say. "I need to get the hell out of here and disappear for good."

"Wait," Travis says. "That's a bit dramatic. We didn't do anything wrong. Not really. We just need to lie low while we head west."

"No," I say. "We need to disappear. *And* head west."

"What's out west?" Fia asks.

"I'm trying to find my father. I think he's in California, so that's where I need to go."

"You dad's in California, but you don't know where?"

"I have an address."

Fia shakes her head. "Okay, look. I have cash. I have a car. Those are things you need." Then she turns to Travis. "But I don't know who you are. Maybe Milkshake here is all the help you need."

Travis ping-pongs his gaze back and forth between the two of us, exasperation bleeding over his face. "Can the two of you shut the hell up and tell me what's going on? How do you even know each other? And why the fuck does everyone have to disappear?"

I take a step up to him, take him by the elbow, and lead him over by the door. I lower my head and my voice. "Remember I asked you if you overhead the conversation at the club between Arthur and the men he was with?"

Travis nods.

"Well, I heard it," I say. "And I heard them specifically say they were coming here to Willmar to kill the woman who owns the Out to Lunch Diner. Arthur got angry, and I think that's why the shooting started."

Travis pulls back and jabs a thumb in Fia's direction. "Wait, are you talking about her? They're coming to kill her, and we just casually went and ate in her place last night?"

I have no good answer. "You were hungry."

"Jesus. So you, what, drove out here based on some conversation you think you overheard?"

I don't tell him that I walked the last few miles, what with his car being at the bottom of Solomon Lake.

"It was west," I say. "And yes. I felt I had a responsibility." Then I turn to Fia. "And I did warn her, but she didn't want to hear it. But now she's in our room asking if she can trust me."

"I was wrong," she says. "*Dios*, I was wrong." Fia walks toward me until we're less than a foot apart. "You said you're the smartest person I'd ever met. How smart are you?"

"I have talents," I say. "But they haven't been doing me a lot of good lately."

"You said you could help me. I didn't believe it then, and I'm not sure I believe it now. But something happened this morning, and now I suddenly find myself...in need of assistance. So maybe I'll give you a shot. You do what I need, and do it right, then I'll agree to help you out. Take you away from here. But if you fail...well, if you fail, we're probably all fucked."

My heart rate inches up. "They're here, aren't they?"

Fia jabs a thumb to the door. "They're standing outside my diner right now."

SEVENTY

IT'S MY TURN TO peek out the window.

There they are.

Fifty feet away, just outside Fia's diner. Two men lean against a black Oldsmobile, the car's shine matching that of their slicked ink-black hair. One wears his in a ponytail; the other has his long and straight to his shoulders. They're wearing monochromatic clothes, just as they did the other night: Ponytail in a black T-shirt and his partner in a crisp white button-down, each shirt tucked into dark suit pants with black belts.

And the boots.

Matching snakeskin boots.

Ponytail smokes, his focus fixed on the ground. The other man sweeps his gaze back and forth over the parking lot, slow and steady, like a prison spotlight.

"It's a miracle I wasn't in there," Fia says. "The diner was dead, so I stepped out for a walk. I locked up and put a sign on the door saying I'd be back in fifteen. When I came back, I saw them just like they are now, so I backtracked behind the motel and found you."

Travis eases in next to me and stares out the window. "Those are the same guys from the other night?"

"Yes," I say. "Same guys."

I release the curtain and turn around. "Do you know who they are?" I ask Fia.

"No. But I'm pretty sure I know who they work for."

I recall Arthur's words verbatim: *Your boss and I go back. We've been very happy with his product. But I'm not telling you where she is.*

"What did you do?"

Fia doesn't answer the question. I don't blame her. "I think the first time they showed up, they just wanted to make sure it was really me. I should have left at that point, but I didn't take it seriously enough. And then you warned me, and I still didn't leave. How the hell can I be so stupid?"

"Call the cops," Travis says.

Fia turns to him. "To do what? They haven't done anything. The cops show, they'll just tell these guys to leave. But these assholes will be back, I promise you. I don't need these guys to go away. *I* need to go away." Then, to me: "Whatever your talents are, I need you to use them to make these guys disappear."

"I'm not a magician."

"I hope you're wrong about that." Fia shakes out her hands, as if releasing built-up electricity. "Look, there's a safe in my apartment. It only opens by using both a combination and a key. The key is in my purse, along with my wallet and car key. The purse is in my diner, which I can't get to right now. But you can."

"What's in the safe?" Travis asks.

"Money," Fia replies. "A lot of it."

I nod at the window. "*Their* money?"

Fia admits nothing.

"We could just wait," I say. "They'll leave eventually."

"They look like they have a lot of patience."

"Hell, I'll do it," Travis says. "Just go in and grab your purse? That's easy."

"No," Fia said. "Not you. It's going to take more subtlety than just going in and grabbing my purse. The diner is locked, so whoever unlocks it must work there, right? Or at least know the owner. That means they'll ask about where I am, I'm sure of it. And if I had to pick between the two of you to pull this off, I'm going with the genius."

Travis furrows his brows. "How do you know I'm not a genius?"

"If you have to ask that question, Milkshake, then you've already answered it."

Travis and I exchange glances. He looks how I feel: freaked out. I dig deep to summon confidence.

I can do this.

This is followed by a question.

Can I do this?

"Where's the key to the diner?" I ask Fia.

Fia produces it from her front jeans pocket and hands it to me.

"And if I do this," I say, "and do it successfully, then you take us with you?"

Fia takes a deep breath. Lets it out with the weight of life. "You said you overhead a conversation and that's how you knew to warn me. Where were you?"

Travis and I look at each other.

"Might as well be honest," he says.

I nod. "At a comedy club in Minneapolis."

Fia's eyes widen. "Wait. *Arthur's* comedy club?"

"Yes."

"Why were you there?"

"Travis knew Arthur's son. He was lending us some money."

"And the Snakeskin Boys were meeting with Arthur?"

"Yes."

"Fuck me." Fia squeezes the back of her neck. "So they know. They know I'm connected to Arthur. Which means they might know everything about me. Like where my children are."

"What *is* your connection to him?" Travis asks.

Fia starts pacing. Small steps.

"Let's just say he's a friend who's helped me over the years."

"Then you don't know," I say.

"Know what?"

I hesitate, weighing how much to say. But I decide this is a moment to lay the cards out on the table.

"The night we were there, right after I overheard this conversation, there was a shooting. Those guys out there, waiting for you, they shot Arthur and his son, Leo. They're both dead."

"*What?*"

"In the conversation I overhead, those guys told Arthur they were coming for you, and he got pissed off. I think that's what the shooting was about."

More pacing. Bigger steps. "Fuck, fuck, fuck, fuck, fuck."

"I'm sorry for your loss," I say, kinda meaning it. "Were you close?"

Fia doesn't answer. Instead, she says, "This is real. This is totally real. Even seeing them at my diner, it didn't feel real." She stops pacing. "Yes, if you help me out of this, we'll all disappear together."

I take a step closer to her. "So you're just going to walk away? From your diner? From everything here? You can do that?"

"I should have done it months ago," Fia says. "I've had a sense for a long time that something was wrong. But I got lazy. Too used to my routine. I should have done it yesterday, after you warned me. But it still didn't feel real. Kept telling myself things would be fine. But now? Yeah, I'm ready to pull the plug on everything."

"Will you take us to California?"

She nods. "Yes."

I squeeze the key in my hand, wondering exactly how this is going to all go down.

"Look, this is dangerous," Fia says. "I shouldn't be sending you in there. I mean, they want me, not you. But who knows what they'll do?"

"I said I can do this," Travis interjects. "Give me a shot."

I know Travis wants to make up for leaving me behind in the club, but this isn't the way. I don't know why I think I can fix this situation, but the feeling doesn't ebb.

"Like you said," I tell Fia, "they aren't looking for me."

"The purse is in the office in the back," Fia says. "Hanging on the chair. Hopefully, you can just get in and out."

Travis shoots me a hard stare. "Jesus, Penny, don't do this."

I turn to Travis. "It's *okay*. And we need her help, right?"

Travis seems ready to keep arguing but gives in and falls silent.

"One other thing, Penny," Fia says. "In the kitchen, next to the grill, there's a photo taped to the tile. If you can, please take it with you. Please."

"Yes."

"Thank you."

"I haven't done anything yet."

"Just…thank you."

"You're welcome."

I turn, steady myself, then open the motel room door.

Morning sunlight washes over me, making me feel dangerously exposed.

After I close the door, I imagine myself as one of the yellow metal ducks at a county fair shooting gallery, moving slowly and steadily while people with BB guns try to blast me out of existence, hoping for a prize.

SEVENTY-ONE

ON THE BRIEF WALK to the diner, I try to figure out what the hell I'm going to do. If I just rush in and out of the place in silence, that'll seem suspicious and could trigger the men. Like Fia said, this is going to require subtlety. I need to be someone I'm not: outgoing and warm.

I walk up to and then whisk past the Snakeskin Boys, my gaze straight ahead, posture erect.

I catch a scent, heady cologne.

After unlocking the diner's door, I turn to them and say, "Back open again. Sorry for the wait. Assuming you fellas are looking for some breakfast?"

I've never used the term *fellas* in my life.

Ponytail turns to the other and nods, and they both follow me into the diner.

Inside, the smell of grease pulls at me.

"The owner," Ponytail says, his words spoken with an accent. "Is she here?"

"Who, Fia?"

"Yes. Fia."

"Y'all friends or something?" Now, apparently, I'm Southern.

"Something like that."

I'm not really sure how to answer this, but assuming I can get out of here in the next couple of minutes, it doesn't really matter.

"She's on her way," I say. "Had to run an errand."

Ponytail leans over to his partner and mumbles. The partner then leaves the diner. I watch as he slides into the front seat of their Oldsmobile and stares out through the windshield.

"He's not hungry," Ponytail says. "Just me."

"Well, all right."

I spy the office where Fia said the purse is but don't move for it yet. This man's energy…it feels unforgiving. He doesn't trust me because he doesn't trust anyone. And with him in here and his partner in the car, the last thing I want to do is create suspicion.

I go to the host station, grab a menu, hand it to him. "Sit wherever you want."

He does, and to my dismay, does so at the grill's counter, directly in front of the photo I'm supposed to take with me.

"Eggs, bacon, toast. That's all I want. Some coffee, also. *Please.*"

"Okay, hon." I think of the waitress Flo from *Alice* and do my best to channel her. "How you want them eggs?"

"I want them cooked."

"'Kay, then."

Just get the food cooking, I tell myself. *One step at a time.*

I head inside the kitchen area, between the counter where the man sits and the grill where I'm supposed to know what I'm doing.

Lots of big equipment, but maybe it's nothing more than a large-scale version of what I cooked on at home. Still, it's like looking at the cockpit controls of a 747 and being asked to fly it.

Coffee. At least that's easy.

I beeline over to the coffee station, two pots half-full. Grab one and pour it into the mug next to Ponytail, feeling him watching me as I do. That same feeling as when Bain nestled next to me in his tighty-whities.

"That's decaf."

I look up. "What?"

"You're pouring me decaf. The orange around the top of the pot means it's decaf. American coffee is a crime against humanity. American decaf is a crime against God."

"You want regular?"

"I want regular."

I had no idea about the orange/decaf relationship. I take the other pot, pour some in a fresh cup, hand it to him.

"So you're not from here," I say.

He smiles. I don't like it. "No."

"Where you from?"

He takes a sip and doesn't grimace. "Nicaragua. It's a...a small country."

"Central America," I say. "In between Honduras and Costa Rica."

"That's right." He glances behind me, surely seeing Fia's Nicaraguan flag on the wall. "I see she's educated you on our mutual home."

"Fia? I don't know her too well. Just started here last week."

"But she's told you about Nicaragua."

"No. I knew about your country on my own. I know lots of things."

Ponytail shifts in his seat, and I wonder if he's armed. If he has a gun or knife, it would have to be on his ankle. Either would have been obvious anywhere else.

"Know things?" he says. "That hasn't been my experience with most Americans. Tell me what you know."

And, for better or worse, I do.

SEVENTY-TWO

"THE CAPITAL OF NICARAGUA is Managua," I start. "Colonized by the Spanish in 1524. Independent in 1821 and then occupied by us ignorant Americans in the early twentieth century. A smatter of military dictatorships after that, then, in the sixties, full-scale revolution. Still going on. Ortega is the current president and the leader of the Sandinistas, but many countries—including our own—see it as a sham election."

Images appear. An encyclopedia page here, a newspaper article there. I'm doing little more than reading the words flashing in the front of my mind.

"Your national flower is the sacuanjoche," I add. "Their heavy fragrance at night lures sphinx moths, which pollinate them. Your national animal—"

He interrupts by holding up his hand. "Enough, please."

I go quiet, cutting short my recital about the turquoise-browed motmot.

"What is your name?"

"Nellie."

"Nellie. I'm Sebastian." He doesn't offer a hand to shake.

Nor do I.

"You know a lot about my country. More than me. Who knew there was a national flower?"

"Most countries have them."

Sebastian rests his elbows on the countertop and folds his hands together. When he looks at me, I swear his brown eyes turn black. Not even black, but a pure absence of light. "You were saying about Ortega? That his election was... What did you call it? A sham?"

"Yes. That's the word I used."

"And where are you getting that information from?"

"The *New York Times*. July twentieth, 1984, a Friday. Article by Steven Weisman."

He exhales a low whistle. "This is how your brain works?"

"This is how my brain works."

"So you recall everything but know nothing."

"Excuse me?"

Now he rests both his hands flat on the countertop, straightens his spine. "What do you *think* about the election? What do you *know* about the election? Have you lived on the streets of Nicaragua, on the streets of Managua? My *city*. The city where ten thousand people died in the earthquake of 1972, including my father. And the president's own national guard embezzled all the aid money sent from other countries. Have you lived through that, Nellie? And this sham election, were you there to count the votes? Did you see the hope on the people's faces for removing a corrupt government and putting in one that promotes literacy and health care for everyone? Were you there for all that?"

"No."

He steadies his gaze at me, and it's like sinking into quicksand. "This is what I think. I think you are smart but not wise. And there is a vast difference between the two."

I say nothing.

"I have no doubt you could tell me Nicaragua's national anthem, word for word. But you don't know orange means decaf. You don't know to put on an apron or hairnet to start cooking, and I'm guessing any meal you make for me would be terrible. You seemed to have lost your awful Southern accent in midsentence. But most of all, you don't know how to lie, *Nellie*. You think you do, but you don't. The wisest of all know how to lie."

I admit the truth. "I have no idea what Nicaragua's national anthem is."

Sebastian straightens on his stool and smooths a shirt that needs no smoothing. "Where is Fia?"

"What do you want with her?"

"That isn't your concern. And I promise you don't want anything about me to be of your concern."

I take a step back, wondering where the knives are. "Your English is good," I tell him.

"Where is the owner of this diner? And don't tell me you don't know."

"I don't know."

He studies me long enough for me to think maybe I passed the test. "What did I just tell you?" he finally says.

"I can try paging her."

"She has a pager?"

I hold eye contact, feeling it's important to do so, but how I struggle. "Doesn't go anywhere without it."

Sebastian takes a long, slow sip of his coffee. "When she calls back," he says, "you tell her there's a small emergency and you need her help. Nothing more."

"Okay."

"Fine, then. Page her."

"The phone is in the office."

He flicks a dismissive hand. "So go. But you come back out here while we wait for her to call back."

"Okay."

I turn and walk to the office. Walk, not run, because predators are triggered by sprinting prey. At any moment I'm expecting him to grab me from behind, but he doesn't.

Inside the small office, I grab Fia's purse.

Then I lift the receiver of the teal phone sitting on the desk.

The call lasts less than a minute.

SEVENTY-THREE

WHEN I RETURN TO the counter, Sebastian is looking at his nails. Doesn't even glance over when he speaks. "So you paged her?"

I reach up and casually pluck the photo Fia asked for off the wall. The picture shows two boys, maybe early teens, shirtless and smiling on a dirt path. I'm guessing they're her sons.

I slide the photo into Fia's purse. "I didn't page her."

He looks up. "No?"

"I called the police."

His face is still, then breaks into another smile I don't care for. "Is that so?"

"Yes."

Sebastian shrugs. "Who cares? I haven't done anything. No matter the story you told, I'm staying here. They'll come, ask three, maybe four questions, then leave. All you've done is make me angry, which was not a good decision for you. Again, smart but not wise."

"I think you do care. Because you did do something," I say. "Something awful."

"Yes? And what is that?"

"Well, like I told the cops, it was just a normal quiet morning until you came into my diner. You and your friend. I was alone. You both seemed out of sorts. Panicked, even. You ordered food, and I overheard you talking. Talking about something too terrible for an ignorant little Southern girl to understand."

Sebastian's smile is frozen, like he's a wax figurine.

"But, being *just* clever enough, I was able to position myself behind a wall near your booth," I say, "where I could hear your conversation crystal clear. You were talking about a shooting you were involved with."

"Oh, yes? And where was that supposed to be?"

"Roasters Comedy Club in Minneapolis."

His expression doesn't change, but I can see his world shifting. "And what would you know about that?"

"I know what I know."

"You were there?" He squares his shoulders to me. "You were *there*. The teenagers who interrupted our meeting."

"I'm not a teenager."

He's squeezing his fist now, and it's not hard to imagine my neck being next. "We should have checked the rest of the club."

It takes everything I have to keep from sprinting to the front door. The only thing stopping me is knowing I'll never make it. "It's all over the news," I continue. "But the police have no leads, so I was able to help. I made it quite clear that although you two were speaking in English, you had an accent. And, by the looks of you, I guessed Colombian. Maybe connected to that Pablo Escobar's drug cartel or some such."

"I'm not a fucking Colombian."

I keep going. "I also told the cops how I overheard you talking about a car you stole that night. Took the keys from the men you shot. You and your partner split up, and he took the car parked in front of the club. You later met up at this motel, exhausted, on edge, maybe on drugs. Hard to tell, since I don't have any experience with that kind of thing."

Sebastian is now nodding, perhaps with respect, but probably not. "And this other car," he says, "why would we steal it?"

"I haven't the slightest idea. It's just what I overheard you saying."

"And where is this car now? Clearly, I don't have it."

"I have no idea about that either," I say. "Y'all didn't say anything about it." I summon everything I have and lean in close enough for him to grab my throat, should he move fast enough. "But between you and me," I whisper, "what happened to that car is directly tied to another horrible thing your partner did. So horrible that I imagine the police will kill you in custody before you ever make it to the electric chair."

"*Puta barata*," he says, his voice controlled but his eyes wild. "What did you do?"

I flinch because I'm human, and moreover I am who I am, a twenty-one-year-old woman completely out of my element and so scared, I could pee myself. But I keep my show of fear to the singular flinch.

I press on.

"XZ7Y24S. That's your license plate. I gave that to the police, along with a description of both of you, all the way to the mole on the left side of your partner's chin. Now you're right. I don't work here, and any food I cook for you would taste awful. Maybe I know a lot of things, but perhaps I'm not wise. I don't suppose any of that matters right now. What I *do* know is the police are on their way. You know who Fia is, and you want her for some reason. But I'm guessing you're sitting there weighing the odds of how badly you need her today against how desperate you are to get out of here." Now I take a step back, just in case. "I don't know one side of that equation. Only you do. But I know the other side, and even with all my brains, I struggle to calculate how you aren't already back in your car speeding as fast and as far away as you can."

Sebastian stands, looks back to his partner in the car thirty feet away, and gives him a nod that could mean a lot of different things.

"Suppose I do leave," he says. "But also suppose I have enough time to hurt you before I do."

Here it is. The moment I should be blinded by fear, only to feel a calm settle over me. Have I always been this way but never been scared enough to discover this trait?

"That's possible," I say. "But maybe I know how to hurt as well."

"Oh, yes?"

I shrug.

"You *are* an interesting woman. Tell me your real name, Nellie. That's all I want to know."

"To make it easier to hunt me down?"

"I want to see if you match your name. Because you certainly aren't a *Nellie*."

Now I take two steps to the right and spy a tenderizing mallet, heavy and wooden. Not a knife, but not the worst option.

"Keep watching the news," I tell him. "I'm guessing my name will be on it soon."

He considers this for a moment and then gives the faintest bow of his head to me, as if conceding a game of chess.

"Normally, this is when I would shoot you," he says. "But I want to spend more time with you than I have right now. Many, many hours with you. So I will find you, and we will have that time together. Besides, it's true what they say. The chase is always better than the kill."

There's a voice in my head, and it's not mine.

"You're the second person who's said that to me recently."

"Oh? And what happened to the first?"

"Like I said, keep watching the news."

He grins. "My, but you are an intriguing woman." Then he produces a pair of sunglasses and slips them on, cool and casual. Then, with no haste in his steps, he turns and saunters out of the diner.

I follow his every movement as he climbs into the passenger seat of the Oldsmobile, and the two of them drive off, kicking up a cloud of parking lot dirt. I keep following, my gaze on them until the car makes its way to the on-ramp for the interstate.

West.

Everyone is going west.

I exhale with relief, not even having noticed I was holding my breath.

SEVENTY-FOUR

"HE CALLED ME A *puta barata*," I inform Fia.

I'm back in the motel room. Sunlight streams through the half-open doorway.

"Cheap whore," Fia says.

"Why does everyone here think I'm a prostitute?"

Travis stands next to the motel TV; he finally got dressed. "Did you really call the police?"

"I did."

"What the hell did you tell them?"

I start grabbing my few possessions and shoving them in my backpack. "I told them they were talking about comedy club killings. Saying they had done them."

"Genius," Travis says.

"Lucky. I thought I could outwit them with conversation, but that was a mistake. Calling the cops was my only chance." I've been back in the room for less than a minute, but it already feels a minute too long. "We need to go. Now."

"Yes," Fia says. "Did you…happen to get the photo?"

I nod at the purse in Fia's hands. "It's in there."

"Thank you. I need to go to my apartment, so we'll have to be on the lookout for them."

"They went west to the interstate. That's all I know."

"Okay. My place is east of here, but that doesn't mean they didn't turn around."

Travis and I finish getting our things together as sirens blossom in the distance.

"Your place," I say to Fia, "then we leave, right?"

Her face is still for a moment. "Yes."

"And you take us with you, right? I've done what you asked of me."

Fia clutches her purse against her chest as if holding a baby. "Sí. You did. It's just…"

"Just what?"

Her eyes glisten. "I don't even like this place that much. But it's…it's the longest I stayed somewhere since I left Nicaragua."

"Maybe you'll be back."

"Maybe I'll be back."

We head outside. The sirens grow louder.

Fia takes us to her car, a sand-colored Impala. It's the blandest, most anonymous car I can imagine, which was probably Fia's intention when buying it.

I ride in the front seat, Travis in the back. We ease out of the parking lot, and Fia flicks her gaze to the rearview mirror, eyeing her diner. The diner with the unlocked door and the regular and decaf coffee still keeping warm. The diner with the temperamental jukebox, the Nicaraguan flag, and the forever smell of bacon.

As we head east on the interstate to Fia's apartment, I spot a string of three cop cars, their lights flashing and sirens blazing, speeding toward the motel. For a moment I wonder if those cops worked with Officer Bain, and if so, if there's an active search for him. Maybe they don't even know he's missing yet.

Maybe.

Maybe not.

Speculation is a waste of time.

Fia doesn't talk. She's processing, I know.

Processing, and perhaps grieving.

Okay, I'll speculate.

My best guess?

She'll never step foot in her diner again.

SEVENTY-FIVE

TRAVIS AND I WAIT in the car as Fia walks up to her apartment building.

No menacing Oldsmobile in sight.

Violent green weeds choke the entrance to the complex, a dilapidated two-story affair framed in wood planks faded and frail enough to have been salvaged from a shipwreck.

"This is fuckin' crazy, right?"

I turn to him in the back seat. "Yes," I say. "It's a bit fucking crazy."

"We don't even know her, and, what, we're just going across country in her car?"

"Well, I don't know *you*, and we're going across country together."

"Come on," he says. "You know me."

I wonder how long it takes for someone to really know someone else. Probably forever.

"We all hide things," I tell him.

"The hell does that mean?"

Of course, I mean Bain, but that's a secret I'm not ready to reveal.

"Do you have a better idea? She has money and a car. You said those were things we needed."

I keep looking at him as he bows his head and stares at the floor of the car, his head swaying in what I interpret as anxiety. Part of me wants to slap him, not to hurt him but to make him confront this stinging reality right in its face. This is no longer a fanciful road trip to find my father; it's an escape that demands our collective attention, determination, and intelligence.

Another part wants him to grab me, hold me, and tell me this will all work out.

Neither of those things happens.

"Look," I say, "we don't need all the answers right now. We just need to keep moving. Get away from here. I don't know where we'll end up tonight, but wherever we do, I'll call my friend and see if he's figured out a way to help us. Okay?"

Travis just keeps swaying his head. "You never told me your friend's name."

"Lance. Dr. Lance Brock."

"You call him *Lance?*"

"Never," I say.

"Okay."

I catch movement in my periphery. I turn back around and see Fia emerging from the apartment building carrying a pink-and-teal backpack, quick about her steps.

"Okay, we're good to go," Fia says, sliding back into the driver's seat. "Let's get the hell out of here." Fia eases the car down the street. She's driving with caution.

"You got everything you needed?" I ask.

"Yes."

"Money?"

"Money," Fia answers.

"How much?"

"Everything I have. I hope it's enough."

"Enough for what?"

Fia blinks twice. "I really don't know."

Control is an illusion, of course. My entire time at Willow Brook seemed nothing if not a mastery of control. Answering every question, recalling every memory, inking each and every dot. And yet the event leading me to the institute was a moment of uncontrollable chaos, a hand to my back. Gravity and stairs. And so it's here, in the wild, that control appears as smoke, without mass and without purpose, swirling with the changing winds before disappearing in a huff, as if this control never existed in the first place.

Which, of course, it didn't.

We listen to nothing but the sound of the car for a few minutes. Then Fia says, "I suppose the two of you are wondering what I'm running from."

Travis leans forward so his face is between us. "We know what you're running from. A couple of motherfuckers with itchy trigger fingers."

"You know what I mean. The *reason* I'm running from them. What I did."

"Does it matter if we know?" I ask. "Will it affect how we make decisions together?"

Fia squints into the rearview mirror. "I don't know. Maybe not."

"We can swap stories later. Right now we're just three people driving west, trying to get some distance between us and anyone looking for us."

Fia glances over. "You think the police are looking for the two you?"

"Maybe," I say.

"No way," Travis counters. "There's no way they know we were in the club. How could they?"

I'm itching to tell them both about Bain but frozen at the thought of actually doing it. I say nothing.

Travis leans back.

A few more minutes of silence.

"You good back there?" Fia asks Travis. "You seem…I don't know. Fidgety. That's a word, right? Fidgety?"

I don't turn, don't want to stare at Travis, because the last thing a vulnerable person wants is others' gazes upon them, burning holes. But I expect he's still looking at the floor of the car. Fidgeting as he does.

"Yeah," he mumbles. "I'm good."

I know him well enough to tell his answer is bullshit.

He's not good.

I'm not good.

Nothing about any of this is good.

SEVENTY-SIX

RAPID CITY, SOUTH DAKOTA.

Why here?

It's the next stop on the treasure map.

There are only four locations on my dad's map.

Minneapolis, Rapid City, Denver, Westlake Village.

I justify targeting each of these cities because they're all on the most direct route to our destination. We aren't going out of our way here. And, my god, how I want to find a note from my father. Not just to know what it says but because it's a piece of my past I don't remember. There's something strangely alluring about nostalgia attached to blank memories.

It takes eight hours and forty-seven minutes to reach Rapid City, including a pit stop to use the bathroom and buy chips and pops from a 7-Eleven.

The motel we choose is on the outskirts of town, and but for the different name (Warrior Inn), it's a seamless substitution for the Star*Lite Inn.

That motel feels like a lifetime ago, I think. *I can't believe I woke up there just this morning.*

"I'll get us a room," Fia says.

"We have some money."

Travis chimes in. "I still have most of what we borrowed from Leo." Then he adds, "Well, not really *borrowed* anymore."

Fia opens her door. "This is how it's going to work. I'll pay for everything. I don't know where we're going or how we'll know when we get there. But sooner or later, we'll know. Maybe that means we're in another country. Maybe it means you've found your dad and Travis has found… whatever the hell it is he's looking for. Or…maybe it means we're dead. Until any of those things happen, I'll pay. Got it?"

"I'm not looking for anything," Travis says. "Just trying to avoid that dead scenario."

"Thank you," I say.

Minutes later we're standing in a motel room that is, by my subjective math, 30 percent nicer than the last one. Two beds, a TV, and a spartan but clean bathroom.

None of us has luggage, just our backpacks.

"I assume I'm taking the floor?" Travis says.

Fia and I reply yes in unison.

"Roger that." Travis stretches out on the floor, raising his arms above his head and bemoaning how cramped his muscles are from the car ride. All I can think of is the filth level of the motel carpet.

Fia looks around the room, as if wondering what to do next. Then she settles her gaze on me.

"How old are you two?"

"Twenty-one."

Travis mutters from the floor, his eyes closed, "Nineteen."

"Babies," Fia says. "Just babies. But also adults. When I was twenty-one, I already had two kids of my own. Now those kids are back home in Nicaragua and aren't much younger than you. My plan was to bring them here one day, but now I don't know. I just don't know." She gives me one of those forever looks, the kind that imprints on the brain and is how you always remember that person. "Something about you both reminds me of them. Even though I can't tell you a single thing any of you have in common."

She lets her thoughts end there. In this moment I realize she's capable enough to be running away on her own and doesn't need any help from us. She's helping *us* because she's a mother, and that's what mothers do.

I shift the conversation by pointing to her backpack. "How much money is in there?"

"A lot." She glances down at her bag. "Used to be a lot more."

I want to know how much but don't ask. "You have any coins in there?"

"Some. Why?"

No way I'm using the phone in this room.

"I need to find a pay phone."

SEVENTY-SEVEN

DR. BROCK ANSWERS BEFORE the first ring finishes, as if he's been hunching over his phone in anticipation.

"This is Dr. Lance Brock."

"Hi."

"*Penny*, I've been waiting for you to call."

"I couldn't do it this morning."

"Are you okay?"

That question again. How does a person define *okay?* Everything is relative. "Mostly."

"Where are you?"

"I don't have many quarters. You said you were going to talk to some people. See if they could help me out."

"Yes, I know." I hear frustration in his voice. "I'm still working on it. It's one person I need to talk to mostly, and, well…she's not easy to get a hold of."

"Who is she?"

"I'm afraid that's not something I'm at liberty to discuss. At least not in the moment."

"That's cryptic."

"I suppose we both have our secrets."

I'm not sure I like the idea of Dr. Brock keeping secrets from me. "I told you everything. You're the only person who knows…about the lake."

"Let's not discuss that. I don't know where you're calling from, and I can't be positive this line is clear."

"You think someone is listening?"

"I think it's safest to always assume that," he says.

"You sound like you've had calls like this before."

He pauses. "Penny, I can assure you I've never had calls quite like this."

I squeeze the receiver, close my eyes. "I don't even know how you can help. How anyone can."

"Listen," he says, "I know your situation seems…untenable. But there are people interested in you. And they could be in a position to help you."

"What people?"

"People with more power than me. Listen, do you have money? A place to stay?"

"Yes. For now."

"Then call me again when you can. I hope I'll have some answers. In the meantime, lie low."

"Yeah."

I hang up, suddenly overcome by a wave of profound sadness.

Hazy dusk light trickles through the dirt-streaked panes of the phone booth glass. I slump, grab my knees, and for once think not of my father but my mother. Is she scared for me? Does she know anything? Or is she ever oblivious in a haze of pills and booze?

This feels like a special kind of despair, one that transcends tears. A sense of loneliness and desperation so perfect, I'm not certain I've ever experienced it, at least not in the adult version of myself.

In that aching sadness, I find, only for a moment, happiness, pure and distilled to its essence, born from the mere fact that, for once, my brain has turned off entirely and I'm as desperately human as everyone else.

Hungry, scared, uncertain, grief-stricken, lonely.

As human as it gets.

SEVENTY-EIGHT

TREASURE MAP.

Location number two.

Oak tree in front of a touristy mercantile store at 622 Main Street.

There's a hollow near the base of the tree, the map reads. *The notes are in their bottles, nestled deep in that hollow.*

As I walk Main Street, alone, I know to keep my hopes in check. There's maybe a 1 percent chance the bottles are still in the hollow of that tree.

Still.

My pace quickens as I hit Fifth Street, and I'm nearly running as I get to Sixth.

I stop in front of the building marked 622.

It's not a mercantile.

It's a pharmacy.

And those hopes fade to zero as I look around.

There's no tree in front of this place.

In fact, there's not a single tree anywhere on Main Street.

I wait a few minutes, just standing here, as if the tree I seek will suddenly thrust itself up through the concrete and present its hollow to me. But, of course, nothing of the sort happens.

I turn and begin walking back to the motel, the setting sun at my back, disappointment in my chest.

As I walk, I'm reminded that everything changes.

And that eventually everything crumbles.

Crumbles and then disappears.

SEVENTY-NINE

FIA GRABS THE BOTTLE of Canadian Club she bought from a supply run and unsheathes a flimsy plastic cup from the motel bathroom. She pours herself a couple of inches, offers some to me. I take a sip of hers, find it disgusting, tell her, "No thanks."

"Suit yourself."

She walks back to the windows and peers around the scratchy and stained curtains yet another time.

"We take turns watching," she says.

"Is that necessary?"

"Probably not. But the worst part of not knowing whether something's necessary is finding out too late it was. We'll each take a shift, then wake up Milkshake to take one as well."

It's nearing eleven o'clock. I take a seat in the one chair in the room. It has a two-inch tear in the seat cushion, and I push the white stuffing back inside with my fingertips.

Travis is asleep on the floor, a sheet pulled over his head and soft snores bleeding through.

"I don't think he wants to be called *Milkshake*," I say.

"Of course he doesn't. No one likes a nickname. That's the whole point."

"That seems mean."

She keeps staring out the window. "Fine. I'll leave your boyfriend alone."

"He's not my boyfriend."

"No? Could've fooled me."

Without prompting, I tell her how I came to meet Travis. The mall. The corn dogs. Watching *Letterman* at his house. Travis agreeing to come with me into the wild.

"That's a big commitment for someone you don't even know," Fia says, sipping at her drink. "Just up and leaving town together."

I smile. "Like driving to Rapid City with some random Nicaraguan lady."

"I don't think any of this is random."

"No?"

"No," she says. "I think all this is happening for a reason. Why we met. Why we're here together."

"And that reason is what?"

Fia shakes her head. "I don't know. But it will become clear to us at some point."

"Pour me some whiskey," I say.

"I thought you didn't like it."

"I don't. But I didn't give it much of a chance."

She does.

I take a taste. It burns. The second sip, not so much.

"I think life is chaos," I say. "I don't think anything happens for a reason. It's all entropy."

"No reason behind anything?"

"No."

"Do you believe in God?"

"No."

Fia shakes her head, but it's not patronizing. Maybe just a little disappointed. "What brings you comfort?"

"Comfort?"

"*Sí.*"

I consider this. "Logic."

"Okay. And where did your logic come from?"

"It's just biology," I say. "Evolution."

Fia quits looking out the window and turns to me. "And all your talents, your *genius*. Who do you think gave you those, if not God?"

This answer is easy. "My mother. She pushed me down the stairs when I was seven, and my injuries made me a savant."

"A savant?"

I take a third sip and tell Fia what happened when I was seven. About the things I've been able to do since then. I tell her about the annual birthday cards from my dad and the broken person that is my mother. I even tell Fia about the conversations I have with my father in my head. How I ask him for advice when I need help.

I say nothing about Bain.

"*Dios,*" Fia says when I'm done talking. "Of course, that's why that doctor of yours wants to know where you are. You're valuable."

"He doesn't own me," I say. "No one owns me."

Fia takes a seat at the edge of the bed. Travis, near her feet, keeps snoring.

"But you're like...I don't know. Like a weapon or something."

The word spears me, perhaps because it evokes some distant thoughts, some hunches, a suspicion or two. Things I never thought too closely on because they weren't facts and were therefore unreliable. But still, there it is, that word, *weapon*, a knife in the belly. Cold steel and sizzling flesh.

"I'm not a weapon of any sort."

Fia stares up at the popcorn ceiling. "I mean, if you were *my* kid, I'd figure out how to make a fortune off you. If you're as rare as you say, you should be a millionaire. Like, get yourself on a game show and win everything."

"My mother wanted to get me on *Jeopardy!* and *$20,000 Pyramid*, but I refused to try. It's cheating."

"Cheating?" She barks a laugh. "I did a lot worse things for a lot less money."

I look at my roommate. My partner. My…accomplice. This woman old enough to be my mother. What *worse things* has Fia done?

I rise and walk over to the window. "I'll take the first watch. You should get some sleep."

"You know what to look for?"

"Do you?"

She shrugs. "Shadows, shapes, the boogeyman. Anything that doesn't feel right. I doubt those guys can find us, probably headed the other direction. I don't know about anyone looking for you, though."

"No one is looking for us."

"Oh, sure. So, if a police car pulled into the parking lot, you wouldn't freak out?"

"I'm not a freak out kind of person."

"Okay, then." Fia strips out of her clothes, revealing a toned, muscular frame. Leaving only her underwear on, she climbs into her bed, reaches over to the nightstand, and downs the remnants of Canadian Club from her plastic cup. "You do an hour, then I'll do an hour, and I'll wake up Sleeping Beauty for the third hour."

A voice emerges from under the sheet on the floor. "Fine by me."

I look down at the lump that is Travis, wondering if he just woke up or was just pretending to be asleep the whole time we've been talking.

Suppose it doesn't matter.

Lights out. The three of us in the silence.

Eight minutes pass. Thirteen. Thirty.

Thirty. Carbon steel.

I pull back the curtain again, peer out to the motel lot, the darkness mitigated by moonlight and a solitary streetlamp that doesn't seem to understand its purpose, alternately powering on and then off every few seconds. Beyond the dark, more darkness, then the sky, the relief of infinity.

I remember the moonlit sky the night the lake swallowed Officer Bain whole, not a single bite taken.

I release the curtain but keep my focus on the deep-green drapes, losing myself in the fabric, losing myself to the moment.

And so I disappear into my mind, and what a dark and unforgiving place it has become.

EIGHTY

HI, DAD.

Silence.

Silence.

You there?

Hiya, Pen Pen. What's shaking?

I stare out the window and on to the dark motel parking lot, imagining the black Oldsmobile easing into a parking space.

Tell me something happy, I say. A happy time when we were together.

Well, we did have a few of those, all right.

I don't remember much.

Nah, you were just a little one. Can't expect you to remember everything.

He falls silent for a bit.

You remember our date? he asks.

It's only the vaguest of memories. *Tell me again.*

It was your fifth birthday, and your mother was a bit under the weather. He means she was drunk. *So I told you I was going to take you on a date, and you wore that green dress with the flowers on it.*

There, now I remember. *Purple and pink.*

That's right. Purple and pink flowers. And I wore my suit. My one and only suit.

A gray suit, I say.

Bingo.

We were dressed to the nines, the two of us. You remember where we went?

Yes. The Howard Johnson's.

That's right, he says. *You had spaghetti, and I had a burger. What a fun dinner. This will probably come as no great shock to you, but I was always happier spending time alone with you. When the three of us were together, well, just seemed like we'd start fighting.*

I believe that.

But the best part of our date, he continues, *was the dessert.*

Orange sherbet. Same color as the roof.

That's right. The color of orange that just grabs your eyes and doesn't let go.

To me it's an eleven. Eleven is that color of orange.

Well, I don't see numbers as colors like you do, but I'll take your word. And you had two helpings of that sherbet.

I know.

Then you remember what happened next?

I summon the scene in my head. It doesn't have the movie-like clarity of all my memories after the fall, but it's vivid enough.

I puked right there on the table.

You sure as hell did! I've never been more surprised in my life. Just a fountain of vomit, mostly orange, of course. You ate too much and too fast, and it caught up with you. And here's the thing when you're a parent: When

your kid is sick in public, you don't care about the mess or the embarrass-
ment. You just want to make your kid feel better. I expected you to start
crying, to ask to go home, and all I wanted to do was tell you everything was
fine and we could still have a fun birthday date. But that's the thing. You
weren't upset. It was just a thing that had happened, and after you were
done, you were trying to figure out how to react. You looked at the mess on
the table, then you looked up at me. You were silent for a good ten seconds.
And then...do you remember?

I do, I tell him.

I can almost hear the laughter in his phantom voice. *You looked up*
at me and said, "Ta-da!"

Now I'm smiling.

The memory feels good, but in the reality that is this motel room,
the cold hand of the forgotten still knows how to squeeze with a firm
and icy grip.

Tell me about that night, I say.

What night?

You know.

Silence. Silence. *The night you fell down the stairs?*

Yes. I can remember hardly anything about it.

For a moment I think he's gone. But then:

That was the worst of all nights. I don't like thinking about it. I sure as
hell don't want to talk about it.

I search for him in the blackness behind my eyelids. Even just a
glimpse would be okay, but of course there's nothing.

I'm really angry you left.

I know, Pen Pen. I know.

You hurt me.

I know.

And then there's something. A spark of a memory, but not enough to catch fire. I have a sudden feeling I'm close to remembering that night on the top of the stairs. I can almost feel myself there, looking down. And shouting. So much shouting. All around me.

"Rabbit hole," I whisper out loud. "Something about a rabbit hole."

Yes.

What does that mean? It just came to me.

Rabbit hole, he says.

What does it mean?

And then I hear him sob in the darkness, soulful and heartbreaking, a lifetime of sorrow in that one fleeting gasp.

Those two words were the last I heard you ever say. Over and over, he says.

Rabbit hole.

Rabbit hole.

Rabbit hole.

EIGHTY-ONE

July 19, 1987
Sunday, Early Morning

SIX DAYS AGO WAS the day before my birthday. I woke in the institute that day, at the same time and with the same disposition as nearly every other day in my highly structured and predictable life.

Now I wake sleep-deprived in a motel room in Rapid City, an older woman in the bed next to me, a teenage boy on the floor, and haunted by a dead cop who, if he could talk, would tell the world Penny Bly killed him.

Chaos theory. A butterfly flapping its wings in Africa and such.

This is all chaos.

We check out of the motel and grab drive-through at McDonald's, Sausage McMuffins all around, along with hash browns and OJ. Fia's stash becomes seven dollars and eight cents lighter. Our last stop before hitting the road for the day is to gas up, ninety cents a gallon.

"I'm paying," I say.

"What did I say? I pay." Fia turns to Travis in the back seat. "Make yourself useful and go pump."

Travis rubs the remnants of sleep from his eyes. "Okay, okay."

We get out of the car, and as Fia heads toward the station attendant, I stop her.

"You don't make all the decisions," I tell her.

"What are you, tough all of a sudden?"

"No," I say. "But I want to have a say in things. And I'm paying for this gas. We have plenty of our own money left."

Fia shrugs and heads back to the car. "Suit yourself."

I go inside and hand cash to the attendant. While Travis pumps, I glance at the TV on the wall. It's dialed to the local news, where a puffy-haired man talks about the weather. The high will be ninety-one—*ninety-one: yellow Starburst candy chew*—and clear, a scorcher. Just the weather. No images of my face with the word *wanted* beneath. The sight of the news alone draws anxiety, but I can handle a weather report.

The worry is Bain, of course. Is he still in the lake? When will the news show Travis's car being dragged to shore, then water gushing as the cops open the doors and discover one of their own bloated and nibbled on by fish?

While waiting for Travis to finish pumping, I thumb through a road atlas of the entire United States to memorize it. Pages twenty-six and twenty-seven encompass most of Minnesota, which includes the little blue blob of Solomon Lake.

I replay that night, even though I don't want to. It's like sitting front row at a horror movie.

The tighty-whities. That's the image that strikes me most. Those disgusting tighty-whities, with just a hint of the man's erection emerging.

"Twelve fifty-seven," the gas station clerk says, pulling me from my flashback. He punches at his register, which chimes as it opens. "Here's your change."

"Thanks," I say, keeping my gaze down.

As I start to head to the doors of the gas station, my brain replays what happened last night. Dad's voice. The repetition of the words *rabbit hole*.

But this mental movie is cut short by the sight of a car pulling into the gas station.

A black Oldsmobile.

I stop moving. I stop breathing.

Two men in the front seat.

One of them, I know, is named Sebastian.

EIGHTY-TWO

THE OLDSMOBILE CRAWLS TO a stop at the pump farthest from Fia, who is now back in the Impala. Travis leans against the trunk of the car, stupidly smoking a cigarette.

I stare through the panes of the gas station door, my stomach crawling inside itself.

Coincidences happen all the time.

I find no comfort in those words. In the institute I once flipped a nickel four hundred times. There was a stretch where it landed on heads fourteen times in a row. Improbable but not impossible. The math of it intrigued me.

The math of that Oldsmobile pulling within thirty feet of my friends, however, is horrifying.

Sebastian's partner emerges from the car and walks directly toward the store where I'm standing.

Do they know we're here?

Did they find us?

No way of knowing—too many variables to calculate. Not that it matters much in the moment. I can only hope this is a coincidence, in which case, they don't know who Travis is, a good thing since he's clearly visible to them.

Please, Fia, stay in the fucking car.

The car.

Damn it.

They probably know Fia's car.

I reverse course and disappear down one of the two aisles in the small convenience store and pretend to look at beer offerings in the coolers.

I sneak a glance at the door.

Sebastian's partner enters, all swagger, confidence, and mild disdain.

I peer over an array of chips as he walks to the counter.

"Number four," he says to the cashier. Same accent as Sebastian.

"You got it," the cashier says. "Need anything else? Smokes?"

"No."

There's nothing in the men's demeanor to indicate they have any idea we're here. So then, it's a monumental coincidence. But perhaps something more.

A test.

My entire time in the wild has been a test. How will a girl like me outsmart predators? And can I continue doing it?

If I believed in any kind of god, I'd carve out time to explore these questions further. And perhaps, if I continue being, you know, *alive*, then this could be the day I start believing in a god.

But now, peeking over the rows of potato chips, is not the time for an internal theological debate.

Sebastian's partner exits the building to pump. The Oldsmobile's tank holds what, fifteen, sixteen gallons? It'll probably take three or four minutes, and then he'll come back inside for his change. There is a chance the entire transaction could take place without them noticing us. A chance. But even then, the two men will still be out there, somewhere. Existential threats. Fia will always have to worry for herself and her family.

Best I can tell, I have two options.

One: hope for the best.

Two: attack first.

I turn back to the coolers full of beer, a shimmering display of Budweisers and Coors, and give myself one minute, no more, no less.

I close my eyes and simply let go, traveling deeper into the recesses of my mind than I ever have before.

I let go of any sights or sounds.

Let go of memories, abandon all thoughts of the future. In this simple minute, I no longer see numbers as colors, nor dictionary pages rendered in fine mental detail.

In this moment I exist in a space of nonexistence. The absence of emotion, senses, thought, logic.

On my deathbed I suspect I'll look back on this moment as my true birth, the time I discovered another plane of existence, not by fluke but by capitulation to all I know, from which springs forth a level of understanding that no one—not even me, one of seventy-five—has ever known.

At the end of it all is father's voice, clearer than I've ever heard it. I can almost feel his breath on my ear.

He tells me what to do.

"Yes, okay," I whisper.

Then I open my eyes, the minute having passed, those cans of beer still glistening in their cooler, Dad's words still echoing in my skull.

But I know, deep down, it isn't him.

Of course it isn't him.

It's me.

Seeing the future all on my own.

EIGHTY-THREE

I SLIP A PAIR of sunglasses off a display rack, then walk directly to the gas station attendant at the counter. "I have to tell you something."

He's older, maybe in his forties. Heavy, bald, whiskered, with faded tattoos on muscled forearms, all beneath a forest of arm hair. "Yeah?"

"You don't have much time," I say. "That guy who just came in? He's going to come back in for his change, and then he's going to put a bullet in your head. After that, he's going to take everything in that register."

This gets his attention.

"The fuck?"

"It's true," I continue. "He's with another man, his partner. Really bad guys."

He turns his head and squints at the Oldsmobile. Both Sebastian and his partner are sitting inside.

"And how the hell do you know this?"

"Me and my girlfriend, we met them last night in a bar. They told us all about the things they do... I swear, a drunk and horny guy will tell you anything. They talked about holding up gas stations all over the place and said it was just easier to kill the station clerks. I said I didn't

believe them, so here we are. Right here, at your place. Seriously, I don't

think they're bullshitting. I think they're actually psychos." I lean forward

and press my waist against the counter, then lower my voice. "They told

me the key is to do it quick, right when the cashier is getting the change.

No warning, just…" I put my finger against my temple. "*Boom.*"

The clerk clenches his jaw and shifts his gaze from me to the front

door. "I don't believe you."

"Believe it or not, mister, doesn't change a thing. I didn't believe it

either until they showed us some Polaroids of the last guy they did.

Looked a little like you, I suppose. Though there wasn't much face left."

"Jesus Christ."

"I don't want to be part of it," I say. "Neither does my girlfriend. We

only agreed to meet them here so I could warn you. So we're going to drive

off, hope never to run into those creeps again. Thought it was only fair to

give you a chance. That's the Christian thing to do, I suppose."

We both turn our heads toward movement outside. Sebastian's

partner is out of the car, putting the gas nozzle back into the pump.

"Here he comes," I say.

"Fuck. I'm calling the cops."

"They won't get here in time. Might as well just call the coroner. Do

you have something to protect yourself with?"

This is when the sweat appears on his forehead for the first time—

all at once, dozens of the smallest of beads.

"You're goddamned right I do." He reaches under the counter and

emerges with a gun that looks a lot like Officer Bain's. The clerk squeezes

it in his right hand, his forearm muscles rippling as if worms are burrow-

ing beneath his skin.

"I'm going," I tell him. "Just remember what I said—there won't be any warning. If you can surprise him first, maybe you have a chance."

With that, I turn, lower my head, then leave the store. I realize too late that I never paid for the sunglasses. Oh well.

Outside, I put on the glasses, which are way too big for my face. Sebastian's partner is headed directly toward me on the way to the store.

Seconds later, our paths cross. I can't resist meeting his gaze behind my shades, searching his eyes for signs he recognizes me. He nods and smiles, and then I see...something.

A flicker of recognition?

Maybe.

He only saw me for seconds once before, outside the diner, and even wearing sunglasses and with my hair pulled back in a ponytail, it's possible he could still recognize me. Maybe he has a memory like mine.

As we pass I catch his scent. Musky.

Moments later I'm in the clear. Almost at Fia's car.

The man calls out to me. "Hey."

I consider not turning.

But I do.

"Yeah?"

He's standing next to the door of the convenience store. I can't see the attendant inside.

"You're sexy." His accent is thicker than Sebastian's. "You should come party with us."

I release a breath of deep relief.

"*Vaya con Dios*," I tell him.

I don't wait to see his reaction, instead turning and getting back in the car. Travis and Fia are inside, with Fia browsing radio channels. I'm guessing she hasn't seen the Oldsmobile.

"What took you so long?" Travis asks.

I ignore the question, reaching out and lightly grasping the hand Fia is using to tune the dial. "I'm going to tell you something, but not until we're driving. Which I suggest we start doing immediately. And head east on the interstate this time, at least for a while."

I'm expecting Fia to question me, but to her credit, she doesn't.

"Okay."

The first sound is the engine turning over as Fia starts the car, followed by the mellow hum of the engine.

The second sound, while muted, is unmistakably a gunshot.

The third is the slamming of the Oldsmobile door as Sebastian races out and beelines for the convenience store, his gun in hand.

Fia's eyes widen in horror with recognition.

"Now," I say. "Go *now.*"

Another gunshot.

As we speed toward the interstate, I stay silent and close my eyes, wondering exactly what kind of person I've become.

EIGHTY-FOUR

TRAVIS IS BESIDE HIMSELF. "What the fuck happened back there? How did they find us?"

It's his third time asking. Fia asked once and has remained silent since.

But I'm not ready to talk about it. I feel like shutting down and trying to process what I felt while listening to Dad's instructions. Happiness, relief, fear, disgust. And I can blame nothing on him, for *I'm* my father, nothing more, nothing less.

I summon the road atlas from my memory banks and give Fia instructions.

"Go east on the interstate until you see signs for Route 79, then head south to that. Then take 79 south to Hot Springs, then south on 18 until you get to Lusk, at which point we'll be in Wyoming. There 18 heads west again and connects to Interstate 25. Then it's a straight shot south to Denver, which we can make by the early evening. Got it?"

Fia looks over, and her expression isn't one of understanding or compliance. "Hell no, I don't *got it*. I heard 79, and at that point, I got annoyed and stopped listening because you won't tell us what you did back there."

I take a breath. "East on 90 then 79 until—"

"What happened at the gas station?"

"They didn't find us," I say. "If they had, we'd be dead. It was a coincidence, but one that's changing my beliefs about coincidences. Maybe fate. Maybe some kind of sign. I don't know. But I need to close my eyes. Take 79 to Hot Springs. That should take about an hour. Wake me up when we're a few miles out from there."

I close my eyes, ending the discussion.

I'm out within a minute, my brain demanding a respite.

———————

Fia doesn't get a chance to wake me.

The chainsawing pain in my head takes care of that.

EIGHTY-FIVE

EVER SINCE I CAME home from the hospital all those years ago, I've been prone to headaches, but I've never experienced one like this.

The image that comes to me is page 47 of the book *Torture Devices of the Early Modern Period*, by John Stinby. For some reason the institute had that book in their library, and as with all other books there, I read it and therefore committed it to my memory.

Page 47 is dedicated to the Renaissance era device simply called a head crusher.

The page contains only 107 words of text, for no more are needed to describe a device so self-evident in its application (and its name) that a child can figure it out.

Forged entirely of iron, a head crusher features a lower plate upon which the victim places their jaw. A metal cap is then lowered millimeter by millimeter using a twisting handle, wide enough to offer optimal torque. Once the cap reaches the skull, every subsequent twist applies pressure equally to the lower jaw and the cranium. The jaw, being more fragile, shatters first. Then the teeth, the mandible, and facial bones, then finally the skull itself. Eventually, it leads to death, but only after the brain shuts itself off due to the incomprehensible agony.

The remainder of page 47 is occupied by a drawing, crude ink, imagining the use of the device.

This memory of the book lasts only seconds, but it's enough for me to reach up and grab my head, finding it solid and not pulp.

But, my god, how it hurts.

I don't black out.

But I sure as hell wish I did.

Fia's voice, somewhere in another dimension. *"What's going on? Penny? Can you hear me?"*

I'm screaming now.

Travis shouts, *"We're in the middle of nowhere! Tell us what to do!"*

Breathe. Just breathe through it.

It doesn't help. This thing doesn't care if I breathe or not.

Nausea swells.

And then, as suddenly as the pain came on, whatever hand is on this torture device eases up. Just a little.

"Pull over," I manage to say.

I feel the car slowing, and I open my eyes, which brings a fresh jolt of misery. I keep my eyes open just long enough to bolt from the car. I run down an embankment and into a field of wild grasses and rolled hay bales. There I collapse, a hay bale next to me, a thing so large, it seems an elephant poised to take a casual step and end my suffering once and for all.

In these wild grasses, I desperately suck in the fresh South Dakota air and, for a moment, find relief. Just enough to let me know things are heading in the right direction.

Eyes closed. Hands by my sides. The grass scratching my neck. The scent of hay attacking my nostrils. The gradual easing of pain is like a hit of morphine snaking through my bloodstream.

Breathing, breathing.

Less than a minute later, the last of it slips away.

A shadow passes over my face.

Travis and Fia look down at me as if staring into my grave.

"Are you okay?"

"I don't know."

"What can I do?" Travis asks.

"Nothing."

"I'll get aspirin," Fia says.

She heads back to the car, and I look up into the mouth of the endless sky, mentally reciting the atmospheric layers.

Troposphere, stratosphere, mesosphere, thermosphere, exosphere, space.

Then heaven?

No.

If heaven existed, it'd be much closer. Perhaps these grasses beneath me, touching my skin, reminding me I'm alive, are heaven.

"Here." Fia's back and hands me three aspirin and a warm can of Coke. I sit up, pop the tablets one at a time, then lie back down.

"I get them every now and then. Headaches. But not like this one. I think my body is finally rebelling against all the stress it's under."

Not just the body, I consider. *The mind.*

"I'm ready to talk," I say.

And, as I keep my gaze straight up toward the sky, I do. I tell Fia and Travis what happened at the gas station. About what I told the convenience store clerk.

"The thing is," I say, "at the time, I didn't care what happened. The sounds we heard? Gunshots, had to be. And logic tells me the station attendant shot Sebastian's partner, which was my intention. But then Sebastian ran in there, could have killed that clerk. I set the whole thing in motion, and I didn't care who got hurt. I just didn't want them after us."

"Are you kidding me?" Travis says. "You did the right thing. Abso-fuckin-lutely."

"I'm not sure." I sit up again, then turn my head and stare out to the highway, where only the occasional car speeds by. All this land. Just land and hay bales.

"We should keep moving," Fia says.

So I get to my feet, brushing off some grass from the backs of my thighs. Then I take a step toward the hay bale, lean in, absorb its smell. It's the musty aroma of simple things, of the natural world, of living in the now. Somehow, of freedom. Such a silly thing, but that's what I smell.

"You go back to the car," I tell Fia. "I need to talk to Travis."

EIGHTY-SIX

I EXPECT FIA TO protest, to say something like, *You keeping secrets from me?* But, to her credit, she nods and heads to the car. She must know that, by definition, secrets are shared with some and kept from others.

"What's up?" Travis asks when we're alone.

My hands burrow in my jeans pockets. "I need to tell you something." Deep, deep breath. "About what really happened to your car."

He shifts his weight. "Okay."

Another deep breath.

Then I tell him.

Everything about that night. About Bain. What he tried to do to me and where he ended up. The brains and the blood and the cold lake water.

I confess partly because the car was registered in his parents' name, tying his whole family to the crime. But mostly I tell him because I need to. I can't hold it in any longer because this kind of secret is the type that'll kill someone after too long. Like a headache that ends up exploding the skull.

Travis stands there.

Listening. Absorbing. Judging.

When I'm done, I shut up. I can't look at him, so I turn my attention to the wild grasses, their tips tussled by the breeze.

Finally, he speaks. "You did what you had to do."

And how that breaks me.

Funny that seven little words can wield such a hammer, but they do, shattering my heart. In those words he forgives me—a forgiveness that isn't even his to give—and I don't think I realized how desperately I've been craving exactly this.

I cry. The kind of cry that seizes the throat, making it hard to breathe. A desperate, murderous kind of cry.

Travis doesn't talk, and when he puts his arm around me, I don't push him away. No. I want to sink into him forever, a shipwreck in silence and peace destined for eternity at the bottom of an endless sea.

When the sobs at last trickle into sniffles, I say, "I'm not sure I'm strong enough for any of this."

He removes his arm. "Part of me wants to tell you I'll protect you and that we can do this, whatever this even is. The other part of me wants to say, 'Me neither.'"

Salt stings my eyes. "So what do we do?"

"What choice do we have? We keep moving. For as long as we need to. For as far as we need to."

In the moment, Travis looks much older than his nineteen years.

"Okay, then," I say.

"Okay, then."

We walk back to the car, and I don't spend time wondering what I'll say if Fia asks what we were discussing.

Instead, I think about Dad and how he seems both closer and farther away than ever.

I need you, I say as I open the car door and slip inside.

This time, there's no answer.

EIGHTY-SEVEN

DENVER, JUST AFTER 6:00 p.m.

Outside the lobby windows of the Brown Palace Hotel, an umber haze wraps itself around the lingering sun, choking it out. Travis and I wait twenty feet back as Fia asks a golden-uniformed front-desk clerk about available rooms.

We don't belong here. Too fancy. Too showy.

"Why Denver?" Travis asks me.

"Because it's on the way west," I tell him. "And it's the only other location on the treasure map until we get to California."

"Oh yeah? What's the location?"

"Another tree." I see the map clearly in my head. "City Park. It's so stupid. I wouldn't bother except, like I said, it's on our way."

"It's not stupid. I think it's cool. I've never been on a treasure hunt before. Unless you count lame-ass Easter egg hunts."

A minute later Fia returns jiggling a pair of keys. "Top floor."

"We can't afford this," I say.

"You know we can. Besides, anyone looking for us isn't going to think we're staying here."

"I think those guys are gone," I tell her. "At least I'm hoping they are. They might even both be dead. Who knows what happened at the gas station?"

Fia wags her finger at me. "*If* they are gone—and I don't believe they are—there will be others to replace them. They won't stop, so the best I can do is disappear forever. Which I thought I already had, but I guess not well enough."

Up the elevator, with its shiny brass and shimmering mirrors. I avoid eye contact with myself, feeling ugly and not wanting to confirm it. I need a shower, some food, and solid sleep.

Eighth-floor hallway: thick carpet and mesmerizing wallpaper. There's a subtle humming menace in these walls, along this floor. So many people have stayed in this century-old hotel. Good things have happened here but also bad, and the bad things are the ones that linger, settle in the floorboards, seeping malignant energy as guests tread over them.

Yes, bad things have happened here.

Bad things will continue to happen here.

"This is us." Fia slides the key into the lock and turns it. The door opens, letting out the faintest of groans.

I'm the first inside.

There's nothing outwardly evil about the room, and its decor is a level of ornateness that matches all we've seen of the hotel so far. Nothing surprising, nothing concerning, and, really, nothing all that interesting. But as I inspect the artwork on the walls—all photos of downtown Denver at the turn of the century—I suddenly realize I'm not comfortable with the past. I don't like old things. Don't care for history. Am made uneasy by events that can never be changed, unalterable courses, rivers of bad decisions.

One photo on the wall shows Denver celebrity Molly Brown. The Unsinkable Molly Brown, who survived the sinking of the *Titanic*.

Another thing that can never be changed.

The *Titanic* sank.

I went down those stairs.

My father left.

I killed a cop.

"So it goes," I whisper to Molly.

The clock on the wall says it's six thirty. My mother, especially when drunk, always went a little dreamy at the six thirty broadcast of the *NBC Nightly News*. Dreamy because of Tom Brokaw.

That voice of his, she'd purr in a most unpleasant way. *Makes me want to do things.*

I turn on the TV in the room and dial it to channel nine.

Then, there he is. Brokaw. Swept hair, curious drawl. The headline story concerns John Poindexter's testimony about the Iran-Contra affair, the diversion of Iranian arms profits to the Nicaraguan Contras.

Nicaragua.

I look over to Fia, whose gaze is fixed on the television. I redirect my gaze before we share glances because whatever is happening in Fia's brain at the moment, she deserves to keep it to herself. I know enough about the Nicaraguan civil war, at least as much as the newspapers cover it, the Contras and the Sandinistas. I always read the paper on the days I was at the institute, finding only a fraction of it interesting. But here, in this hotel room, standing next to my friend, this Nicaraguan, there's this reality, a frequency no newspaper could ever provide. Whatever Fia's story is, I'm guessing it's very much related to the words coming from Brokaw's mouth.

Then the image on the TV shifts from the interior of the Congressional Office Building to one that frosts me over.

"A grisly discovery in Minnesota today," Brokaw singsongs. "The body of Officer Jeremy Bain of the Meeker County Police was found inside a car submerged in Solomon Lake." The footage shows a crane lifting Travis's car out of the lake, water pouring from the open driver's side window, just as I imagined it. "Bain was last heard from Tuesday night, when he was off duty but stopped to assist a motorist. His car was found the next morning, seemingly abandoned, near an interstate exit. Law enforcement and volunteers had been furiously searching for the missing officer since, and the outline of the submerged car was spotted by a helicopter crew this morning. The mystery surrounding Officer Bain is just beginning, as authorities want to know…"

I chance a look at Travis, only to find him already wide-eyed and staring at me.

Brokaw makes no mention of the car's owner and thus no mention of Travis or me. But that will come. The police probably already made all the connections, and this time tomorrow night, the words *Penny Bly* may just lazy-river themselves from Brokaw's mouth for the world and my mother to hear.

Fia's voice is like a knife attack. "What the hell is up with the two of you? You're both whiter than you already were."

I say nothing. Just lower my gaze to the floor.

"Oh, no, no, no. What a minute. Wait a fucking minute." Fia's voice keeps cutting. "Minnesota? Do *not* tell me you had anything to do with this. A *cop*? Please tell me this wasn't—"

"Not Travis," I manage. "Just me."

"Don't say anything else," Travis says.

"It's okay. She should know."

Fia walks up and gets right in front of me. I force myself to make eye contact.

"You can't be serious," Fia says. "A fucking police officer?"

"It was self-defense," Travis says. "He was going to kill her."

Fia remains locked in with me. "We're screwed. We're all screwed. You think the Nicaraguans won't stop looking for us? They're nothing compared to cops looking for someone who killed one of their own."

"You should go," I tell her.

"What?"

"Take your car. Take Travis. Keep going without me. You two shouldn't be tied to this."

Fia leans in, searches my eyes down to each last freckle of pigment. I don't even blink. "He was really going to kill you?"

I nod. "He started strangling me when I wouldn't…do what he wanted."

She takes a step back and puts her hands on her hips. I can almost hear the tornado of thoughts spinning in her head. "Fucking promise me you're not lying."

"Does it matter?" I say. "Innocent or not, they're coming for me. And if you're with me, then for us."

"Yes, it matters. You know it matters."

"What I told you is true."

Fia absorbs the words. "How'd you do it?"

"I shot him."

"*Dios*. Where?"

"In the car. Travis's car."

"No, where on his body did you shoot him?"

"Oh. In the head. Left sphere of the frontal bone. I think. It was dark."

Her face softens. "What did it feel like?"

Feel.

Feelings are the amber trapping the mosquito: a surrounding thickness with no definition, no beginning or end. Just an all-encompassing pressure.

"In the moment, relief."

Fia nods. "And now? How does it feel now?"

"How do you think?"

She says nothing.

I walk a few feet over to the bed, then turn to face them. "I don't want to talk about it anymore except to say two things. One, I feel destroyed by what happened, and I know I'll never be the same person again because of it." I pause, studying their faces. "Two, I'd do it all over again if I had to."

"Jesus, Penny," Travis says. "I can't even imagine what—"

"No," I interrupt. "You can't." To Fia I say, "And I know I told you about my talents and you were hoping my smarts would get us to wherever we're going, but I'm realizing I'm no more special or capable than anyone else. Not out here anyway."

"You got us out of two bad situations already," Fia says.

"You should leave. Both of you."

"You feeling sorry for yourself?"

"No," I say. "I'm feeling sorry for you and all the additional trouble you'll be in if you're found with me."

"*Ay, Dios mío.*" Fia shakes her head. "I didn't take you for the dramatic type."

I start to respond, but Fia holds up a hand.

"Enough. There are three of us. I say we vote. Raise your hand if you vote to stay together." Fia keeps her hand held high.

I look to Travis. His hand is in the air, and there's a ghost of a smile on his face.

"Then it's decided," Fia says. "Now put your big, beautiful brain to work, and figure out the next move."

"That's easy," I say.

"Oh, yeah?" Travis squeezes the back of his neck, exorcising tension. "So what do we do?"

I nod at the phone on the nightstand. "We call for help."

EIGHTY-EIGHT

AFTER EXCHANGING FIVE DOLLARS for quarters at the front desk, I walk out into the diminishing sun and find a pay phone on the street corner, deciding to err on the side of caution and not use the phone from our room. I close myself inside the suffocating glass box and dial.

Dr. Brock answers on the first ring. "Hello?"

"It's me."

"Thank god. How are you?"

I scan the streets of Denver, as if that would tell me anything. "I've been better."

"Are you hurt?"

"No."

"Good," he says. "That's good."

"I'm not where I was. We left the motel."

"We?"

"The boy. He found me. And there's one other person."

"Who?"

"I'm not ready to say."

"Well, where are you?"

"Same answer as before."

Dr. Brock takes a few seconds before saying anything. "I don't know if you've seen the news, but—"

"Yes. I've seen it. It's out there."

"Yes," he says. "It is. I don't know if they've figured anything else out yet, but they'll be able to identify the owners of the car. Then it's just a matter of time."

"I know."

"I can't even think about how many people are going to come looking for you."

I hide behind closed eyelids. "You remember when you taught me breathing exercises? I was twelve. You told me how to breathe when I got stressed out. Inhale for a count to four…"

"Hold for a count of two," he adds. "Then exhale for a count of four. Yes, I remember."

"It's not working. I'm pretty stressed out."

"I imagine you are."

"I had a headache today. The worst one ever."

"I'm sorry to hear that. Maybe it's a sign you need help."

A voice tells me to add another quarter to the pay phone, so I do. "You said you were waiting on a woman to call you back. A person who could help."

"Yes." Dr. Brock clears his throat. "She did call back."

"Who is she?"

"Someone who has the power to make things go away."

"Did she say she could help?"

"She did," he says. "But knowing you're with two others complicates things a bit. Maybe substantially."

My face catches remnants of sunlight, which warms me through the phone booth glass. "I'm not leaving them," I say. "And they're not leaving me."

"That's the complicated part."

"So where does that leave us?"

Silence, silence.

"Where are you calling me from?" he asks.

"A phone booth."

"Okay, good. That's good. Well, if we're going to do this, you'll be extracted from wherever you are and sent to a secure location until the details can be sorted out."

My heart rate notches up. "That sounds like custody."

"It's not," he says. "At least not the way you're thinking. To be honest, I don't know all the details. But I trust this person, and if you trust me, then this might be the only safe path for you out of this…situation."

"When you say *out*…you mean freedom, right? Complete freedom."

"I don't know, Penny. I hope so. Like I said, I don't know all the details. But I feel very comfortable saying it's a better option than to be on the run forever."

"I still want to find my father."

There's his sigh again. "You need to let that go. Clearly, your circumstances have changed."

I expected that answer, but it still stings to hear it. There's no logic in continuing my quest, not if there's a real and viable lifeline being thrown to me. But standing face-to-face with my dad remains the thing I want most in the world. Maybe the only thing.

"I'm not used to fighting emotional impulses," I say.

"I know."

"It sucks."

"Well, that's another part of being outside the institute. Being in the real world."

"You kept me sheltered," I tell him. "Too sheltered."

"Perhaps we did. For that I'm sorry."

I open my eyes, look up toward the brown sky, and fight the urge to scream. It would be so *loud* in this phone booth. Might even hurt my ears. But how good it would feel.

Instead, I slump my shoulders. "I'm in Denver."

"Denver, okay. So the three of you kept going west."

There's no point in mentioning the incident at the gas station. "Yes."

"Tell me where," Dr. Brock says. "I can send someone to get you."

"No," I counter. "It has to be you. I only trust you."

"Penny, I don't know—"

"Please," I say. "I need you."

A long pause. "I can get a flight first thing in the morning. I'm sure I can be there by noon tomorrow."

"Okay, then. Brown Palace Hotel, lobby. Three p.m."

"Okay," he says. "I'll be there."

I nod to myself, hoping I'm doing the right thing. Could be it's the worst decision I'll ever make. Or maybe the best. And all that gray area between those two outcomes is enough to drive me insane.

I move to hang up the phone but pull my hand back before ending the call.

I put the receiver back to my ear.

"Thank you," I say.

But Dr. Brock is already gone.

EIGHTY-NINE

July 20, 1987
Monday

MORNING LIGHT STREAMS THROUGH the sheer curtains of the hotel room, and when I focus just enough, I can see dust floating in the beam, thousands of sloughed-off skin particles from the thousands of people who stayed in this room before us. All those lives, floating right in front of me.

"I didn't sleep for shit." Fia's on the floor. She gave up her bed so Travis could have a night in comfort. "The carpet kinda smells like piss."

"I'm sorry," I say. "I should've taken the floor."

She groans and raises herself to a seated position. "I've certainly had worse nights."

Travis sprouts to life in the neighboring bed, stretches, rubs his eyes. He says nothing, and the extended silence feels thick. There's that saying about today being the first day of the rest of your life. I always thought that was a dumb expression, but how true it suddenly feels.

Fia finally breaks the silence. "Back in Minnesota, I had a life, simple and easy, more or less. There was just enough of a routine that I could keep the pain away most of the time. The pain of missing my kids, my mother, my home."

I think about missing my mother but find nothing to cling to.

"I want to tell both of you what I did," Fia says. "Why I'm running."

"That's not necessary."

"Maybe not to you. And I know you're keeping secrets from me, and that's cool. I just feel the need to talk." Fia pivots on the floor to face us, then sweeps her hair out of her face. "Back in Nicaragua, I stole money. A lot of money. From some really bad people." She closes her eyes. Maybe that helps. "Me and my boyfriend. He worked for those people... He's the one who actually stole the money, and we had three bank accounts set up to hide it. We had papers to get us to the States, and the plan was I would go first, and then he'd join me. Later I'd bring my kids, when it was safe."

"Weren't you worried about leaving your kids there?" Travis asks.

"That's the thing. These bad guys? They didn't know I existed because my boyfriend was married. I was a total secret. I'd never met his bosses before, so they wouldn't know me from any other cocktail waitress in Managua."

"How long ago was this?"

Now a tear spills down her cheek, jumps to its death on the bedsheets. "*Tres años.* I haven't seen my babies in three years."

You don't need to be a genius to see the tragedy waiting in Fia's yet-unspoken words.

"Your boyfriend...he didn't make it to the States, did he?" I say.

She shakes her head. More tears sprout. "No. They caught him. At the airport, is what I heard. I don't really know."

"But you know he's—"

"Dead. Yes, I know that." She sucks in a few deep gulps of air, lets them out. "My children are with my mother. I have access to one of the accounts, not the other two. I use it to send money back home, just a little at a time. And next year...*puta*. Next year I thought finally I could bring them all to Minnesota, with real paperwork and everything. And then out of nowhere, those two motherfuckers come to my diner. The *Snakeskin Boys*. The moment I saw them, I should have known they were coming for me. I should have known their boss would keep looking for his money. But I convinced myself I was finally safe. That after three years, no one was looking for me anymore. I got lazy, and I'm very lucky it didn't get me killed."

I replay my entire encounter with Sebastian in my head and silently agree Fia is indeed fortunate to be alive.

"Why did they wait?" I ask. "You said they came into the diner an earlier time. Why didn't they...do what they came to do then?"

"I don't know. I guess they needed to make sure I was the person they were looking for. And I suppose, based on what you told me, to tell Arthur what they were planning to do."

"And what's your connection to Arthur?" Travis asks. "He died telling those assholes to leave you alone."

More tears.

"Fuck," Travis says. "I'm sorry."

"It's okay." She takes a moment to gather herself. "I knew about Arthur from my boyfriend. He was one of many U.S. distributors for the guy we stole from. But it was well known they didn't like each other. Arthur had the power and connections to help us hide, start new lives here in the States. It was a risk, but my boyfriend called him, anonymously, told him our plan to steal the money. Asked if he could help us if we paid him." She looks up, her wet eyes bright and shiny. "Arthur loved the idea. He laughed about it, like a little boy. He was the first person I met when I came here. The diner was his idea, even. Helped me with all my documents, everything I needed to start over again. The only payment he asked for was a small percentage of sales from the diner. Barely amounted to anything. He's a…he *was*…a good man. I know he probably didn't seem that way to you, but he always treated me with kindness."

"Huh," Travis says. "'Cause his son was kind of a douchebag."

"Can you show a little respect?" I say.

"Just saying."

"Your family," I say to Fia, "you must be worried about them. I mean, if they figured out who you are, maybe they know who your family is."

Fia stills. "It's been killing me ever since we left. Yesterday, I went out and called them. Thank God they're okay. My mother said everything was normal. I told them to leave, leave immediately. I told them to drive to the coast, to Popoyo. There's a hotel there that me and Rico—he was my boyfriend—stayed at one weekend, years ago. I told her to book two rooms and stay put until I contacted them again." She gives herself a brief tight hug. "I'm going home. Going back to get my family and find a new place for us all to go. Which means I don't want to be a part of your… extraction, or whatever you've got planned today. I just want to go home."

"Go to the airport," I tell her. "Here in Denver. Fly out immediately."

She shakes her head. "No."

"Why not?"

"Not yet. You might need me today. We have no idea what's going to happen, and I'm not leaving until I know you're safe."

I want to argue but know it won't do any good.

The room falls quiet, the weight of countless racing thoughts attached to no words, a din of internal calculations, what-ifs, and starbursts of regrets.

I get out of bed dressed only in underwear and a T-shirt, and how freeing it is that I don't care.

I'll take a long shower. At least fifteen minutes. Twenty, perhaps. And there will be luxury soaps and shampoos, a washcloth that's actually both thick and soft. I'll be clean, at least on the outside. At least today.

Before heading to the bathroom, I walk to the window, stare out though the sheer curtain. Stare out at this hazy world, its shapes vague and torpid behind the fabric, and I think about all the lives out there, all with their own stories, all with their own joy and tragedy, all unique, not one in seventy-five but *unique*, singular, never to have preexisted or ever repeat again, and how there's something so heartbreaking about that. Whiffs of oxygen, a lifetime of dust, motes in a hotel room, all of us. Every single one of us.

"About the cop I killed," I say, staring toward the outside light.

Travis says, "You don't need to talk about that."

"I'm not going to give any more details except this. It wasn't like in the movies. Not that it should be because movies are just movies. I wasn't just someone trying to figure out how to survive, even though that's how it looks when you break down the chain of events and such. I killed a man, and within a second, he went from being a threat to a lifeless piece of meat. Nothing more than meat. That's all I could think about. *Meat.*" I turn to my friends. "You know?"

Fia holds up a hand. "You did what you *had* to do. Right?"

"Yes."

"Okay. That's all that matters."

And there it is. The acceptance. Just like what Travis gave me.

"Thank you," I say. This time, there are no tears.

Then I head into the bathroom, shut the door, shed my clothes, and take a shower.

It lasts twenty-three glorious minutes.

NINETY

CITY PARK.

Three hours before I meet with Dr. Brock.

It's just Travis and me—Fia elected to stay back in the room. I don't blame her. This is a fool's errand.

I look at the treasure map again, not needing to.

"Where?" Travis asks.

I scan the area. The park is the largest I've ever been in, but the directions my dad wrote are pretty clear.

"Over there," I say, pointing to a group of trees on the south side of a natural history museum. "I'm pretty sure over there."

We walk, the smell of freshly cut lawn drifting into my nostrils. A group of teens tosses a Frisbee while a dad kicks a soccer ball with his son. It's all so easy. So simple. So carefree.

Whether I find the note or not, I'm glad I'm here. Part of me feels like a little girl again, while another part insists I still am.

We get closer, and then it becomes obvious.

The tree.

Holy shit.

The tree.

It's right here, right in front of me. And it's exactly as my father described.

"This one," I say, hardly breathing.

"You sure?"

"One hundred percent sure." I point to a spot about ten feet up from the ground. "There's a group of three trees right off the pathway on the south side of the museum," I recite. "The one in the middle is tallest, and there's a crook about ten feet up where the limbs branch out. Perfect place to stash a little treasure." I point up.

"Jesus," Travis says. "That's it. I see it right there."

"I know." I scan the trunk, which is nearly three feet wide at the base. "I don't know how to get up there."

"Well, how did he get the notes up there?"

I try to access those memories but find nothing specific. A vague sense I've been here before, but that's it.

"Well," I say, "the notes were in pop bottles. Wouldn't be hard to toss them up here. Just hard to retrieve them."

Without a word Travis walks to the tree, wraps his arms around the base, then does the same with his legs. Then, slowly, he shimmies his body upward, inches at a time, a feat of strength I wouldn't have expected from him.

"I climbed trees all the time growing up." He grunts. "Haven't lost my touch."

When he reaches the part where the thick trunk morphs into limbs, Travis straddles two of them and peers down. "Holy fucking hell."

"Don't mess with me," I say. "Don't you dare mess with me."

"I'm not." He reaches down and unearths a Coke bottle, and it may as well be Excalibur for the excitement I feel. "There's another." His arm goes back down and grabs an identical one. "And paper. There's paper inside."

"Drop them. Please, just drop them to me."

He releases them one at a time, and I track the bottles as they fall, then land with soft thuds into the grass near my feet. Seconds later, Travis himself drops, landing with a louder thud.

I pick up a bottle.

Years of grime cake the outside, but it's still translucent enough to see that Travis is right. There's a rolled piece of paper inside. I can't see any writing, but I can tell it's not a crisp piece of paper. The top is curled and warped, as if it was waterlogged at some point.

I peer into the neck and determine the piece of paper expanded enough that it won't just slide out. Then I turn the bottle upside down and shake it a few times, proving myself right.

"Gotta break it," Travis says.

Funny. I don't want to break it. As if that would be destroying an important piece of my past. A stupid and illogical thought but nonetheless true.

"You do it," I say, handing him the bottle.

"Okay." With stunning casualness, he throws it against the concrete pathway, where it shatters.

Travis reaches for the paper.

"Don't," I tell him. "Let me."

I walk over and reach down, plucking the browned and crusty rolled sheet of paper from the path. The second I touch it, I have a rare rush of sentimentality. If this turns out to be my father's note and not mine, then that means he *touched* this. My father wrote on this. In just a moment, I'm going to see the same handwriting I've seen on all my birthday cards over the years. And maybe the words he wrote to me will make me understand something about him. About why he loved me but also left me.

I take a moment before unrolling the sheet. Try to still my mind. But most importantly, try to lower my expectations.

It doesn't work.

I unroll. The paper is brittle, and I'm worried it might just crumble in the process.

It doesn't crumble.

But I almost wish it had.

Because when I open it fully, there are no words.

There once were, that much is obvious. But now there's merely a series of faded blobs, dozens of little Rorschach tests, the ink having been assaulted into something unrecognizable after years of sitting in a fucking tree. Destroyed by hundreds of rainy and snowy days.

"What does it say?"

I don't answer him.

I pick up the other bottle and smash it into the concrete. I already know this paper will be just as damaged, but it feels good to break something.

I pick up the paper, rolled even more tightly than the first.

Doesn't appear as warped, as if perhaps the neck of the bottle was pointed down, insulating it from the elements over all these years.

My heart leaps, but just a little, for it's out of shape.

I carefully pull the sheet open, at first finding nothing, but then I flip it over.

And there, in the handwriting of a little girl, four words:

I love you, Dada.

And a heart.

A single heart, jaggedly drawn by an unsteady hand.

But this heart is at least complete. Intact.

Mine, however, is broken.

NINETY-ONE

TWO THIRTY-THREE.

I lean back into a stiff and large antique chair in the Brown Palace lobby, the back and sides of the chair gently curving inward, making me feel like a bug freshly perched on a Venus flytrap. But the chair is just right. It's not comfort I seek but anonymity, and this piece of furniture offers that better than any other in the room.

I'm here early, just in case Dr. Brock arrives before three. A companion chair sits right next to me.

This'll do. We can talk here.

The lobby fills for a few moments with a flurry of people, and then suddenly they're gone, as if the hotel is breathing guests in and out of its lungs. My back is to the reception area, my gaze directed to the glass entry doors.

Deep breath.

Fia and Travis are waiting in the hotel room. They both volunteered to come, nearly insisted, but I declined. I want to hear Dr. Brock's plans for us before bringing my friends to him.

Two forty-one, and is there anything more maddening than waiting?

My bladder nudges me, telling me I could kill a couple of minutes by peeing. I retort by telling it I arrived early specifically not to be distracted by such things, that I want to keep my eyes on the lobby doors. Besides, I just peed up in the room. My bladder has no reasonable counterargument other than to elevate the nudge to a sharp poke and whisper sweet nothings in my ear. *You know you have to pee. Wouldn't it feel good to pee? If you do it now, you won't be distracted during your meeting. C'mon, it'll only take a minute...*

God damn it.

I take one last glance at the front lobby doors. No one is walking in. So I cross the lobby and make my way to the bathroom.

Inside, it smells of flowers.

I do my business as fast as I can, make my way to the sink, wash my hands. The pump soap is a light purple, but it's not the source of the floral aroma. That comes from a bowl of potpourri on the marble countertop, its contents chaotic and colorful, once-living things now dried to a crisp, and even in death, they emit beauty through their scent. Makes me wonder what other things still smell naturally good after death.

I can't think of anything.

Perhaps only flowers.

I dry my hands and head back to the door. Just as I clasp the handle, it comes to me.

"Freshly cut lawn," I say aloud. Lawn grass still smells good after death. Better, even.

I allow myself a smile of mild satisfaction, then open the restroom door.

Sebastian stands on the other side, a smirk on his lips and fierce, fierce laughter in his eyes.

NINETY-TWO

MAYBE THERE'S A CHANCE, illogical as it seems. A chance he doesn't know it's me, that his memory is naturally fuzzy. That he's standing outside the women's room waiting for someone else to come out.

Those odds fall to zero when he opens his mouth.

"Hello, my brilliant girl."

I'm standing with the door held open, one foot remaining inside the bathroom. "I'm not your anything," I say.

He tsk-tsks me, and how annoying that sound is. "Right now, you're my everything."

"I'll scream."

"No, you won't."

"And why not?"

"Because we have your friend," he says. "And if you make a scene, she dies in a very bad way. Very bad."

I try to calculate if he's lying; his face gives nothing away. It's promising, though, that he made no mention of Travis, which means he's most likely bluffing about having Fia.

But still.

"If you had her, you wouldn't need me."

"Normally, that would be true." His voice is caramel, his gaze poison. "If you had behaved yourself back at the diner, none of this would be your problem. But I have a terrible habit of holding grudges, and the one I have against you is...significant."

A woman and a little girl walk up to the bathroom, each dressed like characters from *Gone with the Wind*. High tea, I figure, knowing that's a thing in this hotel. The woman eyes Sebastian up and down, as his body is blocking their way.

"Excuse me," she says.

"My apologies, please." Sebastian takes two steps back to allow them to pass.

I hold the door open and make a face as the woman walks into the restroom. I'm trying to conjure my best expression for *help me*, but it doesn't seem to work.

Here I am, door still open, Sebastian eyeing me from five feet away, and I'm wondering what to do. How certain do I have to be that Sebastian is lying about Fia for me to start screaming, or tell the woman in the bathroom to call the police? Ninety percent? Ninety-nine?

Funny thing about reason.

It collapses in the face of fear. A beautiful, intricate sandcastle wiped away by the most boorish and common of waves.

I can't chance it.

Can't take the risk that he has Fia and will make her death especially agonizing if I don't do what he wants.

I release the door and walk out of the bathroom.

There it is again, that smirk. So pleased with himself.

We'll see.

"Walk in front of me," he says, then points to my left, toward the back of the lobby. "This way."

And I follow. I have to follow.

And how I hate that I do.

NINETY-THREE

HE STEERS US TO the back of the lobby and through a set of double doors. The doors lead not to the outside but to the parking garage, dark and smelling of damp concrete. When we parked here yesterday, I thought the garage had the feel of a mausoleum. That sense intensifies now.

He's taking me to Fia's car.

When we reach it, I see Sebastian's Oldsmobile in the neighboring space.

"Stop," he says.

He walks around me, his hand brushing my butt. No accident.

He crouches at the back of Fia's car and taps her license plate.

"You didn't change the plates," he says. "A screwdriver and another car, that's all it takes. Thirty seconds of work, and it would have made it a lot harder to find you. Impossible, maybe." He stands, stretches, casual as can be. "But my boss? He has a lot of money, and he's willing to spend that money to get what he wants. There are many people on his payroll, even in this country. Private investigators. *Policía*. And people like me, simple working men. All willing to spread out and check parking garages all over the place. Chances were slim but not zero." He makes a sweeping gesture with one arm toward the car. "And here, like a thing of magic, is the car. Same plate."

"I guess I'm not educated on the criminal mind," I say.

In fact, I've read four books on the criminal mind and can't believe we didn't consider changing the plates.

"Bad for you, good for me."

"I know you don't have her," I say. "You want me to tell you where she is."

Sebastian wags a finger and flashes those teeth. Those shining teeth. "You're right."

"I don't know where she is," I tell him.

"And yet here you are. Here is her car." He takes a step closer. "Quite a coincidence."

"Yes. A coincidence."

He squares off, scanning me up and down, his arms at his sides. If this were a movie, this is when he'd hit me. *Pow*, right in the jaw, just to set my expectations straight.

I summon the memory of a self-defense manual I read when I was thirteen, then take a small step back, split my stance, and shift most of my weight to my back leg. I don't raise my hands—not wanting to appear too aggressive yet—but I think I can be fast in getting my hands up if he tries to punch me.

His smile remains, and he does not punch me.

Instead, he kicks me in the right kneecap.

The movement is sudden, swift. A snake strike.

I fall to the ground, feeling more pain from my hip hitting the cold concrete than the blow to the knee. He delivered enough force to collapse but not to impair me. All calculated.

You're my everything.

"Get up," he says.

I do, slowly, and with pain.

Then I hear something.

Footsteps.

Somebody's running, and from the sound of it, they're closing in fast.

I turn my head and, for just an instant, make out the blur of a man who slams full speed into Sebastian.

Holy shit.

I focus.

Travis.

NINETY-FOUR

SEBASTIAN LETS OUT A grunt from the impact as both men fall to the concrete.

Travis is smaller and lighter than Sebastian and I'm guessing much less experienced in fighting. That means I have only seconds to help him gain an advantage. Problem is, I have no idea how to do that.

As the men flail on the dirty and hard garage surface, I rush over and begin kicking Sebastian as hard as I can. Oh my god, does it feel good to unleash the fury of my right foot against this asshole's body.

I manage to get in three strikes to his back and side before he sweeps out an arm and pulls my leg from under me.

I crash on the same hip from moments ago, the pain searing.

Eyes. Get your fingers in his eyes. Blind him if you have to.

For a moment Travis is on top of Sebastian, his face twisted in rage and fists raised high. I make my move, shoving my fingers forward, just as Travis slams his arms down for the attack.

But Sebastian's too fast, too trained.

He parries Travis's blows and counters with a swift arc of an elbow to the side of his head. The connection is fierce and devastating, collapsing Travis into an instant heap on the ground. In the same movement, Sebastian spins on the ground, away from me, and unsheathes a gun from his ankle.

He remains crouched, the gun aimed at my head.

In my peripheral vision, I see Travis struggling to get to his feet.

"Who the fuck is this?" Sebastian says. He's only mildly out of breath.

I don't move an inch. "An innocent bystander who watched a man assault a woman. There might be others. They might have called the cops."

He spits on the ground. "There are no others." He shifts his aim to Travis, who freezes and raises his hands. "It's just us. And now there won't even be him."

Now I break my gaze and look over to Travis. His expression isn't one of fear. Just disappointment.

"I tried. I'm sorry." He wheezes. "At least I didn't run away."

"No," I whisper. I think my heart will actually burst if he dies right here in front of me. "You didn't run away."

I look back at Sebastian and hold out a hand. "Don't. It's not worth it."

"Worth it? You don't know my value system." Sebastian keeps the gun pointed at Travis's head.

All I can visualize is Bain's shattered skull. Brains on the floorboard.

I wait, saying nothing. Travis does the same. The three of us are frozen in time, silence creeping, death imminent.

Finally, Sebastian slides his weapon back into his ankle holster. "It would be too loud. But you are staying with us."

He gets to his feet and smooths his hair with his left hand. To Travis he says, "I need to decide what to do with you, and you can help yourself by not moving a fucking inch from the spot where you stand. Do you understand me?"

"Yes."

Then Sebastian turns to me. "This is when you tell me where she is. No more games."

The calmer his voice, the more unnerving it is.

I try to push down the throbbing pain in my hip. "She goes by *Fia*," I say. "At least to me. I'm sure that's not her real name, but I like it. I suppose you know her real name, but in a way, I don't want to know. Everyone likes a little mystery, don't you think?"

"You're not telling me what I want to know."

"I'm just telling you the person you're looking for is known to me as Fia, and I couldn't tell you where she is. Not right now, not in this very moment."

I inch back ever so slightly, figuring our best chance comes from an attack by me. He won't expect it. He's a guy who's not afraid of girls.

But hell if I won't try everything in the world to make him scared of me.

My best chance is a punch to his throat. The heel of my hand into his Adam's apple. I have no idea if that's something I can pull off, but I have to try.

I calculate my odds of success at 5 percent.

Five. Violet.

And how close that word is to *violent.*

"I see it in your eyes," Sebastian says to me. "You are thinking of things, I know. Please don't make me hurt you again. I will, but I don't enjoy it. It's disrespectful."

I freeze, but my mind keeps racing. Then my swirling thoughts stop on the image of Sebastian's partner inside the convenience store.

It gives me an idea.

"Your partner, did he die? Back at the gas station. I heard gunshots."

He absorbs the words, taking several seconds to do so. Then he tilts his head and considers me with a renewed focus. "You were there?"

"Yes."

"Wait." He holds up a hand, as if pausing the universe. "You were *there*, at the gas station?"

"I don't like repeating myself. But yes."

He narrows his eyes, tenses his jaw. I can see him getting angry. Perhaps very angry.

This makes him unpredictable. Irrational.

Also vulnerable.

So I poke the beehive.

"I saw the two of you," I say. "Again, you might call the whole thing a coincidence, but I think we were at the gas station together for a reason. I was inside the store and told the cashier you two were coming in to rob and kill him."

"What are you doing?" Travis whispers, but I don't have time to explain. Truth is, I'm not totally sure *what* I'm doing. I feel this is a moment when my instincts take precedence over logic. Maybe I've learned something living in the wild.

Or maybe I'll get us both killed.

I gauge Sebastian's eyes. His pupils are wide in the dim garage light, casting him as feral.

"You knew the shopkeeper had a weapon," he says. "You knew Mani would be coming back inside for his change. You calculated the man would panic, make an aggressive move before Mani even opened his mouth."

"So his name was Mani. I was wondering. He didn't look like a Mani."

Red creeps up Sebastian's neck and spreads across his face, and deep crevasses ripple his forehead. He looks like a man trying to remain calm as fire consumes him.

"*Mani* was my brother. Not my brother in business. Not my brother in friendship. He was my fucking *brother*."

This doesn't surprise me. Nor does it bother me.

"You said *was*," I say, "so I take it he's dead."

He squeezes his eyes shut as if trying to push past the pain, and it's only when it's too late that I realize *that* was my opportunity. In his pain I should have leaped over and punched his throat. But in seconds his eyes are open again, and he's never looked at me with such intention as he does right now.

"I'll find her," he says. "Your *Fia*. You'll help me find her. That was all I cared about until now. I was going to let you go. But now?"

He pauses, but it's a rhetorical question, so I wait for him to finish.

"Our friends down south have what they call a Colombian necktie. Do you know what that is?"

I mentally scour volumes of books and articles, come up empty. "No."

"It's when they slice your throat, reach their hand up through the opening, and pull your tongue back down and through the slit in your neck. And I must tell you, I have a fierce desire to feel my hand inside your neck." He licks his lips like a jackal. "I've never killed anyone this way, but for you, I think this could be a first." He nods over at Travis. "Him, I'll just shoot."

We remain locked with each other, and I put all my energy into maintaining eye contact. Death is near. He will be the last person I'll ever see, and what a strange thought that is.

"I'm sorry," I say, mostly to Travis, a bit to the rest of the world.

Our only hope is to attack. Travis is hurt, and I don't have any fighting skills that I know of. We'd have to coordinate perfectly for even a chance of success. And once either of us makes a move, Sebastian will shoot. But, really, there's no other choice. The whole thing is a desperate bishop-to-queen-four move when checkmate waits on the other side.

I tense, coil. I hope Travis sees this and does the same. But then Sebastian takes his own defensive stance, anticipating an attack. All that remains in me is a fierce will to live, and what little good that did to every soldier killed in every war.

Then...

"Penny, is that you?"

The voice comes from a man, but not a stranger.

I know that voice.

I turn and see the dimly lit shape of him.

And a second shape next to him. Smaller. Feminine.

I've never been so happy to see Dr. Brock in my life.

I just hope Sebastian doesn't kill us all.

NINETY-FIVE

IN MY PERIPHERAL VISION, I see Sebastian swiftly tuck his gun in his pants beneath the small of his back.

Dr. Brock approaches out of the shadows.

He's dressed in his standard institute outfit: gray slacks and a white button-down shirt with his sleeves rolled to the elbows. On his left wrist is the white Swatch watch I gave him for his birthday two years ago.

And the woman…who the hell is she?

As she steps out of the shadows, I can tell I've never seen her before. She's maybe just a few years older than me, though her cream business suit and briefcase give her an air of maturity. Jet-black hair cascades to her midback. And that face, the perfect mix of profound beauty and deathly seriousness. The image that comes to mind is that of a female praying mantis, who devours her partner right after mating.

"Boy, I tell ya, I hardly even recognized you, it's been so long." Brock reaches up and gives my shoulder a firm squeeze, all the while maintaining a dopey grin I've never, ever seen on him. And what is that accent he's using?

"Dr. Brock," I say. I think about blinking a Morse code warning signal to him but decide not to risk it.

Brock puts his hands on his hips and gawks at me. "What're the chances? I mean, what are the chances? Running into you in a parking garage...in *Denver*. What the heck are you even doing here?"

I search for an answer but struggle. "I...I..."

He cuts me off and turns to Sebastian. "Sorry to interrupt, fella. Believe it or not, I was Penny's tenth-grade *chemistry* teacher, all the way back in Wisconsin. I wouldn't even have recognized her except for the way she was standing. Saw her silhouette and just knew it was her. Something about the posture. I dunno; it's weird. But it's unique to everyone, like a fingerprint. I said to my daughter here, by golly, that's Penny. And sure enough—"

Chemistry teacher.

Chemistry.

Dr. Brock used that word before. When I read that self-defense manual when I was thirteen, I was intrigued by a particular passage about subterfuge. Specifically, the wisdom of having a trigger word. I remember discussing it with Dr. Brock, who said, *If you're in a bad situation, you should always have a word that someone else will recognize as a distress call. A good choice is a class you might be taking, a subject you're studying. Physics or chemistry.* Chemistry *is good because you can use it in a variety of ways.*

Now I know he's sending me a message. Telling me he knows this is a bad situation. And this woman? Whoever she is, she's sure as hell not his daughter.

"She called you *doctor*," Sebastian says, his voice monotone. "You are a doctor *and* a teacher?"

Brock laughs in the absence of anything funny. "Well, I'm sure not a medical doctor…faint at the sight of blood every time. I've got a PhD in chemistry, been a high school teacher for fifteen years. Say, where're my manners, anyhow?" Brock thrusts a hand out to Sebastian. "I'm Lance Brock, no *doctor* necessary."

Sebastian doesn't take his hand. Doesn't even look down at it. "I'm afraid you caught us at a bad time. We're in quite a rush."

Brock keeps his hand extended. "A rush?" he says. "Didn't look like it. You all were just standing here chitchatting, far as I could make out." He turns to Travis. "And who's this? This your fella, Penny? Boy, you got some kind of shiner right there, son. Looks like you were on the losing end of a bullfight."

Sebastian takes a step forward. "If you don't mind."

Brock cocks his head to him. "I'd love to catch up with Penny here… she was my star student, you know."

"I'm sorry," Sebastian says, "but I must insist you leave us."

Now I feel it.

The crackle of electricity in the air, energy in desperate need of a violent discharge.

Sebastian takes one step closer to me.

My gaze locks in tight to one thing.

His exposed throat.

I don't think twice.

NINETY-SIX

I LUNGE, THRUSTING MY arm in the direction of Sebastian's neck.

His head turns just as I attack, resulting in him exposing his Adam's apple at the perfect time for the heel of my hand to drive into it.

I can feel his neck move. Not quite cave in but shift in an unnatural way.

A thousand needles shoot up my wrist and travel all the way to my elbow. Painful and beautiful.

His eyes bulge as he grabs his throat, and as he collapses to one knee, the furious gasping begins.

Travis leaps at the opportunity, racing over and unleashing his fists on Sebastian's head and chest, over and over.

"I got this," the woman says. She makes quick work of pulling Travis off Sebastian, then dragging the beaten and gasping Sebastian between two parked cars before rolling him onto his stomach.

She puts a knee in the middle of his back.

His gasping is subsiding, replaced by more normal breathing.

Brock points at Travis and says to me, "Is this the boy you told me about? He's with you?"

"Yes."

"Okay." Brock nods over to Sebastian. "Now tell me who *he* is, but don't be long-winded about it. We don't have much time."

I blink. "Have you ever known me to be long-winded?"

"*Penny.*"

So I tell him, needing only thirty seconds to convey the essence of my relationship with the Nicaraguan.

The woman speaks from the shadows of the garage. "He's coming around."

I look. Sebastian's starting to thrash, a counterattack. The woman remains crouched with her knee on his back, but it won't be long before he throws her. She's so small. She'll stand no chance against him at full strength.

It's dark in here but not so much that I can't see what happens next. The woman wraps her hands around Sebastian's head, seizes his chin with her right, and applies weight on his skull with her left. With a fierce and sudden movement, she twists Sebastian's head until I hear the bones fracture. A rolling popping noise, like walking on a massive sheet of Bubble Wrap.

She releases her hands, dropping Sebastian's lifeless head on the cool and dirty concrete.

"He's defecated," she says. "Won't be long before someone notices the smell. Though it *is* a parking garage."

Travis gags and spits up a glob of puke. "Jesus, fuck, are you kidding me?"

Brock wears a look of horror on his face, which he struggles to erase. "Drag him out of sight," he says. "We need to go."

The woman drags the body with seemingly little effort to the front of a parked car.

"What is happening?" I whisper. "What the fuck is happening?"

"Not here. We need to find a place to talk."

I sweep my gaze along the level of the garage. No one else is here.

"Follow me," I say. Travis and I lead, followed by Dr. Brock and the woman who just killed the Nicaraguan assassin.

We take them back inside the hotel.

I can't help wondering if it's a mistake having our backs to them.

NINETY-SEVEN

THE ELEVATOR DOORS OPEN. The cab is empty.

On the ride up, no one speaks.

I glance over at the woman. She keeps her gaze forward, her face calm, even bored, as if returning to work after a lunch break.

Travis wipes his mouth more than once and pats gently at his swollen eye.

The doors open. There's lingering pain in my hip and knee, but not enough to make me limp as I head to our room with the others in tow.

Fia should be inside.

Please let Fia be inside.

I take the key out and open the door.

Thank god.

Fia's standing at the window. She spins around as she hears us.

"That was quick. How did everything—" She pauses that question once she sees Dr. Brock enter the room. "Oh."

I tug on Travis's arm. "What were you doing there? You were supposed to stay in the room."

"Saving your ass, I'd say. I was watching you from the corner of the lobby in case you needed help."

"You easily could have died."

He shrugs. "And yet I didn't. Told ya I wouldn't run away again." He cracks a grin.

That smile.

Dr. Brock says, "We just arrived and saw you walking with that man, so we followed you."

I turn from Travis to Fia. "Fia, this is Dr. Lance Brock. Dr. Brock, this is Fia. No last name that I know of and very likely not her real first name."

"Nice to meet you," Fia says. "I think."

The unknown woman ghosts in the doorway behind Brock but doesn't enter the room.

"Who the hell is that?" Fia asks.

"Well," Brock says, "while we're mislabeling ourselves, let's assign her a name." Brock turns to the woman. "Any suggestions?"

The woman thinks for a moment. "Eve."

"Eve it is." Brock turns back to Fia. "This is Eve."

"But who *is* she?" I ask. "What happened down in the garage… *Who is she?*"

"She's with me. She's okay."

"What happened in the garage?" Fia asks. "And Travis's eye?"

"So your name is Travis," Brock says. "I'm also curious about your eye, but that'll have to wait. I need to talk to Penny. Fia, Travis, I'm afraid you aren't anyone to whom I can disclose anything."

I look at him. Look at this man I've spent thousands of hours with over the past decade and wonder, for the very first time, who he is.

"Bullshit," Fia says. "I'm with Penny. If she wants me here, I'm staying."

Brock's face is calm on the surface, but oceans roil just beneath. "I don't know you, which means I don't trust you."

"It's okay, Fia," I say, not really believing it myself. "He's here to help. At least I think he is."

Fia shifts her focus back and forth between Brock and me, weighing something in her mind. After a few seconds of this, she says, "Fine."

Brock gestures to Eve. "Take her and Travis and wait in the hallway."

"Wait," I say. "I don't want them to—"

He puts up a hand. "It's fine. You were right...we *are* here to help."

I hesitate, which is acquiescence enough for Eve to turn and open the door.

Travis walks out into the hotel corridor first. Fia follows. "You look like a lot of fuckin' laughs," she says to Eve.

Eve remains silent as she follows them outside.

The door closes.

The hotel room is silent.

"You should sit," Brock says.

I stay put. "I'm just now realizing I've done everything you've told me to do for ten years. I think I'll stand."

"Fine. Depending on how many questions you have, this should only take a few minutes."

"How many?"

"Is that important?"

"You know me better than anyone."

Brock nods. "Okay, let's say...nine minutes. What color is that?"

"I think you know."

"I do." He turns and finds a chair, the uncomfy fancy kind with brass buttons up and down the arms. He sits in it, closes his eyes for a moment, and exhales as he reopens them.

"Black," he says. "Deep-space black."

NINETY-EIGHT

I DON'T WAIT FOR him to start. "How old is she?"

"Who?" Brock asks. "Eve?"

"Yes."

"I don't know. Maybe thirty? I just met her."

"What's her IQ?"

He smiles. "I'd guess lower than yours. Higher than most."

"Is she from the government?"

"Yes."

"Doing what?"

Brock raps his fingers on the arm of the chair. "I don't know exactly. But you can guess from her skill set, it's not the General Accounting Office."

"Why is she here? I wanted you to come alone."

"And I didn't want to come at all because this is not the kind of thing I'm suited for."

"You mean killing?"

His expression remains flat. "Eve works for the person who's interested in you. She sent her along to make sure we brought you back."

"That sounds mildly threatening."

"There's no threat intended, I assure you." He leans forward in his chair and intertwines his fingers, the posture of a parent lecturing a child. "Like you, Eve's abilities drew interest from the government since she was young."

"Like me?"

"I don't know Eve. Like I said, I just met her. But I do know...have known for some time...that there is a small agency within our government that maintains ongoing interest in exceptional citizens. I'm guessing Eve is an exceptional person, and she was eventually recruited to work for this agency."

All this is surprising. None of this is surprising.

"What, like in the CIA? NSA?"

"I have no idea."

"And what was she recruited to do?"

"Again, that's not been shared with me."

"And that's why you went to go work in Washington?"

"Partly. The opportunity arose from Eve's employer, but it's true I'm working at the National Institutes of Health. I'm a doctor, Penny. Not a spy."

I have so many questions, and my nine minutes are rapidly dissolving. "When did they start getting interested in me?"

"Four years ago."

"Four *years?*"

"Yes. And it was the first time I heard anything about it. As far as I know, you are the first person from Willow Brook who has warranted their prolonged attention."

"You've been hiding this from me for four years?"

"There's nothing much to hide. We haven't been grooming you for anything. We've just shared some of our findings about you with them. Your accomplishments."

"What? So they can eventually recruit me to go kill people in parking garages for them?"

"I don't think your talents are suited to that kind of work. But I can see how your abilities could be tailored for a variety of positions in service to the country."

Now I'm pacing because if I don't physically move, my head just might explode. "Why are you sounding like a Marine Corps recruiter? 'Service to the country'?"

"I believe it's an honor to work for the government. That's one of the reasons I left for my current position."

"My god, you've been brainwashed."

"Nothing of the sort. You're exceptional, Penny, but you're young. You know more things than most humans will ever know, but you don't know everything."

"Clearly not." Then something occurs to me. "So when I up and left Willow Brook, that set off alarms, didn't it?"

"There was concern, yes." He straightens in his chair. "But you need to understand something. There was never a plan to *draft* you into some kind of service. You are someone who's going to be in great demand for both the public and private sectors. Should you eventually be in the employ of…this agency…it will only be because you've chosen to do so. So when you went, for lack of a better term, AWOL, they just wanted to make sure you were okay. That you were safe."

I can't stop my mind from racing. "I don't understand. So, what, the government wants to hire me to draw or something? Design the next twenty-dollar bill? Besides drawing and remembering things, I don't see what value I bring at all."

Brock looks at his watch. "I don't know what their designs for you are. Look, we really need to get going."

"But you haven't told me *anything*."

Brock stands, and I know he's out of patience. An uncommon occurrence with him, but I've seen it before. "I've told you as much as I know and as much as I've been authorized to say. I'm just the messenger, and I'm only here because you asked me to be." Brock walks up to me, stands close. "I truly believe if you come with us, you will be safe, along with your friends. I'm worried about you, Penny. I want to help you, but only they can, not me."

"And what if I say no?"

He lowers his voice. "Don't make this difficult. Let them help you. Let them help all of you."

Of all the things I know, what to do next isn't one of them.

"I need to use the bathroom."

At that moment Fia, Travis, and Eve come back inside the room, heralded by Eve insisting it's time to go. As I head to the bathroom, I exchange a look with my two friends, trying to convey both concern and comfort. I have no idea what the next few minutes will bring, but I hope Fia and Travis receive one simple message from my look:

Be ready.

NINETY-NINE

IN THE BATHROOM, THERE'S cold porcelain and gleaming glass. Fluffy towels dangle on chrome bars. Baby bottles of shampoo and lotion stand at attention. I settle myself on the lid of the toilet, then close my eyes.

Deep breath in to four, slow exhale to four. Voices from the other room, but seconds later they're little more than blobs, indecipherable.

And I burrow deep within, the sensation both concerning and comforting, like feeling snug within the belly of the animal that just swallowed me whole.

I'm here.

Silence, silence, silence.

I need you.

Nothing.

Not for the longest time.

In that darkness, that thickness, thoughts of death creep in. Not daydreams of me actually dying, but a consideration of the forever afterward, or most likely the eternal nothingness. When I look back on what

I remember of my life, the idea of death was always more a curiosity than a fear. Sitting in the bathtub as an eight-year-old, dipping beneath the surface, remaining there until the struggle became a sublime tranquility, coming up for air almost out of spite.

But always wanting to know what death would feel like. Never considering suicide as a means of ending pain, but often considering death as a wonder worthy of its inevitable exploration.

I never wanted to kill myself.

But part of me has always wanted to die.

Maybe that's why my mind randomly conjures various scenarios of my demise.

And then.

In the mud of my brain.

A voice.

Well, hey there, Pen Pen. Whatcha got yourself messed up in now?

Dad.

ONE HUNDRED

HI, DAD. MY EYES are squeezed shut so hard, I see stars. *I hear you. I see you. But it's not really you. I'm the one telling myself what to do, not you. I'm the one giving myself advice. I'm not sure you have much to do with anything.*

Well, that hurts a little, baby girl, he says. Maybe more than a little. But I'm willing to hear you out. So here you are in this hotel room face-to-face with another man. A man you thought you knew well. But now you have some doubts. About that woman, Eve, for sure. But maybe some doubts about the good doctor himself. And you want to know what to do next, but you don't want me telling you because I'm not real. So, you tell me, Pen—what's the move?

Voices in the other room bleed through the bathroom door, but I try to block them out. *I'm scared about the headaches. They're getting worse.*

You're right to be scared, he says. That brain of yours is a powerful thing, but even Superman has his kryptonite. Could be all your time in the wild is sending that wondrous mind into overdrive. Maybe you should stop right now. Just use your sense. Go back with that doctor of yours; let him lead you to safety.

I don't want to be saved by anyone.

We all need saving, darlin'.

Did you? Did you need saving?

This is a question he does not answer. After a few seconds of silence, I ask him a different one. *Daddy, why did you leave?*

Oh, we're back to Daddy *now?*

I just want to know.

I know you do. And it breaks my heart that I can't tell you. But maybe it'll come to you. And all I am is a collection of neurons firing in your brain, accessing those long-lost memories. So maybe it'll come to you.

Cool air rushes into my nostrils. *I don't like not understanding.*

And then it occurs to me, for the very first time, that maybe I shouldn't be using these moments with him to ask what to do.

Maybe I should use them to remember the past.

I remember every aspect of my life since waking from the coma nearly fourteen years ago.

But I remember nothing of the accident itself.

I want to know, I tell him.

That night?

Yes. About the rabbit hole.

You sure?

Yes.

Silence.

Could be remembering such a thing will give you a headache you don't recover from. That's a hell of a memory to tap into.

I slowly nod. *I want to do this.*

Well, then, he says. *Well, then.*

ONE HUNDRED AND ONE

IN THIS BATHROOM WITH its cool tiles, fluffy towels, and army of soaps and shampoos, I rise from the toilet and stare into the mirror. Stare into my eyes, past the irises, the blood vessels, the nerve endings. Right into my brain, this brain that's miraculous but, really, unique like all others.

I need to know what to do next, whether to let Brock take me away or forge a path into the wild on a forever basis, with all the risks either choice carries. Yet somehow this is not about Brock but about my father. He's the root of everything, my reason for beginning this journey and perhaps for ending it. Without the need to find him, there would have been no Travis, no Arthur's comedy club, no Bain, no Sebastian, no Fia. There would have been death, for that's one true constant in life, but I wouldn't have *made* death.

Penny Bly, accidental genius, maker of death.

"I want to remember," I say to Dad.

For so many years, all I could do *was* remember. Every sight, sound, smell. Every word on every page. Every chord of every song. The number of ceiling tiles in my room at the institute.

Sixty-seven.

Sixty-seven.

Campfire orange.

But yet there are the gaps. There's the time before and the time after, with a body-crushing fall down the stairs as the marker in between. I remember little of the time before, and maybe this is the moment to access those memory cards.

I close my eyes.

Summon the dots.

Think until it hurts.

And.

And then.

It's as if all the dots in the universe appear at once, and when it happens, it's as brilliant and beautiful as the face of God Herself.

First, I remember.

Next, I die.

ONE HUNDRED AND TWO

THIS IS WHAT I remember:

He was angry that night, the night so long ago when I was seven.

In 1973.

I didn't realize he was a drinker, but here I see it, the Jim Beam bottle and dirty glass. Daddy sits in the vinyl chair at the kitchen table, and the aluminum legs squeak as he shifts his weight.

God damn it, he says. *What am I going to do?*

Not just you, Mom replies. She stands at the other end of the table, staring down with those fire eyes. *Us. This is happening to all of us.*

Where the hell am I gonna find another job?

We're in a recession, Mom says. *So probably nowhere.*

It's the first time the little-girl version of myself hears the word *recession*.

He downs what's left in his glass, pours another.

You know I don't like it when you drink, my mother says. *You get angry.*

You drink a helluva lot more than I do, he replies. *Besides, I'm already angry. This'll take the edge off.*

You know it won't. You know it'll make it worse.

He bolts from his chair, nearly knocking the whiskey bottle over. *Christ, Linda, let me do what I want. I just got fired.*

Take it easy.

I focus on the thump, thump, thumping of the little vein just outside my father's right eye. A little baby snake waiting to burst from its egg.

Don't tell me to take it easy. If I wanted to take it easy, I would. But I don't. I want to put my fist through the goddamned wall. That's what I want. As a starter.

With that, I run from the kitchen and up the stairs.

Those stairs.

I know minutes later I'll be coming back down them headfirst.

Seven-year-old me puts my hands over my eyes, muffling the shouting, but somehow that makes it all the scarier. So I shut the door of my bedroom, and maybe that helps, if only a little. On my bed, crammed between well-worn stuffies, I face the wall, wanting the noises to end. I don't think he's usually like this. Not usually loud like this. Not so angry. Sometimes mad, okay, but not like this. He can't be. This can't be him.

Dad throws the door open, and there's no thingy to keep it from stopping, and the doorknob plunges right through the wall.

You see what you made me do? Now we got a hole in the wall. Another thing I can't afford to fix.

I say nothing.

Your mom's been calling you. It's dinner.

I'm not hungry, I tell him.

I don't care. You're eating. We're not wasting any food, especially not now.

He turns and disappears into the hallway.

I don't move.

Seconds pass, maybe the length of a TV commercial.

And when he returns, he's mad, *so* mad, his face scrunched and red. When he grabs me, all I can think of is that claw game at the amusement arcade, those teeth biting into the toys and candy.

He carries me and puts me down with a thud at the top of the stairs.

You're gonna eat.

I say nothing.

I don't move.

Go on, now. Go downstairs.

I hold firm.

Mom appears at the bottom of the stairs, takes one look, huffs up the steps, and joins us. The three of us are here, occupying a postage stamp of space at the top of the stairs, and it feels for all the world like no one has any purpose other than to rage.

Including me.

I've had it with both of you, my mother says. *Dinner's on the table, but I'm not eating. I'm taking a pill and going to lie down.*

Dad: *Your daughter won't listen to me.*

And my mother's next words may as well be her life motto: *I don't care.*

Dad's voice steadies as he tries to reason. *Penny, please get up now. Go get your dinner. You need to eat.*

I rise from the floor, turn around, gaze down at the wooden steps. Teeth. They look somehow like teeth.

I don't move any more. Not an inch. Not yet.

And there's that energy between my parents, crackling and spitting, a swirling mix of anger, desperation, hopelessness. I can feel it on the back of my neck, searing into my skin.

And I know what happens next.

Sometime in the next few seconds, my mother pushes me down the stairs, into those teeth, forever altering everything about my life.

But then maybe.

Quite possibly.

It will be someone else's hands I'll feel on my back.

After all, it's not my mother saying, *Don't make me ask you again.*

And there it is.

This realization.

All these years.

All the blame.

All the sadness, and I've been wrong the entire time.

My mother never pushed me down those stairs.

My father did.

That's why he left. He ran away out of sheer guilt, out of not being able to own up to what he did. He left before he got arrested, and my mother never told anyone what he did. Always insisted it was an accident, protected this man who tried to murder his own daughter, and why on earth would she do that?

Penny, I'm not joking, he says. *Walk down those stairs right now.*

I wait for the shove, my stomach clenching in anticipation. Wait for the pain, and will there be any in a memory?

And then.

I suddenly *become* my younger self. I *feel* my insides. Feel my heart, my fingertips, my brain. My thoughts and emotions, coming to me in a tidal wave. And this little girl, this poor little girl standing at the top of those stairs, is thinking about happiness. About how she doesn't know what it is, not exactly, and she's worried she'll never find it. She thinks happiness must be like stepping foot into a new world for the very first time, a world endlessly different from her own, one with brilliant colors, exotic creatures, and thick air filled with the aroma of a million flowers. She thinks happiness is a place—*any* place—other than this one.

Happiness is the wild.

As this sad little girl fixes her gaze to the bottom of those stairs, she thinks about one of her favorite Disney movies, *Alice in Wonderland*. Dear Alice must have felt this very thing as she stared into that rabbit hole. In no way knowing Wonderland was on the other side, but surely sensing *something* was there. A different place, wild and untamed, exciting and, perhaps, a little scary. But perhaps happiness can only be born from this exact mixture of ingredients.

Rabbit hole, little Penny whispers.

I repeat those words twice more, my adult self knowing they'll be the last I speak for three days.

I'm going to count to three, Dad says. *Last chance, Penny.*

Then those toothy stairs disappear, and the whole stairwell becomes a hole, sure and sudden, a black void that sucks in all light and memory. My seven-year-old eyes widen not just at the sight of it but at its promise. How real it seems, as if this other world opens to me right then and there, but only for a short time, and if I miss my chance, it'll be gone forever.

The wild.

It's mine for the taking.

No creature ever flies without first standing on earth, then making a leap, and how brave that first force of will must be.

Dad finishes counting to three.

There is no shove.

The adult me always thought there was, convinced myself I could still feel the hand between my shoulder blades if I focused enough, but it's a phantom memory.

With my father so close, I can smell his rank breath, I spread my arms and leap from the top of the stairs.

I do not fly.

The hole disappears, for it was never there, and what a terrible thing to realize when you've already surrendered to gravity.

In the darkness and pain that follows, there is screaming.

It sounds like my mother.

ONE HUNDRED AND THREE

IN THE DARKNESS BEHIND my eyelids, as I stand in this hotel bathroom, there is comfort. Blackness, the kind that exists between memories.

I'm aware. Aware of the darkness, aware of how it very much feels like deep sleep, that place of both safety and sheer vulnerability. I have finally remembered what happened that night when I was seven, feeling a mix of shame, pity, and acute sadness for the little girl who leaped to her almost death.

But the awareness of this sudden memory is on the perimeter of my consciousness. I cannot open my eyes, cannot move, will not let light in. So maybe this is death after all. Maybe conjuring this memory finally completed the job the seven-year-old version of myself could not. This, my last attempt at using my brain to figure out the best course of action, is the thing that kills me.

Perhaps this is heaven, and what a disappointment.

Maybe it's hell, in which case, not so bad.

And then these considerations fade to black, like the afterglow of a shut-off flashlight.

In its place, life.

Life, and the worst pain I've ever known.

ONE HUNDRED AND FOUR

IN THAT LIGHT AND in that pain, screaming.

My screams.

My eyes open now, and I'm nearly blinded by the dull glow from the bulbs above the bathroom vanity. My voice echoes against the bathroom tiles, ricocheting like bullets inside my skull.

"Penny!"

Fia throws open the bathroom door and grabs me by the shoulders. I'm on my knees, my head clutched in my hands, certain I've shattered my brain into a thousand fishhooked pieces.

"Move," I manage, then lunge for the bathtub. What little I've eaten comes up in a single violent burst, splattering against the pristine canvas of the porcelain tub.

Travis's frantic voice is in the doorway. "What's happening?"

Then Brock speaks. "What's wrong with her?"

"Don't you know?" Fia yells. "You're her doctor. *You* tell me what's happening because it doesn't look good."

"Penny." Dr. Brock is closer now. Right behind me. "Can you hear me?"

Through the needles in my brain, I can. But I don't acknowledge him. The initial crippling stab of pain has given over to the sensation of a nest of spiders hatching in my skull. Horrible but manageable. I keep from screaming by moaning instead, something to create a tremor, a buzz I can focus on, and the pain softly abates. If I am dying, *truly* dying, then this reduction in agony is simply my soul succumbing.

Hanging over the edge of the tub, the foul stench of my stomach contents attacking, I wonder this:

Does it matter if I die?

Who would care?

I go through a quick mental list as I keep moaning and clutching my head. There aren't many names to process.

In fact, I only come up with two.

Fia.

Fia would care if I died.

And Travis.

Travis, with that smile. I think he would miss me.

And maybe that's enough. Maybe two people not wanting you to die is the most you can hope for.

The pain lessens another notch, enough for me to fall silent, wipe my mouth, sit back on the bathroom floor, and look up to Fia and Dr. Brock.

No.

I'm not dying.

But I'm scared as hell.

The four of us fill the small bathroom. Eve is still in the bedroom.

"Jesus, you okay?" Travis asks.

"No."

Brock crouches before me. "We need to get you to a doctor."

I don't say anything.

Eve then appears in the doorway, stands there like a wraith discovered behind a closet door. "No doctor," she says. "Not yet. We need to get her, and her alone, out of here. Right now, while we still have things under control."

"Under control?" Travis gets into her face. "You have shit under control. And you're just going to take her and leave us? That wasn't the deal."

"There was no deal that ever concerned you," Eve says.

"Take it easy," Brock says to her. "Penny's health is the primary concern right now."

Words fly all around. I do nothing but sit here, too weak to do anything, too hopeful the pain will keep subsiding if I stay motionless, and still uncertain of what to do next.

Their words glaze until they're just a string of gelatinous sounds I can't understand, and as the four argue, I look up at Dr. Brock.

In all these years, I've never drawn him.

Not once.

Could have at any time, as his face was etched in my mind the moment I met him. But I've never put pen to paper and summoned that face, letting the dots do their business. It's not that I never considered drawing his portrait; I've gotten close to doing so on occasion. The truth is—and it's a hard truth to admit, even to myself—I never wanted to see Dr. Brock's essence for fear I wouldn't like what it revealed.

He's been the only good thing in my life for so many years. The person providing stability. A father figure. And what if I drew him and found the face of a man who might abandon me? It's what I always feared and, after ten years together, what finally happened.

I have no paper, no pen, no strength.

So I try something else.

There, on the bathroom floor, voices swirling around me—angry voices, insistent voices—I close my eyes and imagine that piece of paper. A sheet of ivory card stock, nice and thick. The pen, a Bic black-ink roller that doesn't smear. My hand holding this pen, hovering above the blank canvas. I can see it so clearly. Every detail, even the little blond hairs on the back of my hand, near-invisible wisps.

The pain in my head bubbles up again as I focus, but I keep going. I summon those dots, welcoming them despite the hornet's nest they rattle.

But the dots.

They don't come.

The pain worsens.

Fuck.

But maybe for the best.

I feel myself slipping into unconsciousness.

Seconds before I pass out, I have another thought.

I recall my first phone call to Dr. Brock from the wild. He said something very specifically about how trauma affected my abilities.

Yes. Trauma.

Then everything goes dark.

And what a relief it is.

ONE HUNDRED AND FIVE

WHEN I COME TO, I realize I wasn't out long because I'm still on the bathroom floor with the aftertaste of vomit in my mouth. The throbbing in my head is now just a dull ache, but it's unwilling to let go of me completely.

Travis's face hovers over mine. "Jesus, you look like shit."

Fia shoves him aside. "You with me, girl?"

I squint, bringing Fia into focus. "I'm not sure...I'm with anything."

Brock says, "We need to get you to a hospital."

Eve's voice cuts through the small room. "No. That's something we absolutely cannot do."

"She could be *dying*."

I relax my gaze, stare at the white plaster ceiling with little brown water rings here and there. "I'm not dying."

Brock takes a knee and leans in, eclipsing Fia.

"Talk to me," he says.

It burns as I swallow. "That's the last time I'll ever do that."

"Do what?" He's close enough to whisper.

My gaze returns to the water spots. Things have changed. Everything has changed. I remembered the past, and it nearly killed me.

I'll never in my life ask that much of my brain again.

Better to be simple and alive than all-knowing and dead.

"It's different now," I say.

"What does that mean?"

"Tell me a number," I whisper.

He shifts his weight. "A number?"

"A number. A number I know. You know what I mean."

Eve's voice: "What the hell is this?"

"Be quiet," Brock tells her. Then, to me, he says, "Twenty-four."

I wait and wait. Finally, I say, "Nothing."

"What do you mean, *nothing?*"

"Just…nothing."

"Come on, Penny. You know twenty-four. Magenta, of the neon variety. You don't see that color?"

"I don't see anything. Everything feels empty. Give me a memory problem."

"Okay," he says. "It's okay. The first line of the Magna Carta. In Latin."

"I don't know."

What looks like panic creeps over his face. "How about in English?"

I shake my head.

He places his palm on my forehead. "You're not feverish. What's going on?"

Then I yell, and how good it feels. "I don't know what the fuck is going on!"

Brock stands and turns to Eve. "Get paper and a pen."

Eve heads back into the bedroom. Fia's no longer in sight, but Travis is still standing in the doorway, looking down at me, tight concern on his face. "What's happening?"

I shake my head.

As Brock paces in the bathroom, I lie still on the tiled floor, trying to disappear inside myself, find comfort in my own thoughts. But there's no comfort anywhere.

Eve reemerges. "She was on the phone," she tells Brock.

"What? Who?"

"The woman. Fia. She was just hanging up a call when I walked in there. She wouldn't tell me who she was calling."

"Never mind that." He takes the pad of hotel stationery and logoed ballpoint from her and offers them to me.

It takes as much strength as I can muster to sit up, and as I do, the blood drains from my head, resulting in a tidal wave of dizziness. When it passes, I take the items from Brock.

He squats so our faces are level. "She's standing right there. You don't even need to memorize her face. Now draw her."

"Okay," I say.

"Just like always, Penny. Nothing different. Just like always. Find the dots."

I look down at the pad of paper, the small white sheet that seems without boundary or definition. Pen held in my hand, hovering, waiting for utility. And I stay this way for a minute before he says anything.

"It's there. You see it, right?"

My voice is flat. "I don't see any dots."

"Okay, okay. Give it a bit longer. Sometimes it takes longer than other times. We both know that. But Eve. See her face. Even without looking up at her, you can see it, every last detail, can't you?"

"I don't understand what this is," Eve says. "All we're doing is wasting time."

Brock shushes her.

I wait another full minute before replying, my focus solely on the notepad. "No," I say.

"You're sure," he says. "You're absolutely sure."

I nod. "Nothing."

"Okay." He stands and turns to Eve. "This was always a possibility," he tells her. "Hers is a case of acquired savant syndrome, smart by *accident*. A genius through brain injury. There was always the chance it could similarly disappear through trauma, and that's what seems to have happened."

"What?" Eve's gaze shifts to me, her look one of doubt. "What trauma?"

"The intense stress she's been under," Brock answers. "The violence she's been exposed to. A *part of*. Not to mention lack of sleep. Perhaps malnutrition. Then culminating with the events of today. Her headaches are the result, and that seems to have altered the nature of how her brain works."

"Bullshit," Eve says.

Brock holds firm. "She's broken."

Eve leans down into my face. "Tell me the fourth sentence of *Moby Dick*."

"I don't know."

"What key is Beethoven's *Moonlight Sonata* written in?"

"I don't know."

"What time did you wake up on your fourteenth birthday?"

"I don't know!"

Brock eases Eve back by her elbow.

"She's normal now," he says. "As normal as anyone in this room."

I decide to stand, and my legs are still wobbly after I do. Brock turns to me and places a hand on my shoulder, something he knows I don't like.

"You had a responsibility to yourself," he says, his voice calm but firm. "Really, to humanity."

"It's my life," I say.

"There was a plan for you," he continues. "You'd outgrown me, and Dr. Cheong was going to take you to the next level of your preparations. And then you left. And now you've…I don't know. You've short-circuited yourself."

"I didn't do this."

"Yes, you did. Don't you see it?" He drops his hand and shakes his head, wearing a look of disappointment I've never seen him wear. "You had so much potential."

And those words.

They kind of break my heart.

Fia appears. "I called the police and reported an active assault in this room. So time's up. We all leave now, but we're sure as hell not going with you."

"That wasn't necessary," Brock says.

"Not for you to decide."

"Everyone out of this room," he says. "I need one more minute with Penny."

Travis starts to protest, but Eve cuts him off. "One minute only," she says. And then the three of them leave us alone.

It's suddenly so quiet.

We stare at each other. This man I've been close to for so long. Who, in a way, loves me. But who also was developing me as some kind of tool. Perhaps even a kind of weapon.

Which man will he be now?

"They can help you, you know."

"I know," I say.

"Your problems don't go away just because Eve goes away."

"I know."

"You're sure this is what you want?"

I've never been so sure of anything. "Yes."

He smiles. Just the smallest thing, but in that smile, I see a world of understanding.

"Okay, then."

"Okay, then."

In the distance, sirens.

ONE HUNDRED AND SIX

WE WALK OUT OF the bathroom, me on shaky legs.

Eve and Fia are midargument, but they stop and turn.

"Good," Eve says. "You're moving. Let's go."

"Yes, let's go," Dr. Brock says. "But they're not coming with us."

This solicits a collective *what?* from the other three.

"Penny needs medical attention," Brock explains to Eve. "And her candidacy as a future employee to your agency appears gravely diminished. Maybe gone altogether."

Candidacy as a future employee. God, who the hell does Eve work for?

"That's your professional opinion?" Eve asks.

"It is."

She considers, but not for very long. "I don't care. She's coming with us."

"Just a minute—"

"My orders are to bring her back with me, broken or not," Eve says. "And I don't take orders from you. You were allowed on this trip as a courtesy."

Brock raises his voice, a thing I've rarely witnessed. "No, I'm here at Penny's insistence. And I'm telling you she's no longer the candidate she was a day ago. You and I are leaving. Penny's friends need to take her to the hospital. End of discussion."

Eve's mannequin expression remains unchanged. "This was never a discussion," she says, and to my surprise, she calmly walks up to me and seizes me by the left wrist.

Her grip is so strong, I might as well be in handcuffs. Even at full strength, I know I wouldn't be a match for her, but weak as I am, it feels like I'll be doing whatever she tells me to do.

"Bitch, let her go," Fia says, her feet rooted in place.

But Travis.

Travis doesn't waste a moment.

He's a flash out of the corner of my eye, and suddenly he's lunging for Eve. The Travis who so eagerly fled the dangers of the comedy club now keeps throwing himself headfirst at any new threat against me.

Eve releases me as Travis lunges with his right fist, which Eve dodges with only the slightest movement. That leaves him off-balance and exposed, perfectly positioned for her to strike with full force into his sternum. Which she does.

He collapses at once, gasping as if the earth's atmosphere suddenly vanished.

"Travis!"

"Don't move," Eve tells me.

"God damn it," Brock says. "Stop this right now."

"She's coming with me. I don't care what happens to any of you, but I have a job to do." Then she looks at me, and in her stare, I see a determination I don't think I've ever possessed. "You're coming with me."

And in this moment, I realize the last thing I want is to be part of whatever agency Eve works for. I don't know anything about it, but looking at this woman makes me believe there is no free will as part of the job description.

"I'm not going anywhere with you," I say, my words sounding impotent even to me. I match her fighting stance with my own, but it's just a show. I'm still struggling to remain upright.

We're separated by less than four feet, a distance that can be closed in the blink of an eye by a fast fighter.

I'm guessing she's fast.

The sirens grow louder.

Fuck.

I have to do *something*. There's no choice but to engage, and for a second, I see Bain's face again. The rage. The hate. The sickening desperation.

Here she comes.

Eve advances. She doesn't strike but instead slips behind me. I turn only halfway before Eve has me in a headlock. Her arm around my neck, her bicep bulging against my throat.

I'm helpless. I'm so helpless, and I hate it more than anything. It's like my death dreams all over again.

I reach and claw at her grip, but her arm is cemented in place.

She whispers in my ear, "I'm going to zip-tie your wrists behind your back now. If you put up a fight, I'll squeeze your neck until you pass out, and then I'll tie you."

As an added warning, Eve squeezes a little harder and cuts off my air for a moment. It's horrifying at first and then, weirdly, a bit of a relief. As if it wouldn't be the worst way to die.

"Stop it right now!" Brock shouts. "This is insane."

But it's not insane, I think. This woman killed a man just a half hour ago. It's clear Dr. Brock had no idea what he was getting into with this trip. He was only trying to help me, and now I'm being conscripted into whatever war Eve's bosses have planned for me.

She eases her grip, enough for me to talk.

"I'll scream," I say. "I'll scream as loud as I can."

There's a tinge of delight in her voice. "That scream will last only a second."

Travis, still on the ground, has steadied his breathing but doesn't even seem aware of his surroundings.

I feel Eve's pressure shifting, telling me that she'll have to release my neck in order to zip-tie my wrists. Maybe I can take advantage of that moment. Maybe a sharp elbow to her ribs. I just need more time. A few more seconds to ready myself.

"He told you," I say, "I don't even have my abilities anymore. I don't know what—"

"*Enough!*" Eve's voice booms. "We're getting out of here right now."

I wheeze against the pressure. "Don't do this. You were once where I am. You get it. Please don't do this."

Her breath is hot in my ear. "This is my job."

"Well, I hope you get fucking fired."

The pressure on my neck is back, stronger than before. Eve's not going to take any chances. She'll choke me into unconsciousness and drag me out of here if she has to.

As the air seeps away and my vision blurs and then darkens, I see a flitter of movement.

Fia.

Fia with a gun in her hand.

She must have grabbed it from her apartment back in Minnesota.

Thank fucking god.

"She's with me."

ONE HUNDRED AND SEVEN

THE RELIEF DISAPPEARS AS fast as it came.

A shifting behind me. I have the momentary thought that Eve's releasing me, but this proves as untrue as it is illogical.

No.

She's not letting me go.

Her arms suddenly wrap around my waist, and her hips dig into my own from behind. I think I hear something click, but I'm not certain of anything anymore.

Eve's breaths are hot and shallow in my left ear.

"This is when you leave," Eve says to Fia. "You drop the gun and leave."

Her voice. So calm.

Fia and I lock eyes from a distance of no more than ten feet. I watch her gaze drop a few degrees, and when it snaps back up, there's an upsetting look on her face. A look of resignation.

This is when I look down for the first time.

Eve's using both hands to hold the shaft of a knife.

The tip rests on my stomach.

ONE HUNDRED AND EIGHT

STILETTO.

That was the clicking sound, I realize.

I consider the blade. Five inches. Maybe six. Thin polished steel.

All Eve needs to do is push a few inches. So easy to do. The blade will slip with ease past my flesh and to all important things inside.

Against my will, my brain conjures the anatomical chart from the thirtieth edition of *Gray's Anatomy*. Page 174. If the knife inserts the way it's currently being held, perpendicular, it'll either pierce my stomach or small intestine.

Brock's gaze darts between Fia and Eve. He doesn't know what to do, I think. He didn't see any of this coming.

None of us did.

"Take it easy," he says. "This has clearly gotten out of control. We need to think about the problem of the police showing up at this door. Let's all calmly leave this room together, then discuss what to do next."

All I can think of is the blade.

The thing I've always feared, based on nothing.

But that's how fears work.

I'd rather be stabbed in the heart.

If she stabs me in the heart, I'll die instantly.

Just not the stomach. *Please not the stomach.*

Fia holds firm to her gun, creating with it a rope that connects her eyeline to Eve's.

"No," Fia says. "This is when you drop the knife."

And those words are all the motivation Eve needs to ease the knife into my belly.

ONE HUNDRED AND NINE

SHARP PAIN, THEN ICE.

Did she just stab me? Is this really happening?

"Oh my god, oh my god…"

Eve removes the blade as quickly as she slid it inside me.

"Relax. That was less than an inch." Her arms remain wrapped around me. "No vital organs. You'll need stitches, but if this bitch behaves and puts the gun down, that's all you'll need."

My eyes bulge in shock and disbelief. This horrible thing I imagined for so many years just happened. Cold steel sliding through my hot flesh.

There's still some pain.

But otherwise?

Not nearly as bad as I imagined. Mostly because, if Eve was right, the cut isn't deep.

I can feel the blood running down my skin, into my jeans. I don't want to look down.

"Jesus Christ," Fia says. She glances down to my abdomen, and based on her expression, it's clear the bleeding is obvious. "You're a fucking psychopath."

"I'm an employee," Eve says. "That's all I am. I do my job, and right now my job is to bring her with me. Do not assume I will be deterred by you."

"How about I put a bullet in your head?" Fia says. "I don't imagine your employer would like to lose an expensive toy like you."

Eve shifts her weight, and there it is again, searing pain. Another cut, this one a few inches over. I gasp against the horror of it, try to remind myself the cut isn't deep. Try to tell myself it's not as bad as I always thought it would be.

But this time Eve does not pull the blade out.

This time she twists it.

And this?

This is every bit as awful as I had ever imagined.

ONE HUNDRED AND TEN

"NO...NO..." MY VOICE is half rasp, half shriek.

My legs start to buckle, but Eve holds firm. Seconds later, she removes the knife again.

"Fuck!" Fia screams. But she keeps the gun level with Eve's face.

"Last chance," Eve says. "Put the gun down. She won't die, but she'll suffer. You don't want that."

I look over to Dr. Brock, to his frozen stare, his mouth half-open. He's shut down in disbelief.

The gun quivers in Fia's hand. "What do I do?"

I try to talk as calmly as I can, moving as little as possible. "I don't want...I don't want any more death. Please. Just no more. No more dying."

I lock in tight with Fia, holding eye contact like I never have before, speaking to her through my gaze, not knowing if my message is getting through.

Fia lowers her gun a few degrees. Aims it at the floor but keeps her arm extended.

"On the floor," Eve says.

What I told Fia through the ether was that I'm not scared of death. I don't *want* to die, but mostly I don't want pain. I don't want hurt.

But more than anything, I don't want to be like Eve.

All I want is to be in the wild.

"No more death," I say, this time my voice a whisper.

Fia nods.

Then she lowers her gun all the way.

Damn it.

The message didn't go through.

I am so incredibly tired.

"Put the gun on the floor," Eve says. I can feel the woman's confidence through the relaxing of her grip.

"No more dying," I repeat, hoping she understands what I mean.

Please, Fia, don't put the gun on the floor.

Fia puts the gun on the floor.

It's over. And I lose.

We all lose.

Then I shift my gaze to Travis. He's still on the ground, seemingly invisible to everyone but me.

And in his right hand, his butterfly knife.

He's had it with him the whole time, never revealing it. Not in the comedy club, not with Sebastian, not in his attack on Eve.

But there it is, gleaming steel, still folded, clutched in his right hand.

We look at each other. He smiles, and it's one of pain and uncertainty.

Still.

That smile.

The knife has a very distinct sound as he opens it one-handed, a whoosh and then a clacking of metal as the handle and blade snap into place.

Eve looks down. It's too late.

Travis plunges the knife directly into the top of her left low-heel pump and into her foot.

From what I can see, the blade goes clean through.

ONE HUNDRED AND ELEVEN

THE HOTEL ROOM ERUPTS into chaos.

Eve drops her own knife, screaming, and releases me.

I run over to Fia, who snatches her gun from the floor and keeps it laser locked on Eve's skull.

Eve crouches over her bloody foot, the blade still very much in place. Her screaming quickly subsides into desperate heavy breaths as she labors over her wound.

"*Jesus Christ,*" Brock gasps. "Everyone *stop.*"

Travis manages to collect Eve's knife, gets to his knees, and crawls away from her.

"Good thing it was just her foot," Fia says. "I'd have gone for the heart."

I can't stop staring at Eve. Such a bizarre and unsettling sight, this powerful and capable woman, so perfectly put together, carefully studying the gore on her own body. Then, with fierce determination and the swiftest of movements, Eve yanks the butterfly knife free, stands, and turns toward Fia, the blade held in Eve's outstretched hand. Her composure lasts only a second before her wounded foot betrays her, collapsing her to one knee. The blade doesn't waver in her hand.

A wave of nausea assaults me as a fresh eruption of blood spouts from Eve's foot, but I hold it down.

"I don't think so," Fia says, the gun still aimed squarely at Eve's head. "Drop it."

"I'll fucking kill all of you," Eve says. "I swear I will."

The odd thought comes to me that it's such an unprofessional thing to say. Even given the circumstances.

"Enough!" Brock shouts.

For a moment I expect Eve to attack or even try throwing the knife, but she finally lets it fall to the floor.

I survey the scene.

Eve, bloodied, defeated, angry. Brock, as uncomposed as I've ever seen him. Travis, huddled on the floor, Eve's knife in his hand. Fia, ready to kill at a moment's notice.

"Let's go," I say.

"Don't," Eve says, holding out a hand as if grasping for a life preserver in rough seas. "You can't go. I have to take you back."

"Shut the hell up," Fia says.

Eve eyes the knife she just dropped, clearly contemplating one more counterattack. Fia must notice this because she fires the gun, aiming just above Eve's head. The bullet hits a mirror on the wall, which rains shards.

The sound is jarring, painful, beautiful.

"Okay, okay," Eve says.

The sirens are now directly outside the hotel, blaring for a few more seconds and then silencing. I can picture cops spilling out of their patrol cars and rushing into the hotel lobby.

"Did you tell them our room number?" I ask.

"Hell no," Fia says. "Told them a floor below us. But we need to avoid the elevator. Take the stairs."

"Okay. Travis, can you walk?"

A pause. "I...yeah, fuck. Yeah, I think so." And with that he gets to his feet, a bit unsteady at first and then gaining balance.

I glance back at Eve, who seems to be using all her willpower to fight back tears.

Then I take one last look at Dr. Brock.

And he takes one last look at me.

"Go to a doctor," he says. "Not just for your wounds but for your headaches. I know you won't, but I feel compelled to tell you."

"Okay."

"Call me. I can still maybe help you."

"No," I say. "From here on out, I'm only helping myself."

He nods.

"Thank you," I say. Meaning it. For everything.

Then I touch my shirt and look at the fresh blood on my fingertips. Funny, I can hardly feel the open wounds where Eve cut me. Maybe the adrenaline is masking the pain, but in the moment, I feel like I could run a marathon if I had to.

"You're welcome," he says.

There are no more words. Nothing to contextualize our relationship in this final moment. Ten years of a near-familial bond that ends when I turn and walk to the hotel room door. I open it for Fia and Travis, who pass into the hallway.

I follow and close the door behind me.

No reason to look back.

I'll never see Dr. Brock again.

ONE HUNDRED AND TWELVE

July 21, 1987
Tuesday

ABOUT HALFWAY BETWEEN DENVER and Los Angeles.

Sunrise.

Interstate 15 stretches deep into the far distance, a long asphalt ribbon disappearing west. It feels to me like chasing the tail of a rainbow. Chasing a prize that may or may not be there.

Sometimes the chase is enough.

The three of us haven't spoken much since we left the Brown Palace yesterday afternoon. It's not that we have nothing to say, but rather that we collectively know now is the time to keep moving west and focus on efficiency and execution.

We spoke when we decided to steal a set of plates from another car in the parking garage. Mumbled a few words over dinner in a roadside Denny's. Debated over which radio stations to listen to.

We spoke when we needed to treat my two stomach wounds, which we did on our own after getting sanitizing supplies and a needle and thread at a supermarket. The stitching was painful enough to bring me to tears, but the cuts were actually much smaller than I'd expected. It's a crude job, and I need to make sure to keep the wounds clean, but I hope it's enough to keep us away from a hospital.

We decided Travis doesn't need a doctor. The damage from Sebastian and Eve left painful bruises but seemingly nothing more.

But mostly we've been listening to music in the car and keeping our thoughts to ourselves.

Now, as the sun rises, Whitney Houston longs to dance with somebody for the third time this hour.

Fia turns the radio off.

We sit in silence for another five minutes, the outside air whooshing as the car pushes seventy miles per hour.

Then Fia asks me, "What's the first sentence of the Magna Carta in Latin?"

I keep my gaze fixed on the sunrise as I answer.

"In primis concessisse Deo et hac presenti carta nostra confirmasse..."

ONE HUNDRED AND THIRTEEN

July 22, 1987
Westlake Village, California
Wednesday

WE REACH 1263 HAWK'S View Court.

I check the address once again on the envelope from my father's final birthday card. The same address on the treasure map, the location of the final notes.

I mouth the words over and over, hardly believing the address on the paper matches the house directly outside the car.

"Are you freaking out?" Fia asks.

"Given the circumstances, I'd say I'm allowed."

The car idles at the curb.

"Place is kind of a shithole," Travis says, craning his neck. "At least compared to the other houses around here."

He's right. From what I've seen so far, Westlake Village is a quaint little Los Angeles suburb that definitely skews upper-upper middle class. The houses around town are ample if not mansions, and there are enough tennis courts and swimming pools to give the impression the collars worn here are assuredly white.

But this house.

At 1263 Hawk's View Court.

This one has a grimy edge to it. Weeds in the lawn. Overgrown shrubs. Trash cans in the driveway, while the neighbors' cans are all hidden out of sight. Faded paint and sun-warped siding. The house isn't a blight—it's probably even a tad nicer than my home in Wisconsin— but it's definitely the wart of the block.

"No car out front," I say.

"And all the curtains are drawn," Fia says. "Can't tell if anyone's in there."

"It's Monday. He could be at work."

"What kind of work?" Travis asks.

I try to slow my breathing. It doesn't work. "I haven't the faintest idea."

Fia shuts off the engine and turns to me. "This is a big deal. Like, a *big* fucking deal."

"I'm aware of that."

"You haven't seen your dad in, what, twelve years or something?"

I blink. "Thirteen years, eight months, and sixteen days."

"That's a long time."

"Yeah. A long time. And you're making me more nervous than I already am."

"Sorry." Fia peers out my window to the house again.

"You want me to come in with you?" Travis asks.

"No."

He shifts in the back seat. "You should at least take Fia's gun."

I turn around. "To see my father? No."

"I'm just saying—"

I cut him off by holding up a hand. "No more guns. No more...no more *anything*."

"Suit yourself."

I turn back to the window, back to the house. Try to see if there's anything that connects with me. Some kind of look, some kind of energy, *anything* that suggests my father is in there. That he lives here.

But nothing.

Just a tired, worn-out house most likely belonging to a tired, worn-out person.

I say nothing as I get out of the car.

The day outside is what people from California brag about: sunny, not too hot, and certainly not humid like in Wisconsin. I think I smell the ocean, though that's at least twenty miles away.

I've never seen the Pacific Ocean. Or any ocean, for that matter.

I walk up the driveway, avoiding the occasional crack in the concrete because I don't want to break my mother's back and such.

The front door has a few missing paint chips. It also has a peephole. Dad will get a chance to see me seconds before I see him, and that doesn't seem fair.

What if he looks through and decides not to answer?

That's about as heartbreaking a thing as I can imagine.

"Stop it," I whisper to myself. "What happens, happens."

I've made it this far in the wild after all. Just one last thing to do.

I take a breath and force myself to ring the doorbell before I chicken out.

Then…

Nothing.

I don't even hear the bell echoing from inside. Is it working? Should I try again? Or should I knock?

I'm sweating. Not a lot, but more than usual. Armpits, forehead.

My stomach flips a couple of times for good measure. There's a distinct possibility I might just up and puke right here, right on Dad's doorstep, and what a greeting that would be.

But still, nothing.

I'll count to thirty. If he doesn't answer by then, I'll come back. But how I don't want to. This is fucking excruciating.

I get to twenty-seven when I hear footsteps.

Twenty-seven: elephant gray.

I stop breathing altogether when I sense a figure at the peephole.

He's looking at me right now.

I smile, as if posing for a photo, but how phony it feels.

I love him and I hate him. There's no proper facial expression for such a thing.

The dead bolt clicks.

The knob turns.

He's opening the door.

I close my eyes, escaping into the dark for just three seconds.

ONE HUNDRED AND FOURTEEN

WHEN I OPEN MY eyes, I see my mother, and nothing in the world makes sense.

I blink. Once. Twice.

Well, not *exactly* my mother but close.

The woman standing in the doorway has my mother's eyes and facial shape, including the slight aquiline nose—a feature I didn't inherit. This woman appears younger, though all the alcohol has put at least ten years on my mother's life.

Same height. Same build.

The hair is different. Mom keeps her hair cut to her shoulders, but this woman wears hers long and free, brown kissed with gray, curly and borderline unkempt.

And the clothes. My mother would never wear these clothes. A tie-dyed skirt flowing past the ankles, a thin and loose floral-patterned blouse with intricate stitching and a hole near the left shoulder. Bare feet.

Mom would call this ensemble *hippie-dippie bullshit.*

"Hello," I say, not knowing where else to start.

"Sorry, honey," the woman says. "Maybe you can't read, but the sign on the door says *no soliciting*. That means I don't wanna buy whatever it is you're selling."

Wow. The voice.

There's none of the nasally Wisconsin accent, but otherwise the voice is indistinguishable from my mother's, and that's more jolting than even the physical similarities.

"I can read," I say. "And I'm not selling anything." I clear my throat before saying the words I can hardly believe I'm finally saying. "I'm looking for Jack Bly."

My words must be full of ghosts because the woman's lips part, her eyes widen, and she loses a few shades of color in the seconds that follow.

"My god," she says. "I never thought you'd actually come. *Penny?*"

I hear my mother in those last two syllables. So distinct. So exact.

Why did I name you Penny? Because you're pretty much worthless.

"Who are you?" I ask.

Tears well in the woman's eyes. "I'm your aunt, sweetie. And I haven't seen you in a very long time."

Aunt?

I've been told all my life that I have no extended family to speak of.

Dead, dead, dead. Everyone was dead, according to my mother. Car accidents, cancer, heart attacks.

But it makes sense.

She's too much like my mother not to be related.

"What's your name?" I ask.

She smiles, revealing yellowing teeth. "Gloria, dear. I'm your aunt Gloria." She takes a step forward, one tear spilling down her cheek. "Can I hug you?"

"No."

"Okay. I know you don't like to be touched. But I just thought—"

"How did you know that?"

"Why, your mother, of course."

I shift my weight, feeling a sudden urge to run away. But I force myself to stay in place because there are too many questions.

"You talk to my mother?"

"Not much," Gloria says. "Sometimes."

"She's never mentioned you."

She nods, causing that curly hair to bob. "I know. It breaks my heart."

I close my eyes again, needing to be back in the dark for my next question. "Is my father here or not?"

Gloria's answer comes after several seconds of silence. "No, I'm sorry."

I open my eyes. "Do you know where he is?"

Another tear joins the first in running down her cheek. "Kind of."

"Kind of?"

Then she steps back and opens the door fully. "You should probably come inside so we can talk. Do you want to do that?"

A swirling mix of intense disappointment and crushing curiosity overcomes me. My answer to Gloria's question comes in the form of me folding my arms and walking inside the house.

Shades pulled closed. Most of the lights off. The house is a mess, and I can only imagine how much worse it would look with good lighting.

"Have a seat on the couch," she says.

I head into the living room—and what a disjointed term that is for this space. The room seems more of a storage facility than a place to do any living. Boxes. Clothes. Newspapers. And the smell. In the corner of the room, two litter boxes, but not a cat in sight.

I move a full laundry basket off the couch and take a seat, thinking how incredibly lonely this house feels.

Gloria eases into a folding chair a few feet away.

"Do you live here by yourself?" I ask.

"Three cats," Gloria answers. "They might just make an appearance, though they're skittish around strangers."

"I suppose I am a stranger."

She nods. "I last saw you when you were six. You and your father drove out here to visit. Do you remember any of that?"

"Some," I say. I don't tell her that the recently unearthed memory fragments of that trip are what spawned my entire journey into the wild.

Gloria leans back as much as seems possible in that chair, then looks up at the ceiling. "That was an emotional time. Even more so after you left and headed back to Wisconsin. My sister and I pretty much stopped talking then, and then she broke off all contact with the family for some time after your fall."

"So you know about that?"

Gloria directs her focus back to me. "Of course I do. I know everything about you. What you became. Your years at that school."

"Willow Brook Institute for the Brain."

"Yes, yes." Her eyes glisten as she rubs her hands. "We do have *some* contact, your mother and I. Couple of times a year, we'll talk on the phone. That's as much as she lets me into her life. But she tells me everything about you. She's so proud."

Proud? My nervousness settles into a vague sense of dread. "Do I have other relatives?"

Gloria touches the small crystal around her neck. "My parents live in Oregon, have for some time. They don't talk to Linda at all."

Wow. Grandparents.

"I don't understand," I say.

"I know you don't. I'm sorry."

"Why would she shut off contact with you? What happened on the trip out here? And why wasn't she with us?"

She lets out a breath that seems to contain lifetimes. "Your father left a note here. It's meant for you. I think that will do the best job answering those questions."

The note.

There's a note.

Why is it I'm horribly sad at the thought of it?

I feel a looming conclusion to all I've ever wanted to know, and the thought of reaching it scares me. It scares me because I think there are no good answers to come.

"It was you," I say. "You wrote the birthday cards. All of them."

Gloria nods.

My chest tightens, and the sadness takes a massive bite out of me. I try to steady myself as I ask the one question I never wanted to. "He's dead, isn't he?"

Another nod.

My father's existence vanishes in that tiny movement of Gloria's head.

"What...what happened to him?"

I hold eye contact as I wait for the answer, wondering if my father's fate matches any of the fictitious ones my mother attributed to the other relatives.

Car accidents, cancer, heart attacks.

As it turns out, his is one Linda Bly never mentioned.

"Why, your mother killed him."

ONE HUNDRED AND FIFTEEN

FORTY-SEVEN MINUTES LATER, I leave my aunt's house, and as with my own home in Wisconsin, I'm certain I'll never return.

The note from my father burns a hole in my pants pocket. It's all I can do not to read it. I will later, when it feels right to do so.

I get into the car.

"What happened?" Travis asks. "You don't look so good."

"Can we just drive? I don't care where."

"Sure. Of course." Fia starts the car. "You okay?"

"No."

Fia eases the car down the street; neither she nor Travis asks more questions. Maybe I'll tell them, maybe not. I'm not sure I can even summon the strength to repeat the story out loud.

Dad is dead.

Mom killed him.

Killed him because she thought he pushed me down the stairs.

But he never pushed me at all.

I destroyed my family the night I decided to find out what it felt like to fly.

Gloria recounted the story, a story she'd kept quiet for nearly fourteen years. There was a fight in the Bly house that night, she said. Jack had gotten laid off and was in a terrible mood, worsened by booze. The arguing culminated at the top of the stairs, with Jack yelling at the seven-year-old me for not coming down to the dinner table. Suddenly, I was tumbling down the stairs, and Linda swore her husband had pushed me.

Your mother told me that's when things went fuzzy. She said all she knew was Jack was dead, and she was holding Jack's hunting rifle in her hands. But she didn't deny killing him. She killed him because he harmed the only thing she loved more than anything, and that was you, Penny.

Hard to imagine my mother ever loved me, certainly not enough to commit murder.

But I believe Gloria. It's logical. All these years wondering why he left, not understanding. As awful as the truth is, it's an answer that makes sense.

But fuck sense and logic. Fuck them to high heaven.

She took you to the hospital and left Jack's body in the house, Gloria said. *The following night she called me. I was surprised because, at that time, we really weren't on speaking terms. But we used to be close, and I guess I was the only person in the world she felt she could confess to. I was shocked and heartbroken when she told me what had happened. But…well, together we came up with a plan for her to…get rid of the evidence. I'm so sorry, Penny.*

When I asked where my father's body was, she refused to say.

I've told you more than I promised to already.

Then I asked her why she was telling me at all. And why now, after all these years?

Your mother never recovered after that night. And she got worse, much worse, and there were times I was worried about you, Penny, but then she'd tell me how smart you were and the things you were achieving, and I convinced myself you were fine.

She cut off contact with everyone—I think it was her way of dealing with it all. But she'd still call me from time to time, and she asked me to send you birthday cards from him. At first I thought it was cruel, but then I suppose I saw she was just trying to give you hope. So I did it, every year, sometimes driving long distances just to get a different postmark. It was a strange and heartbreaking way for her to show you a mother's love, but I did it.

And then this year—your twenty-first birthday—your mother told me it was going to be the final card, that she was done with the whole charade. Writing that last card to you was maybe the most painful thing I've ever done. And just before I mailed it off, I made a choice. A choice I kept secret from my sister. I chose to put my address on the envelope, and I told myself if you ever came to my house, I'd tell you the truth.

I had more questions, of course, but decided it didn't matter. Didn't matter if my father was buried in my own backyard all these years, maybe deep in the sand beneath a swing set that had long rusted over.

The knife to my heart isn't that my mother killed my father. It's that she didn't need to. Dad didn't push me down those stairs; it was a flight I was all too willing to take on my own.

And from that leap came a whole family's worth of shattered pieces.

I didn't tell Gloria the truth. I'll let it fester deep inside me, maybe until it eats me inside out.

As broken as I am from the news, there's nothing I can do to change anything.

Everything matters in the now, and nothing matters in the forever.

And I hate it.

The last thing Gloria said to me was this:

I guess I wrote my address down because I wanted some kind of control. But chasing control is a fool's errand, Penny. Letting go is a faster path to happiness than pretending any of us has the power to control anything.

And so here I sit in the passenger seat as Fia drives aimlessly. How I want to let go. And how hard that is to do.

Twelve minutes later Travis finally breaks the silence from the back seat. "So...now what?"

I think maybe all I'm doing is following in my mother's footsteps. Shutting myself off from everyone because it's the only way to cope.

But no.

I'm not my mother.

I'm not shuttered in a house, angry at the world, lost in regret, alcohol, and pills.

I'm in the wild, and there's so much more of it left to explore.

I turn around and look at Travis. "Now we disappear for real."

ONE HUNDRED AND SIXTEEN

July 28, 1987
Los Angeles International Airport
Tuesday

IT TOOK NEARLY A week, many phone calls, and fifteen hundred dollars, but Fia was finally able to get us new identities through some connections she'd used when she'd first come to the States. The documents arrived yesterday by Federal Express and contained instructions on how to paste and laminate our photos in the passports and on drivers' licenses.

We confined ourselves to a pair of motel rooms in Hollywood as we waited for the IDs to arrive. I finally got worried enough about the haphazard stitching of my stomach wounds that I chanced visiting a small walk-in medical clinic. It was all I could have hoped for. No questions asked, a cash transaction, and sutures that look professional. The doctor told me to come back in a week to have them removed. I said I would, but of course I lied. I knew I'd be long gone and will likely just take them out myself.

I ventured out on other occasions, losing myself among the summer tourists on Hollywood Boulevard, thinking how different this place was than I imagined. Crowded, dirty, desperate. I never saw a movie star, but there were plenty of folks who'd quite clearly burned up in the atmosphere.

Before heading to the airport this morning, Fia insisted on dividing her money with us. I refused, knowing my protests would do no good.

Fia simply said, *Take the goddamned money, bitch.*

So it was I found out how much cash Fia had left in her bag: $138,421. This didn't include the coins she had in the car, but those weren't part of the tally.

We split the cash equally.

Travis and I each placed our portions in hollowed-out hardcover books. I chose Stephen King's *The Stand*, and Travis decided upon James Clavell's *Shogun*, both volumes selected for their size.

The smog is bad today. Sky looks like dirty water.

We park Fia's Impala at the airport with the intention of leaving it here until someone steals or impounds it. It takes us two minutes to wipe it clean of prints.

The three of us walk side by side as we approach the glass doors of the terminal, which whisk open at our presence. Inside, the air from the AC gives me goose bumps. Or maybe it's just my nerves.

Fia's headed to Nicaragua. Going home to be with her family. I almost ask her if she thinks it's a good idea, if she can really be safe there. But I say nothing, knowing there's no keeping Fia from her family any longer. Funny, she was in Minnesota for so long, but once the idea of returning home took hold of her, she can't get there soon enough.

Among the throngs of people whisking by with frenetic energy, Fia turns to Travis and me.

"I guess I should go check in," she says.

"Okay."

"You know where you're headed yet?" she asks.

Travis eyes me. Despite the amount of time we spent together at the motel, the *what next?* conversation rarely came up. We knew Fia was heading back home, and all *I* knew was I wasn't. No going back for me. Not now, maybe not ever.

But now we need to figure things out.

First, a goal.

Then, a plan.

Just like Travis said all those lifetimes ago.

"You just going to run forever?" Travis asks me.

"Not forever. I'm going to disappear for a little while, then decide what to do next."

"How long is a little while?"

I shrug. "I don't know. Maybe a month or two?"

"Okay."

I reach up and touch his arm, a simple gesture I never would have made just a few short weeks ago. "You should go home," I tell him. "You had nothing to do with Bain."

"It was my car," he says. "The dude was found in my car."

"I know. But you can tell the police the truth. It was me." I correct myself. "Well, it was *him* because he was an evil piece of shit who deserved to die. But you had nothing to do with it."

Travis shoves a fist deep in his front pocket. "Not sure it's that easy to explain."

I let my hand drop. "What do you want to do? Not out of fear but out of desire. What do you want?"

He looks down at his feet, thinking. After a few seconds, he raises his head, and there it is.

That smile.

"I want to go with you."

My heart leaps. It's getting into better shape. "You sure?"

"Yeah."

"You don't sound convinced."

"*Fuck* yeah," he says.

I resist the urge to kiss him. There will be more opportunities.

Fia shifts her gaze between the two of us. "So where you gonna go?"

"A foreign country, one with a nonextradition treaty." I read an article in the *New York Times* five years ago delineating exactly which countries those were, and I can only hope they remain the same today. "That's as far as I've figured out."

"You two can still come with me, you know."

Travis shakes his head. "My pasty ass would stick out there."

"There are plenty of Nicaraguans as pasty as you. What would stick out is your complete lack of Spanish."

"Yeah, that too."

I step forward and hug Fia. This time human contact feels good, like clinging to a stuffed animal when you were scared in the dark as a child. There is safety in my friend, and I'm hesitant to let go, even if letting go is the only thing I can do.

"Goodbye, Fia."

"Goodbye, Penny."

Travis hugs Fia as well, and that is that. No well-wishes, no promises to keep in touch. We'll probably never see Fia again, and that's sad, but it's okay. There's a comfort in the logic of it all.

Fia walks away.

Travis and I head to the ticket counter.

ONE HUNDRED AND SEVENTEEN

I'VE NEVER FLOWN IN my life.

Now, at thirty-five thousand feet, it's all I can do to pry my gaze away from the vast world outside. I'm not prone to awe, but here I give in to it as if I'm a little girl in a movie theater for the very first time.

The big and small of it all.

We're seated in row eleven, Travis in a window seat, me in the middle, a man on the aisle. We agree to swap seats halfway through the flight so I can stare out the window.

A voice chimes too loudly from the overhead speakers, telling us to put on our seat belts because of some upcoming turbulence. It then repeats in Japanese.

The man next to me lights a cigarette, his fourth of the flight so far. I wonder if Tokyo is his home or if he, like us, is just connecting on the way somewhere else.

The plane gives a small rumble. I decide it's time to read my father's note.

I pull it from my front pocket.

I don't know why I haven't read it yet.

I think because I'm realizing this note is the only thing I have from him that's real. All those birthday cards all those years, fake. And once I read this note, that makes it official. He'll be officially dead and no longer able to ever be a part of my life.

This letter may as well be an obituary.

Still.

Here I go.

ONE HUNDRED AND EIGHTEEN

Pen Pen—

Chances are you'll never read this. And if you are, that means your aunt decided to give this letter to you. And I don't really see that happening.

Maybe I've already told you what I'm about to say. Maybe you grew up to be the kind of kid who became my best friend, and we share the closest of confidences. Man, I hope that's the case. All I want in this world is to be your best friend.

Anyway, this is the last note of our big trip (and what fun we had!). Thing is, I never meant this to be a vacation. It was supposed to be something on the permanent side of things. But it didn't work out like that.

Here's the truth. I'm in love, and I wish I could tell you it's your mother I'm in love with. But life is quirky like that, and for better or worse, a person rarely chooses the person they love. It just happens.

I figured on moving to California with you. A plan that had very little planning, mostly just emotion. And the second we got here, to this house, I knew I'd made a mistake. Not because my feelings for Gloria changed but because I realized I'm just not a person who leaves someone.

Tomorrow we're driving back home. Back to your mother. And, if she takes me back, then together as a family, we'll figure out how to make things work.

Tonight we're going to a campfire on the beach. It'll be the first time you'll see an ocean. I hope you remember.

I love you,
Dad

ONE HUNDRED AND NINETEEN

ALL THIS TIME, HE wasn't the type to leave a person.

And yet that's all he's ever been to me.

An abandonment.

What a fucking tragedy life is.

ONE HUNDRED AND TWENTY

I FOLD THE NOTE, put it back in my jeans pocket, where it feels heavier than a single sheet of paper should.

I want to draw, if nothing else to distract myself. To put some different thoughts in my head.

I retrieve my sketch pad and pen from my backpack.

The dots come fast, and I thankfully lose myself under their command. I decide to do incomplete drawings, loose sketches, because I wish to do several.

Page one is Travis, his eyes glowing in that wolf-beautiful kind of way.

A flight attendant tells a woman to take her seat and points to the illuminated seat belt sign.

Page two is Arthur, a shifty smile on the comedy club owner. The mental image I have of him is from minutes before his death.

I'm halfway through the sketch when the plane rumbles, followed by an actual tumble. The man next to me gasps, mutters something in Japanese, grips his armrest tight. As if that will do anything.

Then the plane heaves and drops again, enough to bring a collective *whoa* from the crowd. No translation necessary.

I look at Travis, whose smile is of the uncertain variety.

Page three is a mess because the turbulence is now relentless, but somewhere in the jagged pen strokes is Bain, a hellscape of inked fury, screaming and screaming, a demon in self-inflicted torment. Perhaps he's meant to be drawn in such a way, by a hand not in control, because he is chaos. Unpredictable, unforgiving chaos.

"You are...not scared?"

The man next to me. At first I think he's referring to my drawing, which I admit does scare me. Scares me plenty. But then I realize he means the plane convulsing six miles above the endless Pacific Ocean.

"It's nothing I can control," I say.

And that is that.

The captain comes on, says they're trying to get above a storm. He sounds confident. The Japanese translation follows. Doesn't sound so convincing.

The man next to me suddenly reaches for his vomit bag and makes full use of it.

"Jesus Christ," Travis mutters.

"Is this normal?" I ask him.

"I've only flown a dozen times or so. Yeah, turbulence is normal. But this seems kinda bad."

Focus. Just focus on the drawings. They will distract you.

Page five is Fia, a welcome face.

As I draw, the plane calms in a way that makes perfect sense because that's what Fia had become for me. A calming presence. A friend. And more than anything, a mother. The drawing materializes, and in it Fia's smile seems bigger than her face could possibly allow. I picture this exact expression when she reunites with her boys.

Finally, I draw myself.

I rarely do this because I don't care for the essence I find in my own image. It's like looking in a mirror and feeling good about yourself, then seeing a photo and finding a wholly unsatisfying version of you in it. Which was the real you? The one the world sees? Do people see the flattering version or the one rendered flat and dull, a mimeograph copied over a hundred times?

For my portrait, I choose to fill in every dot. To render a complete, detailed version of me, rather than a basic sketch.

I begin, and thankfully the plane behaves. I draw with a surprising speed considering how much work my hand has already performed. And when I finish, when that last dot is inked and no further dots come, I lean back in my seat, take it all in, and let out a little gasp.

This picture.

It's the Penny I've always wanted to be. The one I could only ever hope for.

Transcendental Penny, accidental genius.

A Penny who no longer has headaches because she now controls the wild, rather than letting it control her. A Penny whose eyes gleam because she refuses to ever relive her past. A Penny who exists only in the now, the glorious, ephemeral *now*. A Penny who isn't one of seventy-five but one of a kind.

For however long I continue to live, I know I'll keep this drawing because this is the person I need to be.

I close the notebook.

I'm considering a nap when the plane falls out of the sky.

ONE HUNDRED AND TWENTY-ONE

A BRILLIANT FLASH, LIKE the beginning of time itself. A boom, like the world exploding. But there's no smoke, no flames, no gaping hole in the side of the aircraft sucking people out into the icy atmosphere.

Dropping. First straight down, belly first, as if a child just released a toy plane from her hand. The seat belt mousetrapping into my thighs. Then the nose of the plane angling down, not vertical but at least roller-coaster steep, pitching all the helpless passengers forward in their seats.

Screaming, such screaming.

Some voices are lower and controlled, like the man next to me, sounding like a person grunting through minor surgery without anesthesia. Others sound as if they've been set on fire, begging for it all to stop. Someone praising Jesus, as if this was His master plan all along.

Travis, his face ghost white, his eyes filled with terror.

A man on the floor of the aisle, grabbing his head. He was flung straight into the overhead bin with the initial drop. Hadn't been wearing his seat belt.

Oxygen masks deploy, raining down like party favors, jangling and bouncing above us.

And fear.

Among the chaos, of course there is fear.

But there is also calm.

ONE HUNDRED AND TWENTY-TWO

I GRAB MY OXYGEN mask, not needing to recall the exact visual instructions from the plastic card in the seat pocket but seeing it in my mind anyway.

Attach your mask before assisting others.

Travis does the same, and we both check each other's masks to make sure they're snug.

The man next to me stares straight ahead, his jaw clenched enough to bite through rocks. I manage to grab his mask and attach it around his head.

He doesn't even seem to notice.

The woman in the other aisle seat sits with her eyes closed, her face set in stone, no mask. I can do nothing for her.

There is fear.

And also calm.

The fear comes first.

With the initial drop, there was just the visceral reaction. Shock but with no assessment. No calculation of danger. The fear comes with the screams of others, a feral groupthink. All my physiological cues are triggered. Immediate sweats, difficulty breathing, arm hairs standing like daggers, an overwhelming desire to claw at the exit door in a frantic attempt to leave.

"This is bad," Travis says, over and over, rocking in his seat.

When the plane first tips forward and begins what must be an inevitable rocket strike into the sea, thoughts race through my mind.

My first thought is one born of horror.

The scariest part of all this, I realize, is not hearing from the captain. Nothing to calm us, no announcement saying this is bad but under control. Nor even a fatalist declaration telling us to hug our loved ones because this is *it*.

No. Just silence. Radio silence.

I imagine the crew up in the cockpit, furiously punching buttons and grabbing at controls, all to no effect.

After the thoughts of panic nearly burst my skull wide open, a bit of reason creeps in. I've had plenty of occasions to scream over the past two weeks, and I want to do so now more than ever. Announce my death with all my fury and might, to be heard one last time. But I don't scream because logic prevails. I will not contribute to the fear of others, and if that's my final gift to humanity, so be it.

I look out the window, immediately regretting it. The angle. It's steep. It's too fucking steep.

And, I think, this will be my first and last time ever on a plane.

Travis reaches over and grabs my hand.

This is when the calm comes over me.

The calm insists I consider my vision of exactly this moment. Fifteen days ago, the day before I turned twenty-one. My mind conjured a death scenario, as uninvited as it was unavoidable, one of many over the years. I visualized myself in an airplane, plummeting from the sky, falling as fast as Galileo's stone from the Tower of Pisa.

Then, with more gravity, I consider the endless duality of life, in this calm. Terror and beauty. Power and fealty. Cruelty and kindness. Pleasure and pain. Everything has two extremes, and for most of my life, I set myself right smack in the middle of all of them. As smart as I am, I'd never *lived* until I left my house two weeks ago. Never experienced a terrifying extreme, at least not since I role-played flying at the age of seven.

Ten minutes ago, I would've given anything to change some of the events from my time in the wild. But now, with the certainty of death only increasing by the second, I consider that, perhaps, this is all meant to be. That I was meant to experience the extremes of life, of human behavior, just so I can finally see there *is* no logic in the world.

Ten minutes ago, this concept would have horrified me, but now it's a soothing balm. I will go under the water, and that will be that, completing that curious process of death I never allowed myself to experience in the bathtub when I was younger.

In the end, there is no order of things. Nothing makes sense.

What a fucking relief.

I close my eyes, squeeze Travis's hand, and wait for the end.

I hope the pain won't last long.

Then I hear a voice.

I dunno, Pen Pen.

Dad.

I didn't conjure him this time. He conjured me. That has never happened before.

This seems pretty bad, he says.

Yes, I know.

But there's a chance.

Is there?

Maybe. Maybe not. Good news is, if there's not, we get to be together.

Is that true? I ask him. *Is heaven really a thing?*

*Not the heaven you know. It's way more complicated than that. But you?
I bet you would figure it out fast. Took me fucking forever.*

But I would see you?

Then his voice. So steady. So confident.

*My God, yes. And I will hold you like I've never held anyone, for as long
as I can.*

And the tears come, imagined or not. The sobs of joy, of hope, of
fear, and of beauty. They all come.

I'm so sorry, I say.

Me, too, Pen Pen.

Then he's gone.

The plane shakes and shimmies but slowly levels out. But it doesn't
feel normal. The plane seems to be laboring.

The screaming lessens.

At that moment, Gloria's words come back to me, soft and certain.

*Chasing control is a fool's errand, Penny. Letting go is a faster path to
happiness than pretending any of us have the power to control anything.*

How right she is.

I snatch up my backpack, find the postcard of Los Angeles I bought
at the airport gift shop. While the plane is temporarily not plummeting,
I use the opportunity to scrawl eight words on the back of it.

ONE HUNDRED AND TWENTY-THREE

I forgive you.
I love you.
I'm sorry.

ONE HUNDRED AND TWENTY-FOUR

I JOT THE ADDRESS on the postcard, knowing I have no control over whether it will ever reach my mother or not. If the plane lands safely and I'm able to mail it, perhaps it'll be the first of many I'll send her. One a year, just like my birthday cards. An annual message letting my mother know I'm still alive and *out there*. A different postmark every year: Tokyo, Bali, Rome, São Paulo. Maybe even a little town in Nicaragua.

I slide the card and pen into my bag, close my eyes again, then hear a voice. Not my dad this time.

The captain.

He says we've been hit by lightning. Two of their four engines are nonresponsive. That we're farther from an airstrip than he wishes we were, and that all he can do is be honest with us about the situation.

Death and life. Kingdoms of extremes.

"I don't know, folks," the captain says, the most uncertain thing likely ever uttered by a pilot. "I just don't know. But I will say you have the most qualified crew you could possibly want, and we'll do everything we can to get all of us on the ground safely. However, what I won't do is lie to you.

This is a challenging situation. I ask that you keep your seat belts on, but if you need to move about in order to pray or otherwise find comfort, I understand. I'll tell you if I know one way or another what's going to happen, but otherwise I plan to stay off this intercom and focus on my job. My life's commitment is to make sure United 42 gets safely to the ground."

Then he's gone.

But what I heard was:

Forty-two.

Gleaming yellow, sunlight at its most life-giving moment.

And then it occurs to me for the first time that it's the color of happiness.

Pure and flawless happiness, distilled to its essence, not to be doubted, argued against, or diluted.

It's okay. It's all going to be okay.

I turn to Travis. "I'm going to kiss you now."

"What?"

"I just wanted you to know. It would be wrong to surprise you."

He smiles, but now there's fear in it. "That's not usually how it works," he says. "Usually, you just lean in and do it."

I bite my bottom lip, just to fill it with sensation. "Okay."

And I do. Brief but fierce. The taste of him only cements my belief that everything will be fine.

If I'm wrong, I'm wrong.

Won't be the first time.

I close my eyes one more time.

And I feel it.

The most unmistakable sensation in the world.

I'm smiling.

AUTHOR'S NOTE

Since I don't outline, I never know what direction my stories will take. Moreover, I don't set out writing a new book with a particular theme or message in mind. If my subconscious is doing its job, what my book is *actually about* will, fingers crossed, reveal itself in time.

On first consideration, I'd say Penny's journey is about the irony of being so fully capable and incapable at the same time, book smarts versus street smarts, and the fierce, driving need to understand our individual histories.

But on further examination, I realize this story is ultimately about happiness. The questioning of its existence, the endless search for it, and for those lucky enough to seize upon it, the ephemerality of its nature. Perhaps above all, it's about finding happiness during tragedy.

Or, more to the point, *through* tragedy.

I stumbled upon the phase "pure and flawless happiness" in Erik Larson's *The Splendid and the Vile*, a brilliantly written and stunning account of Churchill's life during the Blitz of London. In it, a woman who narrowly escaped a direct hit from a German bomb, reported, "I lay there feeling indescribably happy and triumphant. I've been bombed! I kept saying to myself over and over again—trying the phrase on, like a new dress, to see how it fit. It seems a terrible thing to say, when many people must have been killed and injured last night; but never in my whole life have I ever experienced such pure and flawless happiness."

I read that and got a bit obsessed with the idea that this person would never have known such joy in the absence of such despair. That perhaps these two seemingly opposing forces are, in fact, complementary.

Or, as Penny would have considered:

This tug of war, what she wanted her life to be and how it was, happiness and despair, a zero-sum game in which she was rendered mere bones and decaying flesh at the end because that's what becomes of us all, no matter how special someone is, no matter if you're one in seventy-five or a dime a dozen.

In the end, I think Penny finds exactly what she's been seeking all along. I think she finds happiness. The thing is, I just don't know how long it lasts.

I suppose that's the nature of things and such.

Happiness,

Carter

Erie, Colorado

January 2023

FOR ANOTHER THRILLING STORY
FROM CARTER WILSON, CONTINUE
READING FOR A LOOK AT

THE
NEW
NEIGHBOR

ONE

Bury, New Hampshire
Day One

A LIGHT SUMMER BREEZE kisses my earlobes as I stand in the driveway, taking in my new home, wondering if it's real.

1734 Rum Hill Road.

Bury, New Hampshire.

I blink, questioning everything.

Is she really dead?

Did we really leave Baltimore and move to some town we've never heard of?

Did I really win thirty million dollars?

Before taxes, the universe answers.

Car doors slam. Fast footsteps.

"It's huge," Maggie says, her voice behind me. "This is ours?"

"Aye."

Bo's voice is less enthusiastic. "We don't even have enough furniture to fill one of the rooms."

I keep staring straight ahead as I answer, "Guess we have some shopping to do, then."

Figure your shit out, Marlowe.

Holly said these words to me once. We were freshly married, living in Baltimore, and I was debating what to do after I got my green card. I wanted to go to school, study the things I never had a chance to. But I also needed to keep working because her salary alone wasn't enough.

We were in bed, and I was running through all the scenarios out loud when she punched me in the arm and, with her signature I'm-only-half-kidding grin, said, *Figure your shit out, Marlowe.*

It's her voice I still hear telling me these same words. And her tone isn't half-joking. It's deathly serious. In those words, I hear:

Don't screw up our kids.

Don't let the money change you for the worse.

Make a difference.

Own who you are.

Figure your shit out, Marlowe.

Let go.

I'm not certain I'm capable of any of these things, but I knew I'd be stuck had the kids and I remained in Baltimore. So I made my best effort at one item on the list. I let go.

I shocked our system. Shocked it thoroughly.

And now, standing here in a hot August breeze, the air of which feels nothing like Baltimore, that shock ripples through me. I can either spend the rest of my life second-guessing all my decisions, or I can move forward and do the best I can to create full lives for myself and my children.

It's easy to say I choose the latter.

But I know me.

I'll always be tempted by the former. The past is your true first love, the one that broke your heart more than all the others, and, despite all your lingering feelings, remains the one you can never get back.

Not ever.

READING GROUP GUIDE

1. Our main character is a savant and can remember everything. How does this ability affect her? If you had the ability to remember everything, how do you think you'd feel and why?

2. Penny's father left her after her accident. What does he send her once a year on her birthday, and what made her twenty-first birthday different? How did you feel when Penny received this card? Would you have reacted the same way?

3. Penny sets out on a road trip to find her father, as well as the clues they buried all those years ago in their final moments together. Why is this a risk for her? Would you have done the same thing?

4. Penny and her father "talk" in her head. What are these conversations like, and how do they change throughout the narrative? Why do you think Penny feels the need to have these conversations?

5. Sebastian tells Penny, "You recall everything but know nothing." What does he mean by this? How does the idea of recalling versus knowing play a role in Penny's character transformation?

6. Travis and Penny begin to travel with a woman named Fia. Why are the Snakeskin Boys after her, and what is the reason they decide to all travel west?

7. In an emotional ending, Penny is finally able to "find" her father. What does she learn about him? How did you feel when this was revealed?

A CONVERSATION WITH THE AUTHOR

Penny is a savant, someone with the ability to remember many details, see numbers as colors, and more. What inspired you to write a main character with these abilities?

I didn't set out to write about a savant. For months, I just kept thinking about this character who'd popped into my head, and the more I examined her, the more idiosyncratic she became. Then one day it simply dawned on me: *oh, she's a savant*. Once that idea formed, I had no choice but to write about her that way. And once I started down that path, it became a fascinating process.

This is not only a twisty thriller but an emotionally wrought story about a young woman trying to find herself. Why do you think the thriller genre works for this kind of story?

Any story about someone trying to find themselves works as a thriller because of the unpredictable nature of that process. Add in a time period pre-smartphones and a character very much out of her element, and you will find no shortage of opportunities for unexpected twists and deep emotions. But this story was always first and foremost about Penny's need for discovery and her fear of abandonment. The thriller aspect was a natural outcome once she realized she was getting in over her head.

How did the novel evolve over the course of writing? Were there any major changes?

Major changes, you ask? Hell, yeah, there were major changes. All my books evolve over the course of multiple edits; that's what happens when you don't outline. But this book in particular threw me some curveballs as it went through the editorial process. The biggest change I made (of all my books) was rewriting the entire novel and shifting it from a third-person, past-tense POV to a first-person, present-tense POV. The end result was worth it; Penny truly came alive as a character after that shift. But the actual work of it—literally changing every sentence of the book—sucked mightily.

What does your writing process look like? Are there any ways you like to get creative inspiration?

Writing is a job and I approach it as such. I don't "wait for the muse" or seek creative inspiration before I write. I simply sit down at the same time every day (seven days a week) and write for an hour, whether I'm in the mood to or not. At that pace, I can have a book done in less than a year.

What do you hope readers experience when reading this book?

The greatest compliment I get is when a reader remarks that a book of mine was unlike anything they'd ever read. This doesn't necessarily mean they liked it but that it was memorable. I just hope Penny rattles around in readers' minds for a while once they're done reading. That would make me happy.

What are you reading nowadays?

So many books! I think this year I've been asked to blurb more books than ever, so I've been knee-deep in thrillers as of late (which is rare for me; I rarely read what I write). I can highly recommend Emily Smith's debut, *You Always Come Back*, and Wendy Walker's *What Remains*. I'm also currently reading *American Pain*, a nonfiction account of how two young felons built the largest painkiller clinic in the United States. Fascinating stuff.

ACKNOWLEDGMENTS

This story is dedicated to my daughter, Ili. Unlike her father, she's exceptionally bright; like her father, she's a bit dark-minded. Ili is about to start her junior year at Michigan State and is pursuing two simultaneous degrees, one in criminal justice and the other in psychology (and, still bragging here, a minor in law, justice, and public policy). In ten years, she's either going to be a top profiler for the FBI, a renowned law professor, or a master criminal. I'll be proud no matter what.

As I suspect happened to other authors who wrote books during the pandemic, this story initially took a different tone than my previous works. All I had was this image of Penny and a little knowledge about who she was. I sure as hell didn't know where the story was going to go, and I took *a lot* of time figuring it out. The initial draft was a beautiful mess. The book ultimately went through many iterations to find the right tone, to establish the appropriate pace, and to make a very complex character accessible to the readers. I owe tremendous thanks both to my agent, Pam Ahearn, and my editor, Anna Michels, for their advice in getting this story where it needed to be. And my endless thanks to the entire Sourcebooks/Poisoned Pen Press team for their hard work, creativity, and enthusiasm in getting this book out into the wild.

Thanks to all the constant support from my family and writing circles. Sawyer, Jessica, Henry, Mom, Dirk, Abe, Sean, Sam, Jim, and Sole—you are my community. Lloyd and Linda, still missing you at critique group.

Dad, I think you would have liked this one.

To all readers, thank you as always. None of this works without you.

Carter Wilson
Erie, Colorado
July 2023

ABOUT THE AUTHOR

© Elke Hope Photography

Carter Wilson is the *USA Today* bestselling author of nine critically acclaimed, stand-alone psychological thrillers, as well as numerous short stories. He is an ITW Thriller Award finalist and a five-time winner of the Colorado Book Award. His works have been optioned for television and film. Carter lives in Erie, Colorado, in a Victorian house that is spooky but isn't haunted...yet.